MID-STRUT

A Novel

Eric Burns

authorHOUSE®

AuthorHouse™
1663 Liberty Drive
Bloomington, IN 47403
www.authorhouse.com
Phone: 1 (800) 839-8640

Published by AuthorHouse 04/28/2018

ISBN: 978-1-5462-3466-1 (sc)
ISBN: 978-1-5462-3465-4 (hc)
ISBN: 978-1-5462-3464-7 (e)

Library of Congress Control Number: 2018903650

Print information available on the last page.

Also by Eric Burns

Broadcast Blues:
Dispatches from the Twenty-Year War Between
a Television Reporter His Medium

The Joy of Books:
Confessions of a Life-Long Reader

The Autograph:
A Modern Fable Between a Father and a Daughter

The Spirits of America:
A Social History of Alcohol

The Smoke of the Gods:
A Social History of Tobacco

Infamous Scribblers;
The Founding Fathers and the Rowdy Beginnings of American Journalism

Virtue, Valor and Vanity:
The Founding Fathers and the Pursuit of Fame

All the Things Unfit to Print:
How Things Were . . . and How They Were Reported

Invasion of the Mind-Snatchers:
Television's Conquest of America in the Fifties

1920:
The Year That Made the Decade Roar

The Golden Lad:
The Haunting Story of Quentin and Theodore Roosevelt

Someone to Watch Over Me:
A Portrait of Eleanor Roosevelt and the Tortured
Father Who Shaped Her Life

CONTENTS

Part One
The End
xi

Part Two
The Beginning
23

Epilogue
The Future
169

This book is dedicated to

Francine Appel
Sylvia Bedzyk
David Sabol
Wendy Hawn
Carrol Sichak
Linda Kedzierski
Bill Bufalini

and to the memories of

Tom Stranko
Jay Knafelc

Part One

The End

Friday,
October 1,
1965

IT WAS HALFTIME, and the majorettes led the band onto the field with their shiny white boots hugging their calves like a second skin. They stepped so high and so briskly that the pleats in their skirts never had a chance to settle on the tops of their thighs; the fabric fluttered up with every step they took, as if repelled by the flesh. To the man who watched so intently, it seemed that their flesh was gleaming.

They crossed the goal line, then the five, ten, the fifteen . . .

Some of the people in the crowd were clapping as the girls appeared. Some were cheering. Only a few seemed not to pay attention, having already left their seats to go to the concession stands or bathrooms or simply to move about, stretch their legs, rub their asses after sitting for two quarters on splintered wooden bleachers.

The twenty-five, thirty, thirty-five . . .

And a few seconds later, with the majorettes having arrived at midfield, they turned sharply to the left, their tassels flapping off their boots just as their skirts flapped off their thighs. They swung their arms proudly as they headed toward the home team's bench.

"Oh, Jesus," the man said, "here they come."

The man stood behind the bench, on the cinder track that surrounded the field, just outside the chain-link fence separating the track from the gridiron. The fence came up to the man's waist and he leaned against it, in the process imprinting the bottom of his tattered trench coat with small diamonds of rust. Above the waist, his lining was fastened to the inside of the coat with safety pins, the zipper no longer functioning. He wiped beads of sweat from his forehead with the back of his hand. The temperature at kickoff was forty-one degrees.

When the majorettes got to the sideline they stopped, marching in place. The rest of the band came to a halt behind them. They, too, marched in place. Then the band director blew his whistle and the percussionists pounded their drumheads. One, two!---and all sound and motion stopped. For a few seconds, the scene was an eerie one, perhaps all the eerier because a faint clicking entered the void; someone in the press box was trying to bring the microphone to life.

The man pulled off his glasses. The right temple was attached to the frontispiece by the original hinge, but the left was held in place by a clump of dirty adhesive tape and jiggled no matter how carefully he handled it. He blew onto the lenses, then wiped them on his pants. He gave the tape a squeeze and slipped his glasses back on, pushing them up to the bridge of his nose. The majorettes, all in a line, were about, say, ten yards from him now, maybe less. Or maybe more. He couldn't tell. But, of course, the fence stood between them.

Success in the press box: "Good evening-*ing-ing*, ladies and gentlemen-*en-en*," said the voice over the tinny loudspeaker, "and welcome-*ome-ome* to our special program-*am-am*. Tonight-*ight-ight* it gives us great-*eat-eat* pleasure-*ure-ure* to present to you-*ou-ou*, the Ambridge-*idge-idge* High School-*ool-ool* Varsity Marching Band-*and-and* in tribute-*ute-ute* to that masterful-*ul-ul* maestro-*o-o* of march-*arch-arch* music-*ic-ic*, Mister John-*ohn-ohn* Philip-*ip-ip* Souza-*ouza-ouza*!"

The band director's whistle sliced into the night again. Once such an innocent sound, the man thought, harsh but still innocent. Since Tuesday, though, a whistle was innocent no longer, and the man's next few breaths lurched into him like hiccups.

The musicians sprang back to life with their version of "Semper Fidelis." At the same instant, they turned about-face, heading toward the visitors' side of the stadium in something close to a trot. The man watched the majorettes, who were now the last row of the band, hustle away from him with their shoulders thrown back and their hips wiggling.

He looked up. A narrow trail of smoke drifted over them, slightly lighter than the sky and seeming to weave in and out of the stars. It came from the Beam Shop along the banks of the Ohio River, owned and operated by US Steel through its American Bridge division, the corporate entity that had long ago given Ambridge its name.

The man smiled. The smoke meant that American Bridge was still running three shifts a day. 24/7, as a later generation would put it---that was his hometown for you! Born in steel, raised in steel, shipping its steel all over the country, the world; steel that was made into cars and trucks, airplanes and rail lines, house beams and appliances, tools and weaponry. The Empire State Building started out in Ambridge, as did the Chrysler Building and the San Francisco-Oakland Bay Bridge and the rockets that were exploring space and the pads in Florida that launched them. Even the Superdome, in New Orleans, Louisiana, a football stadium with a roof over it---if you could believe such a thing!---was a product of American Bridge, and it made the man proud. Of course, he didn't have anything to do with the steel industry anymore. Not since the accident. Doctor's orders.

He kept hearing rumors, though. Everyone in town had heard the rumors. It was the Japs, people were saying. The Japs were coming up with newer and cheaper methods of both manufacturing and fabricating steel. They just had a few more kinks to work out, and then they would take over the U.S. market and it would be World War II all over again, only this time the Orientals would win. Forget the battlefield; they would kick our asses in the marketplace. American industry would be the carnage.

In fact, just yesterday he had been told---granted by an unlikely source---that the men on the Beam Shop's graveyard shift, the shift that had begun working about the same time as kickoff, would be receiving their notices within two weeks. It was not a rumor, said the man's source; it was a fact. If it was true, there would be no smoke floating over the field when the Bridgers played their last game of the season.

But was it possible? Would Ambridge and other steel towns along the Ohio River be the twenty-first century's ghost towns? The man shook his head. He could not imagine a world like that. And this was no time to try.

"Stats, m' man." It was the auxiliary cop assigned to game duty, and he was approaching from inside the fence.

"Hey" . . . Jesus, what was his name? . . . "Norm." Yeah, that was it. "How's it going, Normy?"

"Oh, same as ever. Y' know?"

The man nodded and they shook hands over the fence.

"Say, c'mon in, why doncha?"

"It's okay?"

"It is if I say so, an' you jus' heard me," the cop said. He unlatched a gate a few feet from where the man was standing and swung it open.

The man eased through it slowly, not just because every bone in his body ached, but because it was hard to believe he had been admitted to such hallowed ground.

"Looks like you're limpin'. Worse 'n usual, I mean."

"Yeah, sorta hard to tell with me, I guess."

"What happened?"

He needed a moment to search for an answer. The truth would not do, but nothing else came to mind.

"Have a seat," the cop said, gesturing toward the bench.

"Are you sure? What about the players?"

"Aw, they won't be back for another ten minutes. 'Least. Park y'self, Stats."

"I played ball back in high school" he said, lowering his body onto the pine, "You knew that, didn't you? Tackle, went both ways. Hell, everybody went both ways back then. Guess they still do today, some of them. But I mean this is the first time I've ever been on the field since then. Believe that?"

"Lotta years."

"Yeah," the man said, "where the hell'd they go?" and he looked across the field at the band, listening to them play for a few seconds. They were not as good as he wanted them to be. Their version of "Semper Fi" was distorted, uncertain; it made him think of someone rubbing his finger against the edge of a 78 rpm record. The song gradually wobbled to a close. The applause was scattered, unenthusiastic.

"I don't think I seen ya at a game for a long time now," the cop said. "Been workin' nights?"

The man nodded a single time, only that.

From the press box came the news that the band had just played "Semper Fidelis-*is-is*," and would now present its rendition of "El-*el-el* Capitan-*an-an*. You'll know-*ow-ow* it when-*en-en* you-*ou-ou* hear-*ear-ear* it, folks-*olks-olks*."

The band turned around and started prancing back toward him. Majorettes now the first row. The man stared at them until he found the one he thought of as *his* majorette. She was right in the middle, he should've known. He waved at her. She did not wave back. He called her name. "Debbie," he said, cupping his hands to his mouth, "hey, Deb, over here. It's me, the candy man." She did not answer. Probably too far away.

The cop was confused, began to chew on his lip. What he said was, "Fella could get hisself arrested for what you're thinkin', y' know?"

"Huh? Oh no, no, it's nothing like that. She's just a nice girl. I actually met her the other day. We were chewin' the fat for a while. Just me and her. It was great."

Something was wrong, and the man could feel it. His answers were off. Sometimes they weren't even answers at all. Norm the cop slowly formed a scowl, but didn't say anything, not yet.

The scuffling of footsteps on the track. The man did not have to look behind him to know that people were returning to their seats for the second half.

He glanced up at the scoreboard. AMBRIDGE 13, VISITORS 6. "Upset in the making," he said, and he and the cop spent a minute or two talking about the first half, the man having seen just enough of it to vamp the rest.

The band had stopped again, the majorettes still in front, barely in fair territory. It was as close to the man as they had been all night, but Debbie kept her eyes straight ahead. "The Washington Post March" ground to a halt.

"Ladies and gentlemen-*en-en*, the band will conclude-*ude-ude* its performance-*ance-ance* with what is probably-*ly-ly* Mr. Sousa's-*ousa's-ousa's* most famous composition-*ion-ion*, 'The Stars-*ars-ars* and Stripes-*ipes-ipes* Forever-*ever-ever.*' It's goose-*oose* bump-*ump* time-*ime* everybody-*ody-ody-ody-ody* . . ."

The man's lips parted reflexively as the band kicked into gear and he sang along. "Three cheers for the red, white and blue. Da-da-*da*, da-da-*da*, da-da-*dah-dum.*" You bet, goose-bump time for sure! He didn't know how a person---an adult, at least---could listen to the song and not think of that famous painting of the Revolutionary War. What was it called? Oh, right, "The Spirit of '76," although the man always thought of it as the fife and drum picture. He had first seen it in a high school textbook, and later in the office of one of the mill's foremen, who had cut it out of a magazine and masking-taped it to the wall. Yeah, the song and the picture, they really went together.

"The Star and Stripes Forever" was his favorite of all the football songs, more than "The Notre Dame Fight Song," more than "Buckle Down, Winsockie," or whatever the name of that one was. He snapped his fingers to keep the beat, but his legs hurt too much to tap his feet.

"Guess what I heard," the cop said.

The majorettes took a couple of strides toward him, although off to his left about five yards. They were a lot easier on the eyes, he had to admit, than the wounded fifer and two drummers. The man started to smell hair spray.

Amazing the way music could get inside a person, he thought, as the drums thumped and the cymbals clashed and the brass and reeds carried the melody. Amazing the way it could change a person's entire chemistry, giving him hope again, making him believe, if only for a few minutes, that all would be as it had been once before, that courage bred success, effort led to peace of mind.

Of course, it had to be the right kind of music. And that did not mean just marches. There were also the big band ballads from the forties, when he and Rosa went to the amusement park in Pittsburgh and danced the night away under the covered bandstand, holding onto each other for the sheer joy of contact. He could not remember what *her* hair smelled like, but if his eyes were closed he could still see his face buried in it. The big bands. Now that was the right kind of music for romance. Marches were the right kind for action.

The man wiped the sweat off his forehead with his trenchcoat sleeve.

The cop shivered, zipping up his jacket and stuffing his hands into the pockets. This time the man didn't answer at all. Norm had never had to work so hard before to get Stats to talk, and he didn't understand it. He gave him an elbow in the ribs. Fortunately, considering what was about to happen, the poke was a gentle one. "So, Statsy, I was sayin'---"

"Oh, yeah, right. That's right." But the man paused, squinting at the voice. "What were you saying?"

"I was gonna tell ya there was another protest today."

"Against the war?"

"What else. But guess where it was? Pittsburgh."

"Get out."

"The University of."

"Holy smokers. Damn things're getting closer to home, Normy."

"'Least it wasn't as bad as some of 'em are. Few students got hurt, few cops. They took, maybe, half a dozen people to the emergency room, but I think they all been released now."

"Was it all college kids protesting?"

"Far as I know. Kids that age, anyhow."

"And a lot of them are girls, right? Girls out there carrying signs?"

"Sure, all kindsa girls. Most of 'em look like bull dykes, ya ask me, but---

The term was foreign to the man. "Like what?"

Norm just shook his head, his way of saying, never mind.

"Well, I'll tell you something, and you can take this to the bank." Gesturing right in front of him. "You'd never find our girls doing something like that, I mean, never in a million years. Not our majorettes."

"Couldn't agree more."

"They know how to respect our country's leaders, that's for sure."

"Hey, hey, LBJ, how many kids ya kill today?"

"Huh?" Had the man just heard what he thought he'd heard. "What'd you say?

"That's what the kids are out chantin' when they march. 'Hey, hey, LBJ, how many kids ya kill today?"

"The kids say that?"

"Man, you gotta start payin' more attention to the world, Statsy. Lotta stuff goin' on out there these days."

As if I don't know. But the man just thought it, didn't say it.

The majorettes were marching in place again, with their knees flying up higher than their waists, showing red panties, like bikini bottoms. They backed up a few steps, then made a sharp left turn toward the end zone through which they had entered. The man saw them in profile now. In seconds they would be strutting right in front of him.

Despite the spray, their hairdos were coming undone, strands falling across their foreheads and down their cheeks and they looked even better like that than they did when they were all combed and brushed. Without moving forward yet, the girls twirled their batons first in one hand, then in the other; then they grabbed them with both hands and brought them

7

up over their heads from side to side, like champions acknowledging an ovation for their supremacy. The batons caught some of the stadium's cheap light and threw it off, gleaming for a few moments like pieces of five-and-dime jewelry.

"Statsy, you feelin' all right? It's like you're sick or somethin'."

He couldn't make a sound, not for the moment. He was preoccupied. But it was not what it seemed.

"Maybe y' oughtta pay a little visit t' the nurse, let 'er give y' the once-over. Whatta ya say, pal?"

The stream of smoke from the Beam Shop. It wasn't there anymore. Where had it gone? Had it gotten darker and blended into the night, or had the night gotten lighter and hidden it from view? Or had the shift already ended, the future somehow bleeding into the present?

The majorettes started forward. They were just a few feet from him now.

What a sight it must have been if you were looking down on Ambridge from an airplane. A totally dark landscape---black hills, black town, black river, black blending seamlessly into black---and then, right in the middle of it all, this big bowl throwing off so much wattage it looked as if the sun had fallen to earth. There ought to be a post-season football game for colleges called the Light Bowl, the man thought. Play it at night. That would be perfect.

"You wouldn't believe how hard she worked, Norm."

"What? Who?"

"How much she put into it, all the time and energy and sweat and heart. I mean, she's an athlete just as much as the football players are. Hell, she's better than a lot of them. More dedicated, that's for damn sure."

"Okay, ace," the cop said, "I heard enough," and, slapping a hand on the man's forearm, he dug his fingers in and pulled him up. "Christ, yer practically sweatin' through yer coat. C'mon, we gotta get y' to the nurse."

No. Not the nurses' office. Not now. "Debbie!" the man bellowed, and yanked his arm from the cop's grip as he leaped off the bench like a fourth stringer called into the first game of his career. His majorette had passed him by and was getting away. But then she and her mates stopped another time for the band to swing around behind them. Debbie took a step forward, setting herself apart. She stood with one leg on the ground and the other in the air, bent at a forty-five degree angle at the knee. Her arms were bent forty-five degrees at the elbows, and her baton was tucked under one of them. Her back arched slightly backward. As for her smile, it seemed to extend from one earlobe to the other. It was the pose a person would think about most often when he thought about a majorette.

The man sprang at her. Threw his arms around her and laid his chin on her shoulder.

"Mr. Castig!" she shrieked, dropping her baton. "Lord Almighty, what're you *doing*!"

What he was doing was making his first tackle in almost half a century. He didn't mean to, but with the majorette balancing herself on only one leg, she had no way of steadying herself. The two of them toppled over, and the man suddenly found himself lying on top of her, crushing her under his heft. Christ, what *was* he doing? The missionary position was what it looked like, but having sex was the furthest thing from his mind. It was something that no one would believe in the years ahead, though. No one, not ever.

"I just want to hold you, that's all," he said, almost pleading, "Just hold you, really. Just for old times' sake, you know?"

"We don't *have* any old times, you creep! Are you *crazy* or something? I can't breathe!"

"Only 'til the teams come back out," he said. He tried to peek at his watch behind her neck, but could not do it without choking her. "It can't be long now."

He rolled over without surrendering his hug. Now it was girl on top, boy on the bottom. He thought it looked more innocent that way.

"I just want to hold you, that's all." He whispered it so faintly he could barely hear the words himself.

The cop hadn't moved. He knew he should have, but although a message to intercede on the girl's behalf had formed in his brain, it got stuck there, unable to complete the circuit necessary to translate itself into action; some relay, some synapse, had been clogged by the unexpectedness of what he was seeing. After a few seconds he stood. But he went nowhere, simply stopped and stared---nothing like this had ever happened at one of the games before. It was, finally, the majorette's voice that unclogged him.

9

Let *go* of me!" she screamed, catching her breath, her lips vibrating on the man's ear and exploding into his head. "Let *go* of me! Let *go* of me! Let *go* of me! Let *go* of me!"

The man wanted to. Sort of. He would tell his psychiatrist that later. Or his psychologist or social worker or witch doctor---whomever the hell it was at the time. He wanted to let go of her and then help her up and resume their embrace vertically. But for the moment, he couldn't figure out how to shift his bulk beneath her; everything hurt, throbbed. He rubbed his stubbled cheek against the smoothness of the majorette's neck, now beginning to sob in frustration, wanting her to understand what he could not understand himself.

"*Mis-ter Cas-tig!*"

By now the band had stopped playing "The Star and Stripes Forever," a few instruments at a time trickling out as the musicians saw what was happening and, like motorists at the scene of an accident, nudged their way forward for a better view. The cop had by now pushed his way through them and knelt beside the man, hollering at him. "Get the hell away from her, you son of a bitch!"

The man shook his head as he held onto her with one of his hands clasped in the other.

The cop began to pry them apart. "Get your lousy stinkin' paws offa her!"

Instead he pressed her closer to him, if that was possible, his adrenalin surging. He had no idea what he was doing.

The cop looked at the band members, encircling him with slack jaws and instruments lying in the grass at their feet.

"Don't jus' stand there, ya friggin' fruits!" he bellowed. "Somebody gimme a hand!"

Only the band director moved, but not much; he was stuck at the middle of the throng, squeezed in on all sides. Yet he pushed, inching forward, jumping up and down every few seconds to see how much more ground he had to gain.

The fans on the cinder track, with their Cokes and coffees and snack foods, as well as those who had remained in the stands for the halftime show, saw the commotion on the field and, in what seemed a single mass, bolted toward the fence, bumping into one another as they stumbled forward, struggling for a better view.

"Who is it?"

"What happened?"

"What are they doing?

"Somebody get injured?"

"The second half start yet or what?"

As it happened, one of the first people to stake out a position at the fence was the best friend of the majorette hugger, the person with whom he had originally planned to go to the game tonight. George Szuchinski was his name, but to all who knew him he was Zook, plain old Zook. When he realized that his soulmate was the fellow who had clamped himself onto the young lady, his mouth went slack and he accidentally squeezed his hot dog out of the bun, a projectile dripping mustard.

"Holy shit!" Zook said, after a few coughs. "He's dry-fuckin' 'er! I can't believe it! He's dry-fuckin' a majorette on the forty five! Hey, Statsy! What'd she ever do t' *you*?

The band members were gradually snapping out of their trances and one of them went to the cop's aid. He bent over and tried to help Norm pry the man's right hand out of his left.

"Jesus, Stats," Zook shouted toward his friend, "I know you're supposed t' be sick, but I din't know ya meant sick inna head! Ya gotta stop this, man, it just don't look good. An' everybody's watchin'.'"

The cop and the musician finally freed the man's grip, and the cop grabbed him by the coat collar and jerked him out from under the majorette. He flung the man backward, pushing him onto his side and then ramming his knee into the small of his back, forcing him over onto his stomach. The man's adrenalin was gone. He had no more fight in him. He let out a sigh that sounded like a dying man's last exhalation.

The majorette flipped onto her side in the opposite direction and curled into a fetal position, beginning to gulp out the wildest of tears, her stomach heaving and legs quivering---an electric shock might have been passing through them. The other girls swarmed around their fallen comrade, some of them screeching so loudly in sympathy that it was they who sounded like the victim of the man's clumsy assault.

The cop unfastened the handcuffs from his belt and hooked them over the man's wrists. "The fuck got *inta* y', asshole?" he demanded, angling the cuffs to bring maximum pain to the man's wrist bones. "Y' fuckin' wanna tell me that!"

"I shouldn'ta done it," he whimpered.

"No shit, Sherlock!"

"My heart, my heart."

"What say?"

"I feel somethin'," he said. "It's like my heart's slipping down into my chest."

"Yer *heart!*" Norm went up an octave on "heart." He took a fistful of the man's hair, yanked his head off the ground, then slammed it back down. He would have broken the man's nose if he hadn't turned his head at the last instant. "Y' tryin' t' tell me y' never shoulda jumped that poor little girl 'cause yer afraid you'll get a *heart attack!*"

"I'm not supposed to get all excited." The man wiggled his wrists, trying to make them comfortable in bondage. "It's bad for me."

The cop was speechless.

"What a week," the man said, and closed his eyes against the humiliation of his behavior.

Then, faintly at first, as if they were the initial vibrations of a railroad track with the train still half a mile away, there came a rumbling of the earth followed by a trickle of applause. It might have been just a few people pounding their hands together at first, then several others joining in, then a few more after that. Soon everyone in the stands started to cheer and those at the fence, with the wrestling match now over, joined in. The trickle became a roar.

"Let's go, you guys!"

"Let 'er rip, fellas!"

"Kick some ass, now. Make us proud."

And from several voices, scattered about. "C'mon, Bridgers! Hum, you Bridgers!"

The cop looked back toward the end zone from which the majorettes had emerged. The Ambridge High School Varsity football team was chugging back into the stadium, a train that was long and winding and derailed. Norm seemed to be the only one aware of the danger.

"Hey," he cried, "somebody stop those guys! Don't let 'em out here yet!" But there was no one to obey the command; he was the only policeman at the game, and the coaches and officials who might have been able to help were still in the locker room. "Jesus, Mary, an' Joseph!"

What Norm had realized was that the majorettes and musicians had packed themselves so densely into the area around the Bridgers' bench that there was no path for the players who, supercharged from their halftime pep talk, not to mention an unexpected lead over a tough Ellwood City squad, did not notice the congestion. Instead, they pounded their hooves along the sideline, heads down, slapping one another on the butts and shoulder pads and growling like suddenly uncaged animals. Before them, no more than a few feet away, were trumpeters and trombonists and accordionists arrayed like a storeroom full of tackling dummies.

An offensive lineman ran up to a clarinetist and, probably not even seeing him, gored him in the stomach with his helmet, setting off a chain-reaction collision that sent more than a dozen band members tumbling into their mates. Players tripped over them and some fell onto the hard edges of the band's instruments. But it was the musicians who took the brunt of the attack. Their cheeks and hands were bleeding, eye sockets beginning to swell; they groaned, whimpered.

But when a linebacker dumped a bucket of water into the bell of a French horn, its owner promptly whacked him in the hip with it, putting him out of action for the next three games. The music makers were striking back. A trombonist lashed out at the quarterback by poking her slide back and forth into his face until she broke his chin. Meanwhile, the majorettes began swinging their batons wildly around them, wreaking one injury after another on the football players who had not yet slipped on their helmets.

It would be another ten or fifteen minutes before order was restored to Bridger Stadium on that star-crossed night in 1965. Four musicians had to be taken to the hospital and three were kept overnight. But there were seven injuries of note among the athletes, seven players who would see no action in the second half and five who were out for the season. But even those who could play did so with an unaccustomed listlessness, a lack of hustle. They might not have been pummeled by music makers, but were weary from retaking their position on the sideline; they were fresh out of stamina for another sixteen minutes of football. Ellwood City ran back the second half kickoff for a touchdown, and went on to pile up four more TDs while holding their opponents to one. Final score: AMBRIDGE 19, VISITORS 40. The Bridgers fell to last place in the conference. Their season, for all practical purposes, was over.

None of which the man knew, for as the final whistle blew, he was being led docilely to a jail cell while the entire Ambridge police force tried to figure out what to do with him.

ARNOLDO CESIDIO "STATS" CASTIG had gotten his last name at Ellis Island, when his father told an immigration official that they were Americans now and didn't want to sound so Italian anymore. It wasn't a matter of shame; the issue was one of appropriateness. The family had been Cas-til-ee-*o*-nay, from the village of Popoli in the southern province of Abruzzi. But their parents and aunts and uncles, their siblings and nieces and nephews and one cousin---they had all stayed behind. It was their choice; they had enough money for steerage. But they preferred the imperfect homeland they knew to the unknown across the sea. Only Salvatori, his wife Henrietta and their only child had decided move on, and they wanted a name that would allow them to fit into their new nation.

The immigration man, who probably would have changed their name anyhow, agreed. He picked up his pencil and crossed out five letters, three syllables---and what had once been musical, like part of an opera's libretto, Cas-til-ee-*ooo*-nay, was now clipped, chopped off, a steel man's name. The old name, foreign. *Ca*-stig, American.

As for Arnie's nickname, it had come from friends when he was a teenager, the result of his preternatural ability to remember the statistics of sports. How many triples did Pie Traynor have in 1922, how many strikeouts for Babe Adams, how many passed balls for Walter Schmidt. Arnie didn't try to memorize the numbers, made no kind of special effort at all. He just watched the games and listened to the announcers and read the newspaper articles about them the games the next day, skimming the box scores---and all of a sudden, there they were, all those numbers, piled up in his brain, as if he had his own special lobe for storing them. Arnie knew all the stats for the Pittsburgh teams, not just the Pirates of baseball but the Pirates of football, who would come along during the Depression and later be known as the Steelers. He knew the stats of the hometown Ambridge teams, and this year, for the first time, he would know at least some of the figures for another team, a team he had never cared about before, but had now become even more important than the Steelers---the New York Jets.

Just that should have been enough to mean something to the woman with all the letters after her name who wrote about him in a journal called the *Psychiatric Review and Forum.* But she was not interested in any of it, did not think it was relevant to the story she would call "The Battle of Bridger Halftime: Psyche and Psychology."

She probably didn't even know who Roberto Clemente was.

No, the story she wrote was about the man and the majorette and nothing else. She was certain, she told Arnie, that there was something special about what he had done, that it fit into a category of behavior little studied before, and even less understood. It wasn't, after all, a case of rape; both male and female were fully attired and the man had never attempted to unfasten either his clothes or hers. He kept saying he wanted to hold her, nothing more salacious. But why her, someone so young, young enough to be his granddaughter? And why there, at halftime of a football game?

The woman who wrote the article had no answers. She simply--- actually, there was nothing simple about it---posed the problem of why "a male of a certain economic class and vocational and ethnic background had chosen to interpret the imminence of cultural change in a manner so dispositionally inappropriate and seemingly incongruous that it seemed to edge into the realm of the psychotherapeutic."

Ambridge auxiliary policeman Norman Jankowicz did not read the article. He would not have read it even if it had been written in English. He had his own opinion of Arnie's behavior and would state it whenever he was asked and volunteer it on occasion when he was not. "Guy was a sicko, a fuckin' sicko, a maniac, a jerk-off. Case closed."

But even if Norm's analysis had been a sound one, it did not answer the question. Why did the man jump the majorette? Arnie would be asked so many times by so many people in the days and months ahead that he became numb to the subject. And as a result, his answers, not particularly perceptive at the start, became more and more irrelevant.

As for Arnie's wife, Rosa, she became the town's principal object of pity. Or so she feared. After a few days she pleaded with a neighbor to do some of her shopping for her, so she could stay home and cook, avoiding the stares and whispers. And avoiding the question, from the few who dared ask her. But it didn't work. There was shame in the kitchen no less than there was the rich, life-sustaining odor of tomato sauce. But at least if Rosa stayed home all day, no one saw her and she was safe. She could not spend the rest of her life in hiding, of course, but neither could she imagine a future.

Her husband was gone for most of October and the first week of November, an in-patient at the Western Pennsylvania Psychiatric Hospital in the Oakland section of Pittsburgh. After that, he became an out-patient, ordered to present himself once a week through 1966. Then bi-monthly until the fall of 1967, and once a month from that point on. In 1968 he had pneumonia and missed a few weeks, but his social worker was not concerned. By that time he was thought to be virtually cured. "Cured." The word did not make sense to him. It meant he had been sick, but had he? Was he *still* sick? What was his disease? No one could say. No one seemed to be able to say anything.

However, the consensus among the mental health professionals familiar with his case was that he would never make an ass of himself at a high school football game again.

Yet none of the pros understood why he had done it even once. They kept asking, asking, but the man could not answer---not *would* not, *could* not.

One week, midway through the summer of 1967, the social worker at Western Psych in charge of his rehabilitation reached retirement age and a new one, fresh out of the masters program at the University of Pittsburgh, was assigned to him. She had been the class valedictorian not only at Pitt but, two years earlier, at tiny Carlow College, just up the road from Pitt in Shadyside, where she had received her Bachelor's degree. Also in her favor was her appearance: young and slender, long-haired and pretty, rather than old and dumpy as her predecessor had been. In other words, she looked more like a majorette. Maybe that could lead to some kind of breakthrough.

Unless Arnie decided to hold her, just hold her.

Furthermore, although coincidentally, she was a *paisani*. If *she* couldn't get through to him, no one could.

With the permission of the hospital director, Clara Santarelli would try something different with her patient. She would come to him for the first few visits rather than requiring the patient's presence at Western Psych. She would spare him the bus rides to Pittsburgh and the clinical atmosphere of the hospital, and instead talk to him in the comfort of his own home. She would try to put him at ease, adjust herself to his surroundings. She was proud of herself for coming up with the idea. She was optimistic about the outcome. She could hardly wait to go to Ambridge.

They talked on the Castigs' front stoop in the first week of July. It was a hot day, and damp breezes lay in the air like washcloths, not moving.

Miss Santarelli began by telling Arnie that she was more interested in knowing what kind of person he was than why he caused such a ruckus at that football game.

"You are?"

"Yes, I am, Mr. Castig."

"Geez," he said, and although pleased, he wondered whether this was just another one of those tricks that his interrogators played to get their patient to say something he didn't really mean. Or *did* really mean. Arnie was beginning to be as much an expert on them as they were on him.

"Uh, please," he said with a gesture, "make yourself comfortable."

Miss Santarelli sat on a small metal porch swing and Arnie on a matching chair, facing her. There was room for little else on the stoop except another chair and a small table, on which Rosa had placed two glasses of iced tea atop cardboard coasters.

Miss Santarelli opened her three-ring binder. Taking a ballpoint pen from her purse, she clicked down the top and poised herself to write. Arnie watched her, suddenly uncomfortable. This woman, he realized, was all business.

Now then, she said, had he seen the majorette around town since the night in question?

No.

Did he have any idea what she was doing with herself these days?

She was in college, he supposed. She had been a senior in high school when the . . . incident occurred, and he had seen her name in the paper in

17

a list of graduates who were going on to higher education. Her picture was in the paper, too. She had won some kind of scholarship. She was planning to be an elementary school teacher.

Why did he remember all this so clearly?

It was in the paper. You remember stuff about people you know if it was in the paper.

Did he really think he *knew* her?

Nit-picking, Arnie thought. Dumbass stuff. He said no.

When he saw that picture, did the sight of her fill him with longing?

The patient pursed his lips, shook his head. He was right. The young lady had no more intention of getting to know him, the man behind the deed, than any of the others had been. He was a fool to have thought so. He drank some of the tea that Rosa had made from a package of Lipton instant.

No, he said. No longing.

Had the sight of her filled him with anything else?

Anything else?

Lust.

Aw, Jesus Christ. Sorry, I didn't mean---

That's all right. Actually, it was good, a telling reaction, very good.

Arnie put his iced tea glass down.

Did he ever think about her?

Yeah. Sure. Sometimes. Not *that* way, though. You know, the way people might believe.

In what way *did* he think about her, then?

Well, it wasn't really thinking about *her*, he guessed. It was thinking about what he did to her.

She leaned toward him, getting chummy. Next, she said, she was going to tell Mr. Castig what puzzled her most about the whole situation. But first she sipped some tea. Slowly. Building the suspense. Making Arnie wonder, tense up, even though he had had so much experience with these people.

Finally Miss Santarelli spoke. She said she could not understand how Mr. Castig had come to like his majorette so much after having met her only a few days earlier, less than a week, and why he had decided to express his affection---if that's truly what it was---precisely as he had, precisely *when* he had.

It was, of course, the same old question---nothing new under the sun, as people liked to say. But there was something about the way the woman put it this time, the way she had gradually worked up to the zinger and the quiet earnestness of her manner. There might have been something as well about his own need to unburden himself, something even about the moist mellowness of a summer afternoon nearing the end of the Steel Age, most of the American Bridge Company's mills down to two shifts a day now, a couple of them to one, and the Wire Mill shut down completely except for the rats on the night shift---maybe the way all of these circumstances came together the way they did made the man more responsive to the topic than he had ever been before, enabling him to react with a certain detachment, as if it were someone else's bizarre misdeed he were describing, not his own.

He bent forward in his chair, being chummy himself. His social worker---not trusting him, he assumed---backed up, holding the iced tea glass in her lap with both hands and practicing the patience they had no doubt taught her in college. Neither of them spoke. In his head, Arnie considered various combinations of words, combinations he had never tried before. He wanted her to like him.

Finally the silence got uncomfortable. Miss Santarelli asked again. Why did you---?"

"It seemed like a good idea at the time." That quickly the answer came out, a flash, a streak of lightning, so quickly that the question remained unfinished. Arnie did not think about it before he said it; the words were a reflex, something less than a reasoned analysis.

Miss Santarelli stood up. She set her glass on the stoop ledge and slapped her binder shut. She slipped the pen into her mouth and bit down which made her look as if she were snarling. Maybe she was. She took a few steps toward the front sidewalk and, ultimately, her car, a 1965 Dodge Challenger, blue with white trim. She dug her keys out of her purse and spit the pen into it. Turning back to him, she no longer spoke with her previous restraint. She told Mr. Castig that an answer like that was worse than merely facetious; it was appalling, repulsive, a sign that his rehab was not proceeding nearly as well as it seemed to be on the surface.

Arnie looked at her blankly, a scolded schoolboy who did not know what he had done wrong.

Miss Santarelli fumed. She took a few seconds to regain control, then conceded that he had not attacked any majorettes since the Bridgers lost to the Wolverines that night. But something was still percolating inside him, something vague and mysterious, something that just wasn't good, wasn't healthy, and might erupt again at any time. "It seemed like a good idea at the time," she repeated disgustedly.

Arnie stood. "Maam. Miss. Hey, there. I'm sorry."

She kept walking toward her car.

"I didn't mean to upset you. I wasn't being a smart ass, I really wasn't."

She ignored him, reached for the handle.

"It's just that you just asked me why---"

"Damn you! Goddamn waste of time driving here! Shit!" Miss Santarelli slammed the car door behind her, turned on the ignition, and lead-footed the gas pedal down Maple Street to Fifth, where she made a tire-squealing right toward the Ohio River Boulevard and back to Pittsburgh.

Wow, Arnie thought, girls sure didn't talk like that when *he* was her age.

Rosa had watched the whole scene from the living room. She could not hear anything and so had no idea what it meant. But it did not look good.

The next time Arnie showed up at the hospital, he found out that Miss Santarelli was no longer his social worker. In fact, she was no longer anybody's social worker---not at Western Psych, at least. She had been fired on the grounds of unprofessional behavior. Arnie was stunned. He pleaded for her, insisting that he was the one who had been unprofessional; it was his fault, not hers. She was a nice girl.

But no one wanted to listen to a pervert. Besides, what was done was done. Clara Santarelli had cleared out her office the previous Friday. She was no longer an employee of the institution.

His next social worker was a man in his mid-thirties. He had never heard of John Philip Sousa, never heard of either the New York Jets or Joe Namath.

And they were supposed to develop a relationship! Jesus Christ!

ARNIE "STATS" CASTIG was bewildered. He supposed he always would be. He had already answered the question so many times and would answer it again and again, although with decreasing frequency, in the time left to him. But maybe Miss Santarelli *did* deserve to be fired for speaking to him as she did. Her reaction notwithstanding, he knew the moment the words had left his mouth that afternoon on the stoop---"It seemed like the right thing to do at the time"---that he would never answer the question more accurately.

Part Two

The Beginning

Sunday,
September 26,
1965

THE HEADLINE in the sports section of the *Pittsburgh Press* said that, because of injuries, four Steelers would miss today's game with the San Francisco Forty-Niners, two of them starters. But he did not read the article. Halfway down the page was another headline, this one telling of a home run by Ernie Banks that had given the Cubs a 7-6 victory over the Pirates yesterday in one of the most exciting games played at Forbes Field all season. He skipped that article too, even though on a normal Sunday these would have been his top two priorities. Today, however, he did not want to read about the ineptitude of the local teams

Instead, he turned to the inside pages of the sports section and Phil McIntryre's column. Near the end of it, under the heading "Local Boy Makes Good," he found was he was looking for.

> Joe Namath, the $400,000 rookie quarterback who threw his high school passes just a few miles up the river for Coach Larry Bruno's Beaver Falls Tigers, gets his first start as a pro today for the New York Jets. The Gotham Eleven of the fledgling American Football Leagues plays the powerhouse Buffalo Bills in B-town, and the fray will be telecast in Pittsburgh and environs on Channel 11, WIIC-TV, beginning at 2 p.m.
>
> Western Pennsylvania high schools have produced a plethora of outstanding gridiron warriors down through the years, especially QBs, but the one they call "Broadway

Joe" just could turn out to be the cream of the entire crop
before he finally hangs 'em up somewhere down the road.

"Ha, right on the money, Phil," Arnie said, flicking the paper with his
thumb and middle finger. But it was too early to think about what might
happen somewhere down the road. Instead, Arnie was focusing on today's
game, and could not keep his reservations to himself. It was as if he were
talking to Zook. "But I don't know. The Bills defensive line, they're about
as tough as they come. They could eat a young quarterback for lunch, no
matter how good he is. The best thing'd be for Joey to make his first start
against some doormat, like the Oilers or Broncos or one of them."

He was lying on the sofa in his living room, holding the paper in
outstretched arms and about to provide some more commentary when a
shadow appeared on the bottom of the page. It quickly slid its way up, first
assuming the shape of a head lumpy with hair curlers, then revealing a
solid neck and broad shoulders and finally the top of a torso that was soft
and stocky and untapering. In a matter of moments the entire page was
darkened, but he started in on her before the shadow could start on him.

"I thought I told you to quit sneaking up on me."

"Wouldn'ta make no difference."

"C'mon, Ro, I was barely whispering."

"Uh!"

"I *was.*"

"How many times I gotta tell you," his wife said.

"I know."

"Not to---"

"I got it, Ro."

Both of them in unison: "Not to talk to the sports paper."

Arnie: "I know, I know."

"Sports paper never talk back. Is always only you."

"You just don't get it, you never will."

"You should talk to me as much as you talk to newspaper," Rosa said.
"Besides, time for church."

"Already?"

"Twenny after ten."

"Holy smokers," he said, and confirmed the fact with a glance at his watch."

"Father Daniel today?" he said.

"Suppose to be."

Arnie brushed the paper off his stomach and struggled to a sitting position. He took his clip-on tie from the sofa arm and attached it without buttoning the top button of his shirt. He stood, tucked the shirt into his pants, then tried with less success to do the same with his stomach.

"You change your mind, come with me to Vinnie's this afternoon?"

"We've been through this, Ro. He's *your* cousin, *you* go see him."

"We all family. Make no difference he's my cousin. Same as your cousin anyhow. Besides, he gonna have the game on. You could watch it there."

"He's gonna have the Steelers' game on, not the Jets."

"What's wrong with that?"

"I don't want to watch the Steelers today. Today's different."

"You watch the Steelers every other Sunday."

"Yeah," Arnie said, "and what've I got to show for it. Squat, that's what." He had just gotten a new pair of glasses and kept trying to adjust them, to get the top of the frames parallel to his eyebrows. But they wouldn't stay there; one eyebrow was hidden by the frame, the other was slightly above it. He'd have to go back to the optician. Little things like that annoyed him sometime. "The Steelers're the only team in the whole National Football League that's never won the title. You realize that? The only one."

"You tol' me once, you tol' me that hundred times."

"The only team. And then you throw in the Pirates and what've you got. City of losers, that's what. Losers everywhere you look. I've had it. I mean it, Ro, I'm at the end of my rope."

The years had pressed down hard on the woman Arnie addressed, the woman he used to dance with in the summer darkness. Her center of gravity wasn't in the center anymore, and her breasts had dropped so smoothly into her waist that it was hard to tell where one part left off and the other began. Her girth made her a difficult woman to hug. Her husband's girth had the same effect, and so the two of them seldom embraced anymore, and never with passion.

As for Rosa's hair, it was long and thinning, strands of gray alternating with a fading brown. Her ankles had thickened; her calves bore the tell-tale, broken-veined patterns of one who has had to carry too much weight for too long a time. But there was a surprising vigor to her face: her eyes still clear, the line of her jaw firm, her chin only double. She was not one to quit.

"Maybe Vinnie going to watch the Jets," she said.

"Vinnie's living in the dark ages."

"Uh!"

Arnie took his wife's hand in both of his and squeezed. "Ro, try to understand, okay? It's Namath, the quarterback. You know, the kid from Beaver Falls. I've told you about him. That's why I wanna see the Jets. He's magic, this boy. Got a $400,000 signing bonus---he's a millionaire, for crying out loud! And he's one of us, don't you see?"

"I don't see where *we* got a million dollars."

"You know how far Beaver Falls is from here? Less than ten miles, that's how far. And it's just like Ambridge, you know that. The kid's dad, he worked in the mill, same as me. That's a kind of family too, when you think about it. Except Joey's dad, he was at Babcock & Wilcox, I think. Him and his old lady, I hear they're divorced now, but the two of them are supposed to be really good people individually. Szolnicki, her name was. Rose Szolnicki, almost your name. We lived in Beaver Falls, we could be friends. Maybe I'd still have a job. You can never tell how things might've worked out."

"Arnie, we never met these people."

"*Could* be friends, I said."

"So we live in Roma *could* be friends with the Pope."

"Gimme a break, willya," he said, dropping her hand. "I'm talking about folks just like you and me, just like us, only they happen to have this kid who's gonna set the whole world on fire. A champ of a kid. If we'd've been lucky enough to have one of our own, he's just the kind of boy we'd've wanted. We'd be so proud, Ro. Can you imagine! We'd be sitting in the stands, cheering like crazy, telling everybody sitting around us, 'that's our son, that's our son.'"

"You don't know nothing 'bout this boy 'cept what you read in the paper."

"I can just picture it, maybe ten, fifteen years ago, me and him out in the street playing catch after work, zipping that ball around. I was young enough back then I could've even run some routes. Down to the light pole in front of the Torelli's, then a buttonhook back toward the line of scrimmage and whomp! He hits me right in the breadbasket." He extended both arms over his head. "Touchdown!"

"You crazy."

"I just see things you don't."

Rosa threw Arnie's overcoat at him. She had gone to early mass today so she had time to do her hair for Vinnie's and cook the veal piccata she would bring. Her husband would meet Zook at the church.

"Okay," she said, "you want me to understan', I understan'. How's this? You don't want to be with your family for dinner today because the son of some people we never met who come from this town we never been to is playing football on television for some team we ever heard of. I get that right?"

Arnie did not reply. Instead he applied his lips lightly to Rosa's cheek and told her to give his best to the family. "Remember, tell everybody I said hello. And I mean it. Hell, we're Italians, our family's our life. Don't let anybody think I'm pissed off or something. 'Cause I'm not. I just got different priorities."

"Uh!"

"I'll see everybody next Sunday," he said, then hustled off to eleven o'clock mass at St. Veronica's Roman Catholic Church, in the shadow of the mill where Arnie's father got him his first job at American Bridge, back in the days when what he did for a living made a difference.

ARNIE PUSHED OPEN the church door a few minutes before eleven and dipped his fingers into the bowl of holy water on the near wall. "In the name of the Father, the Son and the Holy Ghost, amen." But then, instead of proceeding down the middle aisle with an usher who would show him to a seat, he walked alongside the confessionals behind the last row of pews. Ahead of him, leaning against one of the booths, was his best friend, wearing his only suit coat over his only sports jersey, Steelers' safety Paul Martha's number 20. His pants were wrinkled corduroys, his shoes a pair of black wingtips so scuffed they looked as if someone had taken a knife to them.

"Hey-hey, Statsy babe." He held out his palm and Arnie slapped it and Arnie held out his palm and Zook slapped it.

"Shhh." It was the usher a few feet away.

Arnie apologized.

"There are plenty of seats, gentlemen" the usher told them, approaching. "No need to hide back here."

"We'll stand," Arnie said.

"We ain't hidin'," said Zook.

The usher backed away from them with a frown, gritting his teeth to emphasize it; these two were always trouble in football season, always chattering. He seemed about to say something else, but knew better. Besides, a young married couple with a baby were waiting for him. He escorted them to a pew midway through the church.

"Know what I was thinkin'?" Zook whispered.

"What?"

"Maybe we got to go to one of the big sports stores in Pittsburgh to get us a Jets' number twelve. That might be the only chance we got. I even went down to Penney's in the Beaver Valley Mall yesterday. No luck. Hellfire, maybe we gotta go t' New York!"

George Szuchinski was one of those people whose age and appearance had never managed to coincide. He had looked thirty when he was fifteen, had continued to look thirty when he was forty or so, and now, on the downside of fifty, was visibly beginning to disintegrate. His sandy hair was divided into two equal clumps by a swath of scalp down the middle, and his shoulders drooped from his neck at a pronounced angle, as if he were carrying weights in his hands. His eyes were their usual rheumy selves and his nose had been broken so many times---fist fights as a boy, more fights or accidents of one sort or another as he grew older---that it was almost flush with the rest of his face; Arnie sometimes wondered how he managed to breathe through a contraption like that. He had recently given up smoking---maybe in time to save his lungs, his doctor told him, but too late to do his teeth any good; they were almost the same shade of brown as a football.

"Well, today's the big day, huh?" Arnie said, softly.

"You surprised they're startin' 'im?"

"Naw. Taliaferro's the only other quarterback they got and he's no good."

"How ya think he'll do?"

"I don't know, Zee." It was what Arnie had been talking out on the sofa, trying to be as objective as he could. "The Bills' defensive line can rush a passer like nobody's business and their secondary, well, this guy Saimes is the slowest guy back there an' he intercepted three passes against the Oilers last week all by himself."

Two women in the last row of pews, directly in front of them, turned around and reminded them they were in a house of worship, not a beer garden. Arnie grinned back sheepishly and put a finger to his lips.

Zook waited a few seconds, then leaned into Arnie. "I seen Father Daniel before I come in this mornin'. 'E was walkin' over from the sacristy. Guess what 'e said."

"What?"

"You ain't gonna like this, Statsy."

"Tell me."

"He said Namath's a asshole."

"What?"

"Yeah, you know, the old story. 'Cause he signed with the A.F.L. 'stead of the N.F.L. Father said in his book that'd make the Archbishop a asshole."

"Get outta here."

"You know how 'e talks sometimes. But e's okay, ya know that. 'E's a pretty good guy t' have a drink with."

"But still, saying something like that."

"He ain't done yet, though." Zook kept trying to whisper. "No sir, 'cause then 'e says the A.F.L.'s not even a real pro league. Said Namath's wastin' his time an' disgracin' the whole Valley in the process. Best player we ever had aroun' here, an' where's he end up? In the worst league."

The usher was back now, stepping between the two troublemakers and looking from one to the other. "Gentleman, please. It's the same every Sunday. I have to---"

"But the mass ain't started yet," Zook pleaded.

"We'll keep it down this time, sir. Promise," and Arnie elbowed Zook and the two of them bowed their heads. A few seconds later, the church

31

organist, seated on a small, raised platform next to the altar, produced the first few powerful chords of the introduction to the opening hymn, "Praise to the Lord, the Almighty." They bounced off the walls of the old church, and rather than ending, just faded away, as if the walls had absorbed them, drawn them in slowly. When the chords were finally gone, they were followed a pitchpipe, a pipsqueak of a sound, and the church choir followed its lead.

> *Praise to the Lord, the Almighty,*
> *The King of cre-a-tion;*
> *O, my soul, praise Him,*
> *For He is thy health and sal-va-tion.*

AFTER THE SERVICE, Arnie and Zook stood with Father Daniel outside the church.

"Nice sermon," Arnie said.

"Did you think so, too, Zook."

"One of yer best, Father. Really."

"What was it about?" Father Daniel asked.

In the pause that followed, the priest nodded goodbyes to a few of the people leaving St. Veronica's. Then he looked back at the li'l rascals.

"Well, it was just . . . you know, you were saying that a person's got to, um, follow the teachings of the Lord, be holy and all that."

"Yeah," Zook said. "Took the words right outta my mouth, Statsy."

Father Daniel laughed. "You guys're the worst, I swear. Anyhow, what do you think? Do the Jets have a chance?"

"Probably not."

"But we don't really care 'bout the Jets, Father," Zook said. "We're just interested in Namath."

"I know, I know, he's your boy," the father said, nodding. "Everybody needs someone to root for. For you guys it's Broadway Joe. For me it's Jesus. Good luck, fellas," and he began to make small talk with other parishioners.

Arnie and Zook looked at each other. Arnie smiled at his friend, who would have smiled back if he could. If his face would have let him. They had decided not to watch the game together, either at a bar or one of their homes. Each man was afraid that the other's excitement or frustrations would make it hard for him to concentrate, and it was crucial to both of them that their concentration not be broken this afternoon. They wanted to study the plays the way a scientist studies molecules under a microscope, and they wanted silence between the plays so they could listen to the announcers on television tell them what they had just seen and take it under advisement as they made up their own minds about the action. That way, they would be able to discuss the game with each other intelligently tonight at the Excelsior, even before they watched the highlights on the eleven o'clock news.

Arnie held out his hand for Zook's slap and Zook returned the gesture. They said their hopeful goodbyes to each other, then went their separate ways to their separate televisions to carry out their identical missions.

THE JETS WON THE TOSS and elected to receive.

"Shee-owtime," Arnie said, and sat on the coffee table, which was closer to the television than the sofa. He craned his neck, getting his eyes closer still, and rubbed his hands together.

"The Bills are lining up to boot it away," said the play-by-play man on television. "We're just about ready for action here at War Memorial Stadium."

But the action was minimal at first. The Jets ran the ball three times, got stuffed three times.

"Jesus, Joey, throw the goddam thing" Arnie said, knowing full well that coach Weeb Ewbank was calling the plays, not his young quarterback. "They're not paying you four hundred grand to stick the ball in other people's stomachs."

Curly Johnson came into punt for the Jets and a few minutes later, the Bills had a 7-zip lead. That quickly.

Arnie stopped rubbing his hands together, instead smacking them. "Damn!"

Buffalo's old pro quarterback, Jackie Kemp, had completed passes of seventeen and twenty yards in the drive and scored the TD himself when he rolled right on third and goal from the three.

Namath threw one pass on the Jets' second possession, but it was just off the fingertips of tight end John Mackey.

"Christ, Mackey, reach, willya!"

"Curly Johnson in again to punt," said the play-by-play man. "Two possessions for the New Yorkers, no first downs yet."

But the second possession for the Bills went nowhere either. They fumbled once, although recovering themselves for a small gain, and were twice called for being offside. The quarter ended a few minutes later with no more scoring, and Arnie hustled to the kitchen for some of Vinnie's homemade wine, a strangely syrupy drink about which Rosa's cousin like to say, "Twice as thick, twice the kick." Arnie filled an old Huckleberry Hound jelly jar with the beverage, then returned to the living room.

Early in the second quarter, Pete Gogolak, one of the new soccer-style kickers in pro football, who approached the ball from the side, booted it between the uprights from the 34.

10-zip, bad guys.

And then things got worse. Shortly after the Jets had taken over, Joey found himself with a critical third down deep in his own territory and the Bills in an all-out blitz. He had to throw too quickly and the pass drifted behind the intended receiver. George Saimes, who had been a fullback in college but was a safety in the pros, picked off the errant throw for the Bills and ran it back fifteen yards to set up another Gogolak trey.

13-zip.

"Fuckin' Saimes again! What is this?"

Joey was telegraphing his passes, looking only at his primary receiver from the instant the ball was snapped. A rookie mistake, Arnie knew, but a bad one.

And then, in an instant, the kid from Beaver Falls found his groove. On the Jets' third play after the Bills kicked off, he completed his longest pass of the day, 32 yards to Bill Mathis. Then he hit Matt Snell looping out of the backfield for another 21. The Jets were now on the Buffalo 24, their deepest penetration of the game so far.

"Yeah, baby, yeah." Suddenly remembering the wine, Arnie downed his first glop.

But the Bills defense stiffened at this point, intensifying the pass rush, dropping the linebackers, and the Jets had to settle for a field goal from Turner, who approached the ball straight on, like a normal human being.

13-3.

"It's a start," Arnie conceded.

The Jets kick off. Bills fumble the return. Jets recover, offense takes the field. Joe fires a first-down bullet to Snell in the seam of Buffalo zone. Snell lugs the leather for 26 yards. He's tackled on the Bills' eight. Falls forward to the five. First and goal, Jets!

Arnie pumps his fist in the air.

Namath---calm, cool a rookie no more---barks out signals. Fakes handoff to Snell off-tackle. Lobs ball to Mathis in end zone. He's all by himself. Touchdown, Jets!

13-10.

"Yessss!"

And that was the way the score stood at the midway point, when the two teams jogged off the field to tweak their strategies for the second half. The play-by-play man urged everybody to stay tuned for the famed Canisius College Marching Band and a halftime show they'd never forget. They were known, he said, for their dazzling corps of majorettes.

"I was watching them practice yesterday," the color man said. "They're like the Radio City Rockettes."

In his head, Stats had Joe at 6 for 15 for 113 yards, one touchdown and one interception. A shitty percentage, but a lot of yards, almost twenty per completion.

That was when the doorbell rang.

"Oh, no," he said. "You *gotta* be kidding me." If it hadn't been halftime, he wouldn't have budged. Still, he proceeded warily, getting up and going to the window. He folded back a corner of the curtain and looked out. What he saw did not seem possible. He shook his head, blinked, and looked out again. Still there.

"What the *hell?*"

Standing on his front stoop was a true-life majorette.

He carefully closed the curtain, hoping he hadn't been spotted.

He recognized the uniform. The girl was a Bridger. He even thought she looked familiar, that he had seen this particular girl's face before. She was decked out in full Friday-night regalia: the off-white outfit with red epaulets and red piping, the boots that almost reached her kneecaps and the skirt that barely covered half her thighs.

She rang the bell again.

"Holy smokers," and he turned down the volume on the television, hustling to the front door, turning the knob. He forgot to pat down his hair, but didn't think he had enough to matter. He opened the door.

The majorette hit him full force.

"Hi there, sir."

"Hi." He brought his hand to his mouth and cleared his throat into it. "I mean, well, hello."

"I hope I'm not disturbing you."

"Oh, no. I---"

"I know everybody watches the game on Sunday afternoon but the last house I was at it was halftime and the Steelers were already losing 23-3. I guess you know that, though."

Her hair was long and honey-brown, falling in bangs to the middle of her forehead and hanging down to her shoulders, where it flipped up an inch or two. Eyes big and dark brown, and aimed right at him, beaming like a pair of flashlights. Her lashes were so long that Arnie imagined them making a sound when they fluttered, a kind of whooshing.

"You look like you used to play football," she said.

Arnie nodded. "Tackle, offense and defense. Long time ago."

"For Ambridge?"

"Bridger through and through."

"Well, that's good" she said, "because I'm selling candy for the Ambridge High School Band. We're trying to raise money for new uniforms next year. Do you think maybe you might be interested in buying some?"

"Candy?"

"Uh-huh. And it's really delicious, too. One hundred percent milk chocolate."

"Oh, chocolate. I thought you meant, you know, candy-type candy."

She smiled back at him: perfect white teeth framed by delicate pink lips. Could someone who looked like that possibly be real?

"And, of course, it's for a good cause, too. Our uniforms are in awful shape."

Yours isn't, he had the good sense not to say aloud. The girl's breasts seemed to squirm under the uniform's constraints, stretching the fabric beyond what the manufacturer had ever intended. He didn't think it was such a good idea for him to notice her like that, and was an even worse idea for her to notice him noticing, but what was a man supposed to do, especially one who so seldom came into contact with a beautiful young woman possessed of such gravity-defying mounds of flesh. As quickly as he could, he forced his gaze elsewhere, but he was not as quick as he should have been.

"So what do you think?"

"Huh?" Was it a trick question?

"The candy, silly."

"Oh," he said, exhaling with relief. "Well, it, uh . . . it doesn't sound like the kinda decision a person ought to rush into. Would you like to, um, come in for a little bit?" He calculated that he had another fifteen minutes, max, until the second half started.

The majorette followed Arnie into the living room, a room whose predominant feature, it suddenly hit him, was doilies. They were everywhere, and browning with age like parchment: doilies on the arms and back of the sofa, on the coffee table in front of it, on the tables that flanked it; doilies on the arms and back of the chintz-covered wingback chair across the room, on the small mahogany table next to it, atop the television. Centered on the TV doily was a ceramic donkey hitched to a ceramic cart full of ceramic African violets. The lampshades were covered with cellophane and a dimpled plastic runner made the path from hallway to sofa. It was a woman's room, he realized, so much a woman's room.

Thank God there's a football game on.

"Is that the Steelers?" the majorette said, slipping the purse from her shoulder and setting it on the coffee table.

"No, that's the Jets and Bills. I'm watching the A.F.L. today, not the N.F.L. It's a real change of pace for me."

"Oh, right. The Jets. That's Joe Willie Namath's team.

Arnie nodded.

"My dad was telling me about him the other day and he said he might turn out to be the greatest athlete who ever came out of the Valley."

Arnie kept nodding. "Sounds like your dad really knows his oats."

37

The wine glass was still half full and the majorette picked it up, turning it around in her hand. "Hey, Huckleberry Hound."

Arnie took the glass from her. Doilies, cartoon characters---not the impression he ought to be making. "Have a seat, miss." He slid the glass behind the base of the lamp on the end table.

The majorette displayed herself on the sofa, pushing up her sleeves, curling some hair around her ears, and tugging at her skirt, which kept sliding above her knees regardless.

On television the halftime show was well underway. Arnie lowered himself into the chintzy chair. He had a bad angle on the screen, but could still see the Canisius College majorettes marching across the field, flinging their batons into outer space and catching them effortlessly, spinning them behind their backs, around their necks---doing all sorts of tricks, some of them executed so quickly that the batons disappeared and blurs took their places.

Then he looked back at the majorette in his living room. Then back at the TV, the living room, the TV, quick flicks of the eyes. Majorettes everywhere. On television, on the sofa---it was dizzying. He squeezed the arm of his chair, tightening his grip on reality as much as on the furniture. How many people in the whole Beaver Valley were going through something like this!

"Do you think you might want to buy some?"

"Oh, yeah," Arnie said. "The chocolate. How much is it?"

She screwed up her face to soften the blow. "It's a dollar and a half a bar."

Arnie did his best to ho-hum the news. Dollar and a half, no big deal.

"But they're really big bars, not like the kind you get in vending machines. Like this," she said, and held her hands apart like a fisherman exaggerating his catch.

"Dollar and a half a bar . . . dollar and a half a bar . . . Do I have to pay now, today?"

"You pay when the candy's delivered." The majorette folded a leg under her and sat on it. "Thursday, it'd be."

"Most people, when you stop at their house, how many bars do they buy?"

"Oh, the average person buys one or two, I guess. I had one woman give me an order for four, that's my record so far."

"Four?"

"Uh-huh."

"Okay," Arnie said, "I'll take a dozen."

The majorette's gulp was audible. "What did you say?"

"A dozen. Twelve."

"Are you serious?"

"Sure am."

"Oh, my God!" Then her smile sank into her jaw. "Wait just a minute." She was suddenly cautious, stroking her chin. "You're not one of those people who . . . I mean, one of those . . . You're really *serious*?"

Arnie was nodding yet again. "I'm totally on the up and up, miss, and that's the truth. You ask anybody about Arnie Castig. They'll tell you. When I say I'll take a dozen bars, that means I'll take a dozen bars."

The majorette's smile re-appeared in an instant, and she batted her eyelids. "Oh, my God. You know, this might make me the top seller in the whole band. I never thought I had a chance to be tops, but now maybe I do. Thank you so much, sir."

"Do you get anything for being tops?"

"Free passes to the movie and a hundred dollar scholarship to the college of your choice from the Lions Club.

"Oh, so you want to go to college, do you?"

She confirmed that she did, but was not certain which one yet.

"Well, I'm sure that any school would want to have someone like you as a student."

"Anyhow," she said, getting down to business, "twelve bars---this is just too much," and she dug into her purse for an order pad and pen. "Wait'll I tell M.A."

Arnie glanced over at the television. The band had finished its halftime show and was marching off the field. As it departed, the first half statistics were flashed on the screen and the play-by-play man recited them. Arnie could barely hear him, but didn't need to. "Joe Namath, the rookie quarterback getting his trial by fire as a pro, was 6 for 15 for 113 yards. One TD, one interception."

The majorette began to write. "Okay, then. Quantity, twelve. Wowee! Now, could you just give me your name again? I'm sorry, I should remember."

"Castig. Arnold Castig. Well, Arnie. What's---?"

"And the address here, Mr. Castig?"

"Four-twenty-two Maple. What's your name, miss, if you don't mind me asking?"

"Debbie."

"Oh, I see. Debbie what?"

"Savukas. And your phone number, Mr. Castig?"

"Congress 8-4874."

"Four-eight-seven-four. Well, I guess that's all I need to know. Oh, one more thing. Do you want your chocolate bars with or without almonds?"

"Without, definitely. I don't like nuts."

She checked a box on the order form. "Almonds are an extra dime a bar anyhow. I should've told you."

"Debbie Savukas. Why does that name sound familiar? Oh, I know," Arnie said, "you're the girl who had her picture in the paper the other day."

"Mmm-hmm. It was for publicity for today. Trying to get the word out we were coming. I'm the captain of the majorettes this year, so I'm the one they chose."

"Captain? Hey, that's terrific. Congratulations."

"Aw, it's not big deal. It's just because I'm a senior." She tore the sheet of carbon paper from between the original and the copy of his order and gave him the copy. She clipped her pen to the order pad and tossed it back into her purse. Then she stood and offered her hand. "Thanks again for this, Mr. Castig. I can't tell you how much I appreciate what you did. It's the best thing that's happened to me all week."

"Think nothing of it," he replied, also rising, shaking her hand and delighting in the soft, uncallused feel of it. He led her to the front door and opened it. "I just hope it makes you number one, is all. If it doesn't, you come back and maybe I can buy a couple more bars. We've gotta get you that scholarship."

With the majorettes in Buffalo having left the field, the majorette in Arnie's living room was also about to depart.

The play-by-play man softly announced the second half kickoff. It was an end-over-ender, out of the end zone for a touchback. Holy smokers, he thought, what a halftime it had been for Stats Castig!

"So I'll see you Thursday, then?"

"You bet. I'll be here Thursday with the goodies."

"I guess you'll come after school, huh?"

"Yes, but don't worry if you're not around. I'll just leave the box at the front door."

"Oh, I'll be here. Don't worry about that. What time does school get out?"

"Okay," she said, "see you then. Bye for now."

Did she hear him? Was she ignoring him? No, she wouldn't do that.

"And, really, thanks again."

"You're welcome again."

She giggled, a tinkling sound as she began skipping down the sidewalk toward the street. "I keep thanking you," she said over her shoulder.

Arnie closed the door behind her and watched through a small, circular pane of glass as she crossed Maple to the Borgia's. They were a bunch of tightwads; he should've warned her. She'd be lucky if they even bought an almond. Debbie knocked at the Borgia's door and as she waited, turned to Arnie and waved. She couldn't have seen his face in the window from that distance, but knew it would be there anyhow. Arnie couldn't figure it out, but there was no time to try. He hustled back to the television.

The Bills had the ball. As he turned up the volume, he learned that it was "second down and seven. Fullback Cookie Gilchrist the deep man in the 'I.' So much had happened at halftime, and yet he missed only one play. "Kemp drops back to pass---no, it's a fake. He gives it to Bake Turner on an end-around . . ."

ON SEPTEMBER 26, 1965, the Buffalo Bills beat the New York Jets 33-21. But Joe Namath, the rookie quarterback from Beaver Falls, Pennsylvania, in the heart of steel country, completed 19 of 40 passes for 282 yards and two touchdowns. It averaged out to 14.84 yards per completion, although Arnie needed a pencil to figure that one out. In the second half, after Joe Willie got his bearings, he hit on 13 of 25 for 169 yards, a touchdown, and no interceptions. It was, as one of the next day's papers would put it, one of the most auspicious performances ever by a quarterback making his first start in the pros. And he didn't have to look up "auspicious." He knew it. Come to think of it, he had probably known it even before he started his new job and gotten pretty good at crossword puzzles.

On the same afternoon, the San Francisco Forty-Niners beat the Pittsburgh Steelers 31-17, making the latter's record 0 and 2 for the young season. As for the Pirates, they eked out a win over the Cubs, but still were nowhere near .500. They had just three more meaningless games to play before going home for another long winter.

City of goddam losers. It's all they were.

He thought about taking a nap. Usually, that's what he did after the Sunday football game. But not today. Today he was too charged up.

Monday,
September 27,
1965

ZOOK WAS IN THE ALLEY behind his apartment, hosing down a white, 1959 Ford Econoline van through which circles of rust had begun to spread like mold through pieces of stale bread. The grill had rusted, the fenders had rusted, the bumper had rusted---the rust had rusted. There were parts of the body you could push a finger through; the radio antenna had been snapped in half and only a few shards remained of the plastic taillight covers, so that the bulbs underneath glowed clear instead of red.

Zook did more to the van than just wash it. He drove it on the job, drove it off the job, paying for a percentage of the gas, oil, maintenance and insurance, and kept it parked in his garage at night. But he did not own it. The van was the property of his employer, the Spee-Dee Diaper Service. Its name appeared in large blue script on the side panels, except that, instead of a hyphen between the *Spee* and the *Dee*, there was the face of a smiling baby, with the word *soffft* in a cartoon balloon over his head. Smaller versions of the logo appeared on the driver's side door and on both doors in the rear of the van.

Zook was due at the laundry at nine. Give or take. Once there he would change into a bright white shirt with the *Spee-Dee* logo on the pocket. And he would slip into a bright white pair of pants with a bright white belt and a pair of bright white sneakers that he was responsible for touching up with soap and water whenever necessary---no stains allowed by Spee-Dee management. He would wear a garrison-style cap of bright white paper, a new one every day. Obviously, "white" was not good enough for *Spee-Dee*; "bright" was also mandatory. In fact, when Zook stepped

43

out of his van at someone's house for a pickup or delivery, he should have been radiant, a vision of purity and innocence.

But it didn't work out that way. There was something about Zook, something inexplicable, puzzling to the eye: surround Zook in white and the white went gray; deck him out in clothes that had just been pressed and in moments they would appear to have been slept in for a week. In the popular comic strip "Peanuts," there was a character who brought his own cloud of dust with him wherever he went, like a satchel always at the end of his arm. His name was Pig Pen. Only when one could tell that Zook was in the best of possible moods could the nickname be used to his face.

It was twenty to nine when Arnie strolled into the alley.

"Hey-hey, Statsy-babe." Zook freed his hands by tossing the hose around the van's antenna, pointing the nozzle at the ground, and flipping the sponge onto the hood. "Gimme five."

Slap.

"How's it goin', buddy?"

Reverse hands, slap again.

They did not have much to say about the game this morning, having thoroughly dissected it over a few Iron City drafts at the Excelsior Tavern last night. But something had occurred to Zook since then.

"Listen, I gotta tell ya. I was thinkin' when I got up this mornin' that, well, see, we both know it's gonna take 'im a while. But maybe, jus' maybe, it won't be as long as we think. 'Cause ya take that second half yesterday---an' Joey was fantastic! I mean, unbelievable, ya get right down t' it. I ain't ready t' put 'im in the Hall of Fame yet, I'm not sayin' nothin' like 'at. But still. Ya know what I mean?"

Arnie did. Don Meredith, Zeke Bratkowski, Roman Gabriel---none of them could have done any better.

Zook turned off the nozzle, stifling a few coughs. "But that fuckin' Kemp, was 'at guy somethin' 'er what!"

"Twenty-two for 37 for 292 yards, two TDs and no swipes. That's some kinda afternoon."

"He was 'specially murder in that third quarter," Zook said, "when the Jets were tryin' t' come back. 'Member?"

"Eight for 10 for 104 and two first down scrambles on third and long," Arnie said, and shoved his fists into the front pockets of his pants and kicked a pebble under the van.

They had been friends, the two men, since the day in kindergarten when Arnie, having gotten a new tricycle for his birthday, pedaled over to Zook's and offered him a ride. It was so long ago, so hard to remember. Was Arnie lonely and, sensing a similar loneliness in Zook, trying to enlist him as a buddy? After all, both of them stood by themselves most of the time at recess. Or it was that Arnie, simply being the nice boy that people always described, was just doing a favor for the new kid in the neighborhood? A little of both, maybe? Well, it hardly mattered now.

"Uh, Zook, listen, there's something I gotta ask you."

"Fire away, pal."

"Anyone pay you a visit yesterday afternoon?"

"Ya mean, durin' the game?"

"Yeah," Arnie said, "did anybody come by your place?"

"Who's gonna come by while I'm watchin' the game? Who *ever* comes by, 'cept you? 'Sides, I hear somebody knockin' at the door, I ain't answerin'. That's all there is to it. You wouldn't, neither."

"All right, another question." Arnie backed up a few steps, half-sitting on one of the garbage cans against the side of Zook's apartment building. "You like chocolate?"

Zook gave it a few seconds, longer than necessary. "Well, I don't know what you're getting' at, but . . . what kinda chocolate?"

"Regular chocolate, I don't know. Big bars of the stuff."

"Sure, I like chocolate bars. Who don't?"

"Good, good, glad to hear it."

"What're ya getting' at, Statsy? Somethin' weird goin' on here."

"Listen, I need a favor from you, okay? Here's the deal. You give me three dollars and I'll give you two of the best-tasting chocolate bars you ever had in your life."

"You'll gimme *how* many?"

"Well, two, but---"

"*Two* friggin' chocolate bars fer *three* cimoleans?"

"Yeah, but it's not like it sounds. See---"

45

"How's about this. How's about you give *me* three bucks, I give *you* two hunks of chocolate, an' I keep the change, like maybe two-eighty. How's 'at sound, palsy?"

Arnie shook his head. "I'm not talking about the normal kinda chocolate bars, Zee. These're big ones, like ingot molds, you know? Probably take you a week to eat one."

"I'm supposed supposed t' believe chocolate bars like ingot molds? I think maybe ya better clue me in here."

Arnie did. He told his friend about Debbie's visit yesterday and how badly the members of the band needed new uniforms and what a great contribution Zook could make by purchasing some of their wares. He also said that, in his opinion, the people who lived in a community had a responsibility to support the schools in that community. The students in those schools, after all, were the leaders of tomorrow, and they should be encouraged in all of their pursuits. Arnie said the more encouragement they got from adults, the better leaders they would be one day and the better the future would be for all concerned. There was, he concluded, a lot more involved here than just chocolate bars.

Zook paused, giving Arnie a chance to catch his breath. "You memorize 'at?"

"It just came out."

"Not bad, not bad." Working a finger into one of his ears, Zook excavated a small clump of wax with what remained of a much chomped-upon fingernail. "Yer really somethin', man." He momentarily examined the wax, then blew it away. He said to his friend, "You buy some?"

Arnie nodded.

"How much?"

"Well . . ." his glasses had slipped down his nose; he pushed them back up. "Twelve bars."

"*What?*"

"Yeah, twelve."

"A dozen?"

"That's what they call twelve, Zee."

"Y' can't be serious."

"I put my money where my mouth is."

Zook slid onto the hood of the truck and wedged his feet behind the bumper. "Man, whattaya gonna do with a shitload of chocolate like that, Statsy? Forget about eatin' it---ya ain't even got room t' store the stuff." He started digging into his other ear. "Rosa know 'bout this?"

"Didn't get around to it yet."

"So when ya gonna tell 'er?"

"I'll cross that bridge when I come to it."

"Aw right," Zook said after a few seconds, "I guess I'll cross it, too." He fished into the pocket of his sweatpants for a small wad of bills, peeling off three of them and handing them over. "Here. What the hell. Easy come, easy go."

"Thanks, Zook," Arnie said. "I'm serious, thanks a lot. You won't regret this." He stuffed the bills into his own pants. "I'll make sure Debbie knows you're the man who bought two of the bars."

"Debbie? Ya even know 'er name, huh? What is she, yer girlfriend er somethin'?

"Yeah, right, a high school girl's my girlfriend."

"Well, ya---"

"I just talked to her for a while yesterday. So I know her name. She knows mine. No big deal."

"How do I get my share of the stash?" Zook said.

"I'll have the whole load of them at the end of the week. I'll bring yours over to you. Don't sweat it."

"Okay, jus' tell me one thing."

"Name it."

"This Debbie, that suckered ya inta---"

"Nobody *suckered* me, Zook."

"This young lay-dee what suggested ya buy 'er product?"

"Yeah?

"She a looker?"

"What the hell's that got to do with anything?"

"Scale of, say, one t' ten, where's she at?"

"All I wanna do is help the band, Zook. That's the only thing I'm thinking about here, being a good citizen."

"One t' ten."

"Fourteen, easy."

"Two touchdowns."

"You got it, pal."

"Hah!" It might have started out as a single syllable, but after Zook coughed once or twice more, he broke into an eruption of laughter. He slapped the parts of his fender that were strong enough to withstand such a blow without flaking away. "I knew it. Goddam, I jus' knew it. Whattaya gonna do next, Stats, take 'er t' the sock hop? 'Member that song? 'Let's go to the hop, oh bay-bee, let's go to the hop . . .'"

"That's it, I had enough, I'm out of here," and Arnie dropped down from the garbage can and began departing from the alley more quickly than he had entered. He stopped long enough to wave over his shoulder at Zook, a sign of amicable parting more than of dismissal.

"Hey, Stats. Statsy. Hang on, I just thoughta somethin'."

He didn't stop, didn't ask.

"Maybe Debbie's on my route, ya know? Fer the super-size diapers? What's 'er last name? I could drop off her undies an' pick up the candy myself. Save ya a trip, huh?" and his laughter was as at least as loud now as it had been before.

Arnie did not look back again. He had heard enough of his friend's laughter for one day; it was among the world's most offensive sounds, and he could not bear it anymore. Nor could he bear any more of the sight. For Zook had a quirk, more like a physical deformity. He was the only person Arnie knew, the only one he had ever seen, who could laugh without smiling. He could chuckle---no smile. Could guffaw---no smile. Just about burst his sides open---still no smile. The result was a sound that conveyed menace more than mirth, one that seemed to be coming from someone else while Zook tried to figure out what was so funny.

He explained when the two of them first met, on that kindergarten tricycle ride, that there was something wrong with the muscles in his face, that they could not pull his lips up. Especially deficient was his zygomaticus major, the most polysyllabic term Zook could ever master, although he would not be able to do so until junior high. It was the muscle that determined the angle of the mouth, front and back, and in Zook it was frozen, unable to rise; ergo, no smile. But Jesus, Arnie thought sometimes, how strong does a muscle have to be to elevate your lips half an inch? Couldn't he do exercises or something? No, Zook, insisted, and stuck to his story.

The queer, throaty chortle of straight-lipped laughter trailed Arnie through the alley like a stray animal, one of those creatures that simply cannot be shooed away. It was unusual for him to hear his friend laugh like that. He didn't laugh very much at all---maybe because he knew how bizarre the sound and sight were---and almost never so enthusiastically. It made Arnie feel better about the whole transaction, even though he was the butt of the joke.

AT TWENTY MINUTES TO FOUR, as Zook was making his last few stops of the day for Spee-Dee, Arnie returned home from a quick hike to the drugstore. Rosa was in the kitchen making the meal he would take with him to work. He called a hello to her, then climbed the stairs to their bedroom. He tossed his purchases, the early editions of the two afternoon newspapers, onto the bed. Then he turned on the radio atop the dresser: the Ambridge station, WAMB, 1420 on your dial.

". . . always a heavily requested song here on 'Melodies and Memories,'" said the disc jockey, a man even older than Arnie. "It's G.I. Jo herself, Miss Jo Stafford, ably assisted as usual by Mr. Paul Weston and the boys, with a little ditty that takes us all the way back to World War II. The Big One, as we call it now. Do you remember 'I'll Be Seeing You'?"

"Do I?" Arnie said. He had probably heard a dozen versions of the song in his life, but Jo Stafford's was easily the best. The lush violins that started things off, the harp rippling underneath---and then the lady herself, one of Arnie's favorite singers ever, her voice as distinctive a sound as he had ever known, one of the most soothing, and yet, at the same time, the most melancholy. Vocal cords of pure satin. As was his way with the tunes on "Melodies and Memories," he sang along, but quietly, wanting the recording artist to take the lead.

I'll be seeing you
In all the old familiar places
That this heart of mine embraces
All day through.

49

He was . . . what, twenty-eight years old when he first heard the song? Unfit for military duty because of flat feet but more than fit to be a civilian, to work the occasional double-shift at American Bridge without complaint---anything for the war effort. He had a full head of hair back then and only a small paunch; drove a Studebaker that was shiny if not new; hoped to be a foreman at one of the basic mills before long, which would make his dad proud despite his son's having been declared 4-F; and hoped all the more to cement his place in young Rosa Yacovoni's heart.

He would take her dancing in Pittsburgh on weekends at West View, the amusement park with the slightly warped bandstand. The bands were never as good as the ones on the radio, of course, but were good enough; Arnie and Rosa were young lovers, not music critics. They would hug each other as tightly as they dared, sometimes actually grinding at the midsection, while submerging themselves in the music that was the night's only sound. The roller coaster didn't run at after dark; the calliope on the merry-go-round was too far away to hear.

He stopped singing and started humming as he opened the *Pittsburgh Press* to the sports section and began to read.

NAMATH SCARES BILLS
WITH 2 TOUCHDOWN PASSES,
BUT JETS LOSE, 33-21

Buffalo (UPI)---Joe Namath made a $400,000 impression. The New York Jets' rookie quarterback also made his share of mistakes, but he turned in one of the greatest passing shows any rookie has ever put on in his first professional start against perhaps the roughest defense in the entire American Football League. Namath, signed off the University of Alabama campus for a whopping 6-figure bonus, piled up 282 yards through the air, including 169 in the second half. He hit on 19 of 40 attempts, including a pair for touchdowns.

However, Jack Kemp, a 9-year veteran quarterback for the Buffalo Bills had an even better day, perhaps his finest ever in a Bills' uniform, passing his team to a 33-21 triumph over the underdog Jets.

That was it, the whole article. It was good as far as it went, but there had to be more, Arnie thought: detailed statistics, a rundown of the scoring drives, and, what he wanted most to see, quotes from the players. Where *was* all of that? Maybe what he had read was the beginning of a longer story that, for reasons of space, had to be cut. Maybe the *Beaver Valley Times*, being more of a hometown paper for Joe, had printed the whole thing. But when he looked in the *Times* he found exactly the same coverage that the *Press* had provided, the same two paragraphs, word for word.

"Crapola," he said, and folded up the papers, leaving them on the bed in case Rosa wanted to look at them, although she never did. "I shoulda checked out the damn stories before I forked over my money." Tomorrow, though, the New York papers would arrive at the Ambridge library. He had no doubt that they would have the kind of coverage he was looking for. Maybe even a picture on the front page. Wouldn't that be something!

I'll see you in the morning sun
And when the night is through,
I'll be looking at the moon,
But I'll be seeing you.

"There you have it, ladies and gentlemen," said the long-time WAMB disc jockey Lou Czygmont, "Miss Jo Stafford and Mr. Paul Whiteman. 'I'll Be Seeing You.' Kind of ironic, though, because as we've been telling you all day today, that starting Thursday, the very day after tomorrow, we *won't* be seeing you. None of your old friends will be seeing you anymore because we're going to bring you a great batch of new friends. New friends, new music, and you take my word for it, you're going to love it all. That's Thursday, everybody, on the new WAMB."

"*What?*" Arnie stood and stared down at the radio, hands on his hips as if demanding an answer from the little box and threatening violence if he didn't get it. "What kind of shit is this? *New* WAMB? What the hell's the matter with the *old* WAMB?" He couldn't figure it out. Was Lou talking about retiring, about all the WAMB disc jockeys retiring? At the same time? It was the only radio station he had ever listened to, ever since he was a teenager, and the only station that brought back memories of the days when music made his body tingle, created a reaction in him that was almost like floating.

51

"Oh, well," he said, after what he realized was a disproportionately long time spent glaring at the radio, listening to commercials, "they can't be doing anything all *that* crazy. We'll just have to see Thursday."

But somehow, he couldn't get the notion of a new WAMB out of his head. It didn't sound like a good idea. It sounded like a threat.

HIS UNIFORM AND HAT were in the middle drawer of the dresser and, as he usually did, he smiled ruefully as he took them out. A person who wore a uniform and hat often had a prestigious job. Zook didn't, of course, but athletes wore uniforms, and soldiers and policemen, even mailmen---people like that. Arnie looked like a policeman when dressed, at least from a distance, but he wasn't. He didn't carry a gun or a nightstick; he didn't have any prestige; he didn't frighten any bad guys.

He glanced behind him at the clock on the nightstand. Plenty of time yet. He decided to indulge himself, give in to the impulse that struck him once in a while but that he never understood. He fell back on the bed and thought about what he wore on the last afternoon when he could earn a living without a uniform. Those were the days, all right.

You go to my head,
And you linger like a haunting refrain,
And I find you spinning round in my brain,
Like the bubbles in a glass of champagne.

Arnie got up for a moment and turned off the radio. If it had been Sinatra's version of "You Go To My Head," he would have left it on. But it wasn't. It was Russ Columbo or one of those other second-raters, and he didn't want to hear it.

He dropped back onto the bed again, lying supine.

"Statsy!" To this day he could hear Rudy bellowing his name in the Fabricating Mill, although he swore he had no memory of it at the time. "Statsy! Aw, no, man! *Nooo*!" The date was October 3, 1962, a little more than three years ago.

He closed his eyes.

ACTUALLY, THE AMERICAN BRIDGE COMPANY had two fabricating mills back then, and it was late in the afternoon when a monster semi with New Jersey plates on it drove into the "B" mill. Wheezing as if it were on its last few miles, it entered through a side entrance. Strapped onto its platform from bulkhead to taillights, a full load, were steel plates, each measuring two feet by two feet by four inches and weighing in excess of a hundred pounds. Eventually they would be made into coke-quenching cars for the Wheeling-Pittsburgh Steel Company's Weirton, West Virginia Works, but there were too many orders ahead of it; for now, they simply had to be stored.

Arnie watched the semi from a stool that straddled the tracks of an unused railroad siding. He wore a thick flannel shirt with the sleeves rolled up to his elbows and the grease stains dark across the light plaid pattern. His khaki pants were less stained, his iron-tipped workboots new and not stained at all. He had bought them a size too large to accommodate the pair of thick gray sweatsocks he always wore with them.

He waved at the driver, then pointed behind him, showing him where to park the truck. He noted the time on a clipboard. It was when he looked up again, turning around on the stool to watch the semi approach, that he noticed the driver was colored. Arnie had never seen a colored man in charge of such a payload before.

The driver eased the truck slowly along the siding until Arnie ran his finger across his throat. The colored man killed the engine. A few moments later, he opened the door and took a step, then a jump, down to the ground. Over his shoulder was an army issue duffel bag.

"Hey, welcome to Ambridge, bud," Arnie said, approaching him. "You're new on this run."

"Yep," he said, "first time up this neck of the woods."

"Well, it's good to have you here," Arnie said and, after shaking his hand, he gave him the clipboard and pen. Taking a piece of gum out of his pocket, he unwrapped it and slid it into his mouth. Then, as the driver signed off on his cargo, Arnie offered him a stick, too.

"'Preciate it, man, thanks. But I'm so damn tired I don't think I got me the energy to chew." He was a young fellow, probably just a few years out of high school, and he seemed puzzled. Arnie guessed that white men probably weren't very nice to him as a rule, and thought that was too bad.

"If you can just tell me how to get to the Fox, I'd be much obliged."

Arnie gave him directions to Ambridge's only hotel, maybe a fifteen-minute walk from the mill.

"What kinda joint is it?"

"Great if you're starting a collection of bed bugs. That's what I heard, anyhow."

"Just so they crawl on me gentle," the driver said, but played it safe, not offering his hand to Arnie for another shake. A colored fellow never knew how far he could go. But: "Look forward t' seein' you again," he said, and trudged off for a few hours sleep before he would report to a different mill at AB and pick up another semi bound for another factory in another town.

"Have a good nap," Arnie shouted after him.

Minutes later, an ancient crane chugged into the mill through the front entrance. It approached the semi warily, then circled it and came to a stop at the rear. Rudy Battaglia sat high behind the controls in the cab, his Pirates' cap perched backwards, catcher-style, on his head. He looked down at Arnie and shrugged.

Arnie pushed his stool out of the way and pointed behind him, to the remains of a concrete wall that had once been a section of a loading dock. With the toes of his boots, he began to trace a large square in the dirt floor of the mill, using the wall as one of its sides.

"We'll stack 'em here, Roo," he shouted up to his partner. He could barely be heard over the engine's grinding.

"Whatever you say, Stats."

But he should not have said *that*. Arnie should have paid more attention to an old sheave wheel leaning unsteadily against the wall's corner. It was a big one, about three feet in diameter and weighing close to two hundred pounds. It had been part of a grab bucket that was taken apart for cleaning with sandblast shot, and BB-sized pellets of shot lay all over the ground. The men on the previous shift, who had done the cleaning, had not swept up afterward. Arnie should have paid more attention to that, too.

Planting himself a few feet in front of the wall, he signaled up to the crane. "Okay, Roo," he said, "ready to roll."

Rudy flashed a thumbs-up, then cranked the crane into gear; it lurched forward a foot or two and reared up for the moment like a cubist's version of a pterodactyl, ready to strike. Then he swung the cab around so that the arm of the crane hung over semi-load of plates.

"Here we go," Rudy said.

It was Arnie's job to off-load the platform. He would hook the arm of the crane into a hole in a corner of the steel plates and guide them into piles within the square he had marked off on the floor. He had emptied semis dozens of times before in various AB mills, sometimes as crane operator, more often as floor man. There was nothing to it in either role, not as long as you kept your wits about you, and less than twenty minutes after he and Rudy had begun, half a dozen plates had been laid. That was enough for the first pile.

The men started on the second. It was just as Arnie unhooked the new pile's top plate that it happened. His attention had not wandered, he had not gotten careless, had not misjudged the trajectory of the plate as it arched toward him. Nor was he sulking over the fact that, after almost three and a half decades at American Bridge, with not so much as a single black mark to his name, he was still not a day-shift foreman in one of the basic mills, and had in fact been bypassed for such a position, one he had been sure he would get, just the week before.

No, what happened was that he simply slipped on some of the sandblast shot and lost his balance, so that instead of unfastening the hook from the plate, he inadvertently swung the plate into the sheave wheel. It wobbled for a few seconds; Arnie thought it would fall back against the wall. Instead, it seemed to bounce against the wall and toppled in the other direction, away from its resting place and into his left leg, where it met all the resistance of a sledge hammer encountering a piece of plywood. Without so much as a whimper, probably already in shock, Arnie fell to the ground, the sheave wheel following him down and blanketing him from waist to foot.

"Stats!" Rudy cried out. "Statsy! Son of a fuckin' *bitch*!"

He tugged on the hand brake and, ignoring the small ladder built into the side of the cab, leaped to the ground. At that moment, he would later admit, he was not even sure Arnie was alive, so still was he lying, so ashen had his face become in no more than a second or two. He settled on his haunches next to his partner; his chest was still laboring in and out. Rudy Battaglia was a powerful man in the prime of his years, a high school athlete who still lifted weights three or four times a week at the

YMCA---but a sheave wheel! How in the hell was he going to pick up something as heavy as a sheave wheel! Simple, he would later tell the story in a number of Ambridge tap rooms; he did what he had to do because he had to do it.

"Mother Mary, be with me, baby," he said, and then gripped the wheel with both hands, yanking so hard that the violence of his exertion shook his head and arms and jaw, like the last shivers of a man freezing to death. His eyelids squeezed shut and his teeth were gnashing, top row against bottom; another part of Rudy's future tap room tale was that he thought he was making powder out of his enamel. He managed to raise the terrible weight an inch or two over Arnie's legs. But for how long?

"Stats," he gasped, "slide yourself out, Stats! Slide your legs out of there, can you do it?"

Arnie never remembered moving; in fact, he would never recall the moment he lost his footing on the sandblast shot in the first place, or the sheave wheel's falling on him, a weight from the depths of hell. But somehow, numbly, he did as he was told, a voice for self-preservation deep within him joining with Rudy's voice to urge him on.

"That's it, Stats, that's it, buddy! C'mon, now, more, more, a little more, dammit! Do it for me, baby, slide those legs!"

Arnie was clawing the ground with his fingers, digging in for traction. His gray skin turned grayer; his jaw sagged and his head flopped onto the dirt. But he did not quit. He kept scraping his way out, pulling himself sideways toward Rudy, finally hauling out his legs as if it were they, not the steel plates, that had to be put into storage.

"Yeah, man, yeah! You did it, buddy! You're a bear, Statsy, a fuckin' bear!"

It's amazing how things like this work out sometimes, Arnie would later think---proof, perhaps, that God is not the inattentive being He so often seems. The instant, the very micro-second, that his legs were clear, he heard the sheave wheel crash to the ground, throwing up a cloud of dirt encompassing both men. Rudy had run out of adrenalin-induced strength precisely as he needed it no more. He coughed and tried to fan the dirt away. Christian though he was, he dropped onto all fours like a Muslim facing Mecca and whispered his gratitude to Jesus's old lady.

Then he saw the blood on his knuckles and underneath his fingernails. He kept coughing as he wiped his hands on his shirt, beginning to feel the pain in the small of his back; somebody had taken a knife to it and sliced clear through to the chest. He dropped perfectly flat, not even capable of panting. Nor capable of looking over at the man whose life he had just saved.

Arnie did not look at him, either. He did not try to move his body, any of its parts. He did not even try to breathe, but the breaths came naturally, pushing against his battered ribs. The hell with it, he thought, and passed out.

THE REST OF THE DAY'S OCCURRENCES, and there were many, never became part of his memory bank. The next thing he knew it was morning, and he had been tucked into the crisp linen of a bed in a double room at the Beaver Valley General Hospital. The other bed was empty. An oxygen mask covered his nose and mouth and the elastic band fit too snugly over his cheekbones. His leg was in a cast that stretched from crotch to heel and when a nurse pulled back the sheets to give him a look at it, he marveled at all that plaster, so much weight. He didn't have a very good view of his toes---why in the hell were they so far away from him?---but he could see they were blue. He wanted to move them, but could not figure out how. He used to know how to move his toes; he was sure of it. How had he forgotten something like that?

Not realizing he was drunk on pain-killers, the most effective versions pharmacological science could offer, he surprised himself by how good he felt. Maybe he was tougher than he had always thought. Over the crest of the oxygen mask he could see Rosa asleep in a chair in the corner of the room, a set of rosary beads wound through her fingers. At least for times like this, and probably more, every man ought to have a wife, a Rosa for his very own. No man should be alone.

He was cold. The room was bright, too bright, and the light seemed to flutter over his head like summer lightning. He listened to the hum of a machine somewhere behind him and tried to figure out what it was.

Too much trouble. "Shit," he said, maybe aloud, maybe not, and he passed out again. He felt better that way.

A COUPLE OF DECADES LATER, or maybe it was a few hours, a doctor came into the room, followed by a younger doctor and two nurses. The lead man wore his glasses at the top of his forehead, like a large barrette holding back his hair, and had a small mole at the tip of his nose. Arnie remembered no other features.

"Mr. Castig? You're awake?"

Yes to both questions.

"I'm Dr. Washburn."

"Hello, doctor." His voice was muffled by the oxygen mask.

Rosa stirred in her chair.

"Shall we wake her?"

"Yeah."

Dr. Washburn nodded at a nurse, who reached over to Rosa, took her by the elbow and shook her gently. "Mrs. Castig."

"Arnie." She was immediately alert, and went to her husband's side, kissing his cheek and, with the hand that did not clutch the rosary beads, stroking his ever-thinning hair. The other hand moved from bead to bead, her lips moving as well, although she made no sound after calling her husband's name. Watching her lips, Arnie recognized the shapes of a Hail Mary: ". . . the Lord is with Thee. Blessed art Though among women . . ." Not exactly relevant to the present crisis, but for a Catholic, saying the rosary was as supportive as it got.

Dr. Washburn seemed in a hurry. A right-to-the-point kind of guy. He said that Arnie's tibia, the larger of the two bones extending from the knee to the ankle, had been fractured, but because the break was a clean one---"no splinters," as he put it---it had been easy to reset. It would be tough going for a while, but the bone would eventually heal and he would regain full mobility, or something close to it. As for a cut on his knee, it had required seventeen stitches, but it too presented no long-term problems. However, the cut had been made by the rim around the hub of the sheave wheel, and the rim was sharp; in striking the knee where it did and as hard as it did, it had created another problems for the doctors who operated on him.

"Whoa," Arnie said.

"Yes?"

"Operated? Somebody cut me open?"

"Last night," said Dr. Washburn.

Arnie looked at Rosa. She nodded, although continuing with ". . . pray for us sinners now and at the hour of our death, Amen." Her fingers squeezed onto the next bead. "Hail, Mary, full of grace . . ."

"Holy smokers. I never had an operation before."

Dr. Washburn continued: The rim of the sheave wheel had severed a peripheral nerve in the knee, snapping it in two. Before Arnie could ask him what he was talking about, the doctor told him to imagine a rubber band pulled taut, then cut in half, with the two ends flying away from each other. It was like that. But, good news once more. The doctor had been able to find the two ends of the nerve, which was not as simple as it sounded, and suture them back together in such a way that the nerve would, in time, function normally again. Had he not been able to find the strands, Arnie would have a permanent limp, a severe one---in fact, a club foot. As it was, he would probably have a slight limp, but most people wouldn't notice and there wouldn't be any pain.

"Hold on a sec, please," Arnie said. "Just . . ."

"Here," Dr. Washburn said, "let's make things easier on you." He reached over and slipped off the oxygen mask. "You don't really need that now." He handed the mask to the nurse closest to him, who placed it on the bedside tray.

Arnie was sharp enough to ask the following: "I might have a limp because of the broken libia---"

"Tibia."

"And I might have a limp because of the rubber band pieces. So that's two chances of having a limp, and that doubles the odds, right?"

"Well, yes, it probably does. As I said, you'll probably have some kind of limp, but I really wouldn't worry about it."

Yeah, but you aren't the one who's gonna be gimping around town, are you?

Dr. Washburn was not finished yet. All things considered, he said, the patient had been lucky; lucky, that is, as far as the accident itself was concerned. But his "reaction" to the accident---the doctor pronounced with word with unusual emphasis, Arnie thought---was something else again.

"Reaction?"

Dr. Washburn walked around to the side of the unoccupied bed and sat. "Do you have any history of heart disease in your family, Mr. Castig?"

"My dad."

"What happened?"

"Heart attack."

"Fatal?"

Arnie said yes.

"How old was he?"

"Fifty-two."

"And I see you're already in your fifties," the doctor said, sliding his glasses down to eye level for a glance at Arnie's chart. "Anyone else in your family have problems with their heart?"

"I don't know. I don't think so."

"How about yourself? Have you ever had an EKG, any other tests like that?"

"Not that I know of. I . . . well, I can't remember. I probably had one sometime or other."

"You have those physical exams at the mill, Arnie," Rosa said.

"Yeah, but they don't do very much. I mean, they put the stethoscope on your chest and move it around, but . . . I don't know. They always told me I passed, so I figured I was in good shape."

Rosa asked Dr. Washburn why he wanted to know about Arnie's heart. He replied to her husband.

"Because I'm afraid you're a sick man, Mr. Castig, and you've been a sick man for quite some time. Probably, in a manner of speaking, since you were born."

Rosa made a small sucking sound through her teeth, tightening her grip on her husband's shoulder as well as the rosary beads.

"Sick how?" Arnie said.

"In simple terms, you have heart disease. Specifically, without getting too technical, it's a problem with your coronary arteries, and the indications are that it's congenital. What the disease has done is left your heart in a generally weakened condition, making it more susceptible to stress than a normally-functioning heart would be. When that wheel fell on you yesterday, it gave your system, quite understandably, a real jolt. You had a coronary occlusion."

"A what?"

"Like your dad," Dr. Washburn said. "A heart attack."

Rosa made the sign of the cross with the small cross at the end of her beads.

"Was it a bad one?" Arnie said, after a few moments of reflection.

"There's no such thing as a good heart attack, sir. But this one could have been a lot worse. You have an obstruction of blood flow in the coronary artery, but, again, you'll recover. The thing is, though, you're going to have to make some adjustments in the way you live."

"What kinda adjustments?"

"Oh, being more careful about what you eat, cutting back on fatty foods, booze, desserts. You'll have to lose weight, take it easy on how much exercise you do, although it doesn't look like you do very much anyhow. You'll have to reduce your tension levels, see that you get enough rest. We'll give you some pills. They should be a big help."

"Will I have to take them the rest of my life?"

The doctor said he would.

The phrase sent a chill through Arnie. For the rest of my life. There was such a haunting acknowledgment of death in the words.

Rosa interrupted her importuning of the Lord. "His job is pretty tough sometimes, Doctor."

"Well, yes, I'm *well aware* of the fact." That strange emphasis again.

Arnie blinked at him. "So what do I do about it?"

"I'm afraid that your job is *too* tough, Mr. Castig." Dr. Washburn took off his glasses and began to wag them as he spoke. "Too strenuous. The truth of the matter is there's no way a man with a heart condition like yours can work in a steel mill."

"What're you saying?"

"You'll have to find another way to earn a living."

"No, no, you can't mean it."

"I'm afraid I do."

"But I can't get another job. There isn't anything else. I mean, the mill . . . it's been my whole life. A person can't change his life without any kind of warning. I don't know, I---"″

"Stay calm, Mr. Castig, please. Especially right now."

"Maybe I could get assigned to special duties, easy ones, you know. Not everything in the mill's a ball-buster. I could talk to some of the bosses and---"

The doctor was shaking his head. "The mill won't keep you on the payroll, Mr. Castig, not after they find out about the problem. They can't. It's against the law for them to employ someone with difficulties like yours. That's why they give you the physicals, superficial though they are."

Like a child who believes that, when his eyes are closed, no one can see him, Arnie disappeared.

"You're going to have to shift your priorities, Mr. Castig, and I understand that it won't be easy. Like you said, they're the priorities of a lifetime. But I'm afraid you just don't have a choice."

He pointed to one of two intravenous feeding bags attached to the patient, then aimed the finger at the young male doctor. He proceeded to the bag and turned a valve beneath it.

Arnie allowed himself to be visible again.

Dr. God Almighty, the man who had just changed his life forever, stood up and placed his glasses barrette-like again. "Believe me, Mr. Castig, I know how this must seem to you now, but it isn't nearly as bad as it sounds. You're going to get better. You're going to get your health back. You're just going to have to go to greater lengths than before to keep it. Now, I want you to stop worrying for the time being and try to get some rest. Will you do that for me?"

For *you*?

He picked up the oxygen mask and handed it to one of the nurses, who slipped it back over Arnie's head. "Loosen this thing a little, Lorraine." To Arnie: "I'll drop in later and we can talk some more." To Rosa: "And you, maam, you should go home and get some rest. You've been here all night and we've given your husband a sedative, so he'll be asleep in a few minutes. There's nothing more to do for now."

The doctor and his entourage left.

Rosa stayed a few more minutes, but the doctor was right; there was nothing more to say right now, nothing to do, for either of them. Her prayers were probably as good as anything, and she could pray anywhere. Besides, Arnie's eyelids had drooped to half-mast; the sedative was kicking in. Rosa kissed him on the forehead and told him she would come back after she slept for a while. Then she would spend the night with him, a phrase that used to mean something very different from what it meant now. She turned and left, walking slowly.

Arnie listened as his wife's footsteps melted into the other sounds of a hospital corridor: the rubber-soled shoes of nurses squishing on a tile floor, wheelchairs gliding from room to room, gurneys rolling in and out of elevators, the muted voices over the loudspeakers paging doctors. It was a peaceful cacophony. Like ocean waves. They could put you to sleep.

The last thing he remembered thinking was that he wished he could trade obstructed blood flow in the coronary artery for a new zygmawhatsis major, or whatever the hell it was called.

THE FOLLOWING WEEK, despite an uproar from the United Steelworkers' Union, the men who failed to sweep up the sandblast shot were fired without severance. An American Bridge court martial. Arnie had just gotten home when he heard the news, further learning that the decision had created an uproar. Some of the men he had once considered friends were blaming *him* for the firings. He could have been more careful. He should have swept a path for himself. How were men without jobs supposed to support their families?

Arnie was stunned to learn about this reaction. But there were others, definitely a majority, who took his side, and the disputes were so great that fights broke out at the mill. Fists were thrown on more than one occasion and a couple of men got black eyes, others fat lips and swollen cheeks. Some of them men refused to work, sitting down instead, like the coloreds had done in the South. Meetings were called, suspensions handed out---there had never been anything like it at AB before. The story made headlines in the *Beaver Valley Times* ever day.

Arnie did not read any of the stories about the ruckus. He told Rudy on the phone one day that he could not help feeling embarrassed for having lost his balance. Rudy told him he was nuts. Arnie told him that, despite not having had anything to do with the firings, he could not help but feel the sting of his detractors. Rudy told him he understood.

When he got out of the hospital, he sank into a mire of loneliness like none he had ever known before. Of his past co-workers, only Rudy communicated with him, his wife sending flowers and the two of them talking a couple times a week. Both men marveled at the hard feelings, how they seemed to linger; a person didn't have to work in Fabricating Mill "B" to have an opinion about the accident and adjudication.

But it did not take long for Rudy and Arnie to find that they had little in common beside the job, and Rudy soon began to call his old friend with diminishing frequency. From twice a week to once, from once a week to once every several weeks. Then not at all. They still would have identified each other as friends; they had just exhausted the only topic that bound them.

Two months after his homecoming, Arnie began an extensive rehab program. Three months after that he started looking for a new job and found one in less than a week; he had been wearing his uniform and showing up for work without missing a day ever since. When old friends, people who knew about his accident but not the aftermath, asked him how things were going at the mill, he'd always say, "Same as ever, you know." And then he'd change the subject to last night's game, no matter what the sport or who had been playing.

HE TURNED ON THE RADIO AGAIN. The Dorsey Brothers. Or was it just Tommy? Just Jimmy? "Never thought I'd fall," Arnie sang along, "but now I hear love call. I'm getting sentimental over yo-oo-ou."

On the dresser was an ashtray Zook had stolen from a bar near Three Rivers Stadium in Pittsburgh called The End Zone; he had given to Arnie for his birthday a few years ago. In it was a whistle on an old tennis shoe lace. The ends had been tied together to make a loop and Arnie slipped it around his neck, tucking the knot under his collar in back. He patted down the collar so that the shoelace lay flat under it, then patted his epaulets, for which he had never been able to figure out a reason. He slipped into his black pants, the crease permanently blotted out. Then he picked up his cap, straightened the badge in front, and put it on, angling the shiny vinyl visor just so. He liked the hat; wearing it was the only thing he did that was better than working at the mill.

All right, time to forget those thoughts. He was, once again, a man in uniform.

Tommy. It was Tommy Dorsey who played the trombone and that's what Arnie was hearing now, a trombone with a mute on it. Arnie loved the sound of a muted trombone, and Tommy blew into it in such a way that a person could feel the sound on his skin. It was like having a piece of flannel rubbed against you on a cold night; one of the WAMB disc jockeys had said that once and Arnie had never forgotten. Usually they didn't talk fancy, but it was an interesting way to think about one of his favorite songs.

He grabbed his keychain, hooked it to a belt loop, and proceeded downstairs, the keys jingling against his hip, a whole orchestra's worth of them, as he moved.

Rosa handed her husband a paper bag. "Cream cheese san'wich on whole wheat, carrot sticks, an' little piece of cake I bring back from Vinnie's yesterday."

"What kind?'

"Devil's food, but just little bit."

"Thanks, Ro," and he kissed her on the cheek, this old dancing partner of his from the West View Park days, holding his lips there longer than usual.

HE CAUGHT THE BUS at the corner of Sixth and Merchant, and it turned onto the Ohio River Boulevard at Fourteenth. On the other side of the river, stretching as far ahead of him as he could see, was the Aliquippa works of Findlay & Russell Steel, the largest plant in the Valley after American Bridge. Rosa's cousin Vinnie had spent the last nineteen years there, sixteen of them in the Seamless Tube Mill.

After which the bus chugged past the Gauge Mill and the Rod Mill and the Wire Mill and the Blooming Mill, then past rolling dunes of coal in the storage yard, a mountain range of coal. At this point the road veered away from the river long enough to swing around an automobile junkyard, and when it swung back again the Basic Steel Mills eased into view. They were cavernous structures; Arnie always thought they were big enough to store airplane hangars in. Just like the basic mills at AB. Coal chutes joined the mills at diagonals; waste gas pipes wound around them like mazes; conveyer belts ran in and out carrying fifty-pound bags of limestone and the occasional bag of cement or box of spare parts for the machinery. Cut into the riverbank, every fifty feet or so, were concrete pipes that jutted over the Ohio, spewing waste water with such force that the ore barges docked nearby swayed in its wake.

Rising out of the mills were half a dozen smokestacks, and the fumes they flushed into the sky sometimes made the day seem like twilight and the night so thick it would never end. Then the wind would change and the sky would suddenly clear. It was not clear now. The bus, Arnie knew, was at this moment directly across the river from the soaking pit, but he could barely make out the shapes. And the Coke Mill's blast furnaces, just beyond the pit, were hazy, their violent orange flames smudged and indistinct. Even through the sealed windows of the bus he could smell sulfur dioxide, the familiar scent of rotting eggs. He hunched down in his seat, tipping his cap over his eyes, and dozed for the rest of the trip.

Twenty minutes later, the bus was approaching Freedom, named after the signs that had been planted along this stretch of riverbank by abolitionists early in the nineteenth century. At times the signs sprouted so densely that one plea for **FREEDOM** overgrew a few letters of the next. **EDOM. FREED.** Passengers on paddle-wheelers had pointed at the signs, repeating the word to one another, and probably, inadvertently, giving the town that would one day be built on the site its name.

Today, Freedom had no room for a crop of signs, much less a steel mill. The riverbank belonged to the Valvoline Oil Refinery, a small facility with large storage tanks giving the air a scent so acrid and syrupy that some families had to move elsewhere in the Valley to breathe without side effects. An earlier Freedom industry was the rare area enterprise that never fouled the air. But the casket factory had long since gone out of business.

The bus driver was about to approach the storage tanks, when he suddenly took a fork to the right, up a hill and into the larger town of Rochester. He stopped just beyond the second traffic light on the main street.

"Yo, Stats," the driver said.

Arnie shook his way out of a half-sleep, pulled himself up, and shuffled down the aisle, holding onto the seatbacks. He dropped thirty-five cents into the coin box.

"Thanks, Gus."

"See ya tomorrow, old man."

Arnie stepped down to the street and the doors slapped shut behind him. A siren wailed in the distance; a crow cawed on a telephone line directly overhead, then flew away. In front of him stood what had once been the Abraham Lincoln Elementary School, but was now a structure of more varied purpose: offices of the Social Security Administration in the basement, some Beaver Valley Community College classrooms on the first floor, and storage space for the Beaver Valley Historical Society on the second. He limped around to the alley in back of the building. All was peaceful until he reached for the key ring on his belt loop, but then came a small explosion of glass, followed by a burst of nasty laughter and the faint sound of footsteps growing fainter as they ran away from him and into silence. He could not see the vandals, but the late afternoon had suddenly become a little darker, the street light at the end of the alley having just been shattered.

Young kids, apprentice hoodlums. The Abraham Lincoln Elementary School was in a bad neighborhood. Sometimes he thought the whole Valley was a bad neighborhood. Or was he just an old man now, as Gus had said, no longer up to life's challenges as he had once been?

He unlocked the boiler room door, and made certain it was locked behind him. He limped down a hallway, up a flight of stairs, down another hallway and into the room that was his base of operations, the place from which he ventured forth on his nightly adventures. It had once been the lounge for the Abraham Lincoln faculty; Arnie thought of it as his locker room. He played a game with himself as he made his solitary rounds. It helped him get through the hours.

After hanging his jacket on a nail in the wall and putting his meal into a small refrigerator, he picked up the phone. First duty of the night: check for a dial tone. He opened a metal cabinet in the far corner and took out his time clock and a small cellophane packet. Unsnapping the clock's imitation leather case, he removed the back plate. From the packet he withdrew a cardboard disc about the size of a spaghetti jar lid; around the circumference were printed the numbers one to twelve a.m. and one to twelve p.m., and there were a few lines in between to tell the time more precisely.

He fit the disc into the clock, fastened the plate over it again, and synchronized the clock face, on the front, with his watch. 4:42 in the afternoon. He was supposed to start his first round no later than five. The bus schedule kept him prompt, but he would have been on time anyhow. "Early Arnie." Or sometimes just "Early." That's what his boss called him, but he always did so with an edge in his voice.

He slung the time clock over his shoulder by the imitation leather strap and hitched up his pants. End of pre-game drills. Time to take the field. "All right," he said, and the crowd roared as Arnie strode from the locker room for his first round of the night.

He did the following:

Inspected every room on the first floor. If the Beaver Valley Community College day students had left behind garbage, he threw it away. If they had forgotten a book or purse or some other personal item, he put a note on it and left it on the teacher's desk. If they had left the desks sloppily aligned, he rearranged them as they had been at the start of the day, putting the legs precisely on the edges of the floor tiles and making sure there were several inches between the front of one desk and the back of the next. Sometimes he washed the blackboards, even though he wasn't supposed to. But a man who appreciates the exactitude of statistics is likely to be a man who prefers straight lines, smooth surfaces, visible signs of neatness.

Out in the hall, screwed to the doorframe of each room, was a small metal tray with a key in it that was secured by a chain. Arnie removed the key, inserted it into a slot in his clock, and gave it a quarter-turn to the right.

This made a notch in the cardboard disc at the appropriate time, the key for each room leaving its own distinctive mark and thereby establishing Arnie's precise location at a precise moment, proving his reliability. At the end of his shift he would slip the disc under the door of the administration office. Tomorrow would be another day, another disc.

Finishing with one room, he went to the next and did exactly the same things. In exactly the same order. And then into the next room and the next and next---fourteen rooms in all, seven on each side of the first floor corridor, counting the office, which he was not to enter. So there were thirteen rooms demanding his attention.

After giving it, he started up to the second floor. The door from the top of the stairs to the Historical Society hallway had a padlock on it; all Arnie did was jiggle it, determine that it was secure. He did. It was. He put his nose against the pane of glass in the door and framed his face with his hands, looking into the darkness. He didn't see anything. He never did, and wasn't supposed to. A lot less to do up here than there was a floor below.

Click with the key, notch on the disc. Then Arnie descended two flights of stairs to the basement.

There he twisted doorknobs, that was all, just twisted doorknobs--- making sure that the Social Security people had locked their doors upon leaving. They had. They never forgot, and as soon as Arnie had established the fact in front of each office with his time clock, he headed back to the locker room. He entered, closed the door behind him. There were fewer surprises in his new line of work than there were rickshaw driver in western Pennsylvania

"End of the first quarter," he announced to himself. "No score."

Arnie "Stats" Castig takes off his clock and hangs it on a hook on the wall. Removes his hat, his shoes, and opens an old classroom desk next to the sofa. Withdraws a pencil stub and the March, 1963 issue of the *Dell Crossword Puzzle Magazine*. Falls back on the sofa, so battered a piece of furniture that more foam rubber shows on the surface than floral print. He puts his feet up on the table and, in the glare of a shadeless lamp, starts on a puzzle in the medium difficulty section. There are only three and a half more puzzles until "Difficult." He hopes he will be ready when the time comes. It will be like the playoffs.

SECOND QUARTER, starting at six p.m. sharp. The blitz, as he calls it. Arnie would:

Open each door on first floor.

Turn on light.

Run eyes across room.

Turn off light.

Shut door.

Proceed to next room, blitz that one.

Blitz every goddamn room on first floor.

Turn key in clock, turn key in clock, turn key in clock, turn, turn, turn.

Up to second floor, jiggle padlock, peer. Sigh.

Stop, rub knee, aching knee.

Down to basement.

God, but it was quiet in this building! Even talking to Father Daniel about Joe Namath would be better than this. Guy knew his football, though, Arnie had to give him that. He just liked to rag his pals Stats and Zook about the great young QB. He might not have admitted it, but, as a man born and bred in the Valley, he too was rooting for Joey.

Go through boiler room, noting familiar shapes of room's shadows, familiar rhythms of rattling pipes.

Make sure door still locked. Pretty silly.

Still, do the same with Social Security doorknobs.

Back to locker room, get lunch and beverage from refrigerator, sink into sofa, prepare to dine.

Phew . . .

Arnie kept a set of plastic utensils in the desk. For a place mat he used the crossword puzzle magazine, back cover up. His napkin was one of the coarse brown paper towels that went into the dispensers in the old school's lavatories. Outside, the evening was ripening into night, the sun having turned a dull orange and lost its place in the sky, falling behind the horizon as he was partway through the blitz.

Did he just hear something? Something outside? He immediately thought of those kids vandalizing, laughing, up to no good. Was there danger ahead? No. He wouldn't have been able to hear the kids from the locker room even if they *were* running wild outside. Forget it.

"Halftime," Arnie said, with a smile that Zook could not manage, and opened the paper bag Rosa had given him and one of the sodas he bought by the six-pack.

Two rounds down, two to go.

THE BEAVER COUNTY COMMUNITY COLLEGE night school students started to come about ten minutes after seven tonight. The night school people started to come about ten minutes after seven *every* night.

Arnie stood in front of the building like the doorman at a fancy apartment house, smiling and saying hello as the residents entered, touching his visor to the women, inclining his head to the men. But many of them ignored him. He couldn't understand why. They stared off to the side or into their notebooks, maybe speeding up as they neared him, even though classes didn't start until 7:30.

There were two students, though, who Arnie *wished* would ignore him. Chico Marconi and Davey Ignatius were among the men who had failed to sweep up the sandblast shot and were fired as a result. Both landed low-paying jobs afterward; both were fired about the same time. Now, thanks to a government program, they were being paid to take classes that would enable them to become electricians. They glared at Arnie as they passed him, called him a traitor, a son of a bitch, a motherfucker. They kept their faces straight ahead, though, as if they could have been talking about anyone. One night they threatened Arnie with a beating after class, although it was a threat on which they never made good. That was during the first month of the semester.

Now, having run out of epithets, they turned to him without a word, just glaring. Sometimes Chico spit near his shoes. Sometimes Davey pretended to slip, as if there were sandblast shot on the steps. Did they work this out before they came to school every night, Arnie wondered, deciding what each of them would do? It was as if they had a choreographer. Regardless, as they passed him, either entering or leaving, he could feel their undeserved hatred as if it were a poison he had just been forced to swallow.

Most of the night school students, though, were cordial. Some of them, as they entered the building, picked up the threads of the previous night's conversation, and not always about sports. They asked about his health, his wife, his family, his opinion about this or that, sometimes even a national political issue, although Arnie wasn't very good with those. It was the best time of the day for him, the most social, the time when he felt most among the living, the way he used to feel at the mill. But it came and went quickly.

After the last of the night school people was inside, he locked the door to the school, weaving a thick chain around the inside push handles and fitting a lock through the links. Anyone who was late would just have to pound on the door and hope Arnie heard. It happened more than it should have. Arnie always heard. He hustled back to the door, unlocked it without complaint, then locked it again and headed back to his command post, picking up his time clock, and starting the third quarter.

But this time things were different. The third round was his favorite part of the game. Instead of walking into the first floor rooms, which were now occupied, he merely listened outside each one for a few minutes, making sure there were no sounds of trouble, like an argument turning ugly or a student becoming sick. But what he was really doing was picking up snippets of the education he never got in high school, when he and the guys, the guys who were always called "the guys," paid little attention in class and seldom handed in homework on time. They were proud of such behavior; it was as if it were prescribed in the by-laws of an envied social group.

For the most part, he heard about the latest concepts in educational psychology, the majority of the night school students being teachers taking extra credits for their permanent certification---and he had no interest in that kind of thing: "reciprocal information flow," "modular learning environments," "cognitive reinforcement of values." Arnie didn't understand any of that stuff, although he figured he might if it were described without such bullshit language. A history teacher shouldn't learn about teaching; he should learn about history.

But the night school also offered classes in English, math and the manual arts, and Arnie paid special attention outside these doors. For the first time in his life he knew there was a real difference between who and whom; he knew which part of a fraction was the numerator and which the denominator; and he could at least have made a start on installing a toilet without a plumber. Maybe tonight they would talk about that some more in Home Repairs. He hoped so. The toilet at *his* home had been making funny sounds lately.

Once or twice he discovered an odd fact that helped him with his crossword puzzles. It made him feel smarter. It would have been nice to share a feeling like that with someone, but Rosa wouldn't have understood and Zook wouldn't have cared. Father Daniel would have known the satisfaction Arnie got, but he was too busy saving souls.

Auditing, one of the instructors had told him, was the official name for taking classes the way Arnie did---just listening in, not getting a grade or taking any tests, not being enrolled but not having to pay, either. Most auditors, though, would sit in the back rows of a classroom, not stand in the hallway. And Arnie was unique in having to skip out on classes after short periods of time because he had the clock over his shoulder and a disc awaiting its mark. On to the next door, the next snippet.

Turn key, turn, turn.

But he always learned some little thing.

Classes ended at their regular time tonight, between 9:30 and a quarter to ten, and by a few minutes after ten all the night school people were gone. The ones who hadn't said hello to him on the way in didn't speak to him on the way out, either. Screw 'em, Arnie thought. Especially screw you, Chico, and you, Davey. To others he said "Good night, now." "See you tomorrow." "Hope you did a good job on that test." He paid attention to them and they returned the favor. They never said as much to him when they departed as they did when entering, but he could live with that. If you were a night school student after a day spent holding down a job, then sitting through a two-hour class, you were obviously tired, and had other things on your mind than exchanging small talk with a man who was essentially a stranger.

Having unchained the front door for the students' departure, Arnie fastened it again in their wake.

Then, after another locker room break, he made his last round of the night, during which he toted along a plastic garbage bag and repeated all the steps he had taken on the first round, as well as doing a little extra tidying up, like removing cigarette butts, scraps of paper, and beverage cans from the classrooms. He would drop them into his plastic bag. Between some of the rooms, he checked the front door to make sure no one had been locked into the building and was trying to get out, and that no one who had already gotten out was pounding to get back in, having forgotten his car keys or something like that. Neither happened very often.

When he finished the fourth quarter, close to an hour after it began, he removed the disc from his time clock and flicked it under the door of the administration office, for which the overnight cleaning crew had a key but he did not. Then he trudged back to the locker room and freed himself from the burdens of the time clock. He slipped on his jacket and let himself out of the old school the same way he had come in, dragging the garbage bag with him and stuffing it into one of the cans next to the boiler room door. When he clanked the lid down on it, the game, in his mind, was officially over for the night. The action ceased, the fans departed. Arnie sighed. "Another scoreless tie."

But as limped along to the bus stop on the night after Joe Namath's debut, he adjusted his hat slightly, changing the angle, adding a little rakishness. He could not have explained why; it might have been a mark of pride. He had done his job well, and although it wasn't the way he ever envisioned earning a paycheck, there was no such thing as a job being too small to do poorly. Society had to run, after all, and everybody who worked made a contribution. Teamwork.

Soon he was sitting on the last Ambridge-bound bus of the night, looking across the river as it approached the blast furnaces at Findlay & Russell. As always happened at this point in the journey, Arnie stirred a bit, finding the night so much clearer than the late afternoon had been. The images were crisper, appearing closer to him.

A blast furnace, he thought, should be considered a natural wonder, like the Grand Canyon or the Rocky Mountains. Men, after all, are natural creatures and it was men who had invented the blast furnace. Some of them, Arnie had learned when auditing a class in ancient history last year, had lived two millennia ago in China. Two thousand years! The Bible hadn't even been written yet, Alexander the Great hadn't been born---but a primitive version of the blast furnace was up and running on the other side of the world. Imagine!

Put a candle against the night and the night wins. Put a blast furnace against the night and, with its thousands of candles' worth of illumination, it is the night that seems insignificant, nothing more than a background for the powerful, man-made flame.

And now, as the rumors had it, China's neighbors, the Japs, were on their way to reclaiming the steel industry. Fuckin' Japs, you believe that! It was Arnie's last thought before lowering his visor over his eyes and drifting into a nether state for the last few minutes of his journey.

And so another week had started for him, just the way they were always starting for him now. Strictly routine. But nothing else about the week would be routine. Nor would anything else about his life.

Tuesday,
September 28,
1965

THE NEW YORK NEWSPAPERS, he was told by the woman at the circulation desk at the Findlay Memorial Library in Ambridge, were on strike, all except the *New York Chronicle*---and Arnie hadn't even heard of that one. "Holy smokers," he said, too loud for his surroundings.

The librarian gave him a regulation "Shhh," and he was reminded of the usher at St. Veronica's. Sometimes Arnie just let himself be himself regardless of the surroundings, and he knew he was too old for that kind of behavior.

Then again, he looked around and saw no more than five or six people in the building. A steel town library, always the emptiest of the public places.

Well, Arnie thought, he had no choice. The *Chronicle* would have to do. He found the Monday edition on a wooden rod hanging on a rack in the periodical section. Taking it to a seat at a large table under a skylight, he opened it to the sports section with expectations high.

The table had been so richly waxed that it shone; it was surrounded by columns with one of those Greek names and their bases rested on a floor that seemed to be solid marble and shone itself. Brushed gold buffet lamps, a stained glass window on each of the library's four exterior walls---those robber barons sure knew what to do with their pocket change.

Outside, a wide and sweeping stairway led to the front doors. Arnie thought the steps were granite. The building itself, he knew, *was* granite, with more columns at the entrance and a dome, only slightly raised, centered atop it. The Findlay Library was smaller than any of the AB mills, yet was by far the grandest building in town, so much so that it didn't belong there.

Arnie's expectations were quickly satisfied. First there was an article reporting the game, followed by a shorter piece analyzing various performances and strategies. Then came the most detailed scoring summary he had ever seen of a football game that was not some kind of championship.

On another page there was a story putting the game into historical perspective, comparing Joe's performance in his first start to those of such legends as Sammy Baugh, Otto Graham and Charlie Conerly. After that came a collection of quotes from players and former players, giving their opinions of Joe and their predictions for his future. Everybody thought the world would be his oyster.

From the lady at the circulation desk he got a pencil and a piece of paper; he jotted down the more interesting comments so he could tell Zook later. Zook didn't like to go to the library. Too fancy. Besides, he said, he always felt uncomfortable around a lot of books.

When Arnie finally finished, having read each of the stories carefully and a few of them twice, he began to flip idly through the rest of the sports section. On the next to last page, surrounded by stories about minor sports like harness racing and ads for used cars, there was yet another picture of Joe. But unlike the previous ones, in this one he wore a tuxedo, although he was holding his arm up as if to throw a pass. Standing next to him was a young lady holding onto his arm with both hands. The caption began in capital letters: **BROADWAY JOE MEETS BROADWAY BARBRA**, and below that a singer named Barbra Streisand, starring in the musical *Funny Girl.* was quoted as saying, "I just wanted to know what a $400,000 arm feels like."

It took him a few seconds to see the problem "That's not how you spell Barbara."

He stopped, didn't move for a few seconds. The woman at the circulation desk didn't tell him to shut up. He turned back to look at her, but she wasn't there; the circulation desk was unattended for the moment.

Arnie stared at the picture of his hero and the woman for a few seconds. Was her nose really as big as it looked? Were her eyes crossed? Was her hair plastered against her forehead? All in all, he was not impressed.

"Jesus, Joe, you can do better than that."

"What?"

"What?" Arnie echoed, and quickly turned around to find, for the second time in three days, Debbie Savukas, Ambridge High School Varsity majorette, squarely in his line of vision. He was as surprised as he had been on Sunday.

"Debbie!"

"Hiya, Mr. Castig. Did you just say something?"

"Aw, no, not really. I mean, I was just surprised by this picture in the paper, and I sorta made a sound. Gosh, what a surprise. How's everything going?"

"Good, good. How's it going with you?"

"Great. Couldn't be better, thanks."

He could feel himself blushing, a line beginning to descend on his face from forehead to chin, leaving a sweaty shade of red behind it. The descent was rapid. He hoped it wasn't visible.

"Are you off today," Debbie said.

"Off? Oh, you mean from work?"

She nodded. It was then that Arnie noticed the girl standing behind her.

"No," he said, "I work nights. But it looks like *you're* off. You know, from school."

"Oh, I wish I was," she said. "But we just had to look up some stuff for P.O.D.---that's Problems of Democracy. We have a paper due next week, and since this is last period and we have study hall, they let us go to the library."

"Us?"

Debbie moved to the side then, with a certain majorette-ish flair, and the girl stationed behind her stepped tentatively forward.

"Mr. Castig, I'd like you to meet my friend Mary Ann Schiffler. Mary Ann, this is Mr. Castig."

"Hi, there," she said.

"Hi, Mary Ann. How's everything?"

In lieu of a response, she giggled, which made her seem at once more vivacious than Debbie and less poised. Arnie didn't want to stare, but the first thing that struck him about Mary Ann was that she overdid the eye shadow and mascara. No big deal, though. If the result was to call too much attention to her eyes, it was a minor offense; they were a deep, almost bottomless shade of blue. She was an inch or two shorter than Debbie, and not quite as pretty, but her body was similarly configured. Oh, these young girls!

"Are you a majorette, too?"

She shook her head. "I was the last one cut. Well, in the last group."

"Oh, I'm sorry." Had he made a bonehead play by asking?

"Okay," Debbie said, "enough small talk." She plopped herself on the table close to Arnie, setting down the books she had been cradling in her arms. She crossed her legs at the knees, but wore a longer skirt today than she had Sunday. "All right, M.A.," she said, "do it."

"Do what?"

"Come on, you know what. Quit stalling."

"I'm not stalling."

"So ask him then."

"Deborah *Lynn*!"

"You said when I saw Mr. Castig over here and told you what he did there was no way you'd believe it unless you heard it from him yourself. So, go ahead. He'll tell you."

"Yeah," Arnie said affably, even working his way up to eagerly, "go ahead and ask me. I'll tell you. Honest."

"Well, all right." She scowled at Debbie. "I guess I have to now." To Arnie: "Well"---she gave the word a two-syllable boost---"I was wondering if it's really true that you actually ordered ten chocolate bars."

"Twelve," said Debbie.

"Fourteen," said Arnie.

"*Fourteen*!" said Debbie and Mary Ann.

"Bingo," and Arnie reached into his wallet, picking out three dollar bills and unfolding them next to Debbie on the table. He tried to smooth out the wrinkles. "This is for the two extra bars," he said. "Might as well give them to you now, as long as I'm thinking about it."

Debbie looked at them in something close to awe. "But---"

"They're from this friend of mine, Zook. Well, George Szuchinski, but Zook is what everybody calls him. I guess you skipped his house Sunday 'cause he didn't even know about the candy. But as soon as I told him, he went right for his stash. He's a good guy, he goes to all the games."

Debbie slowly picked up the bills, her transaction now having reached undreamed-of proportions. "I can't believe this." She smiled at Arnie and he could feel the heat. "You're the greatest, Mr. C."

Mr. C. He liked that. He was feeling more comfortable with her today than he had on Sunday.

She gently placed the three bills into her pocketbook. "Did I tell you, M.A.?"

Mary Ann was about to concur when the library clock chimed fifteen minutes past the hour. The three of them waited for the last sound to evaporate, then Mary Ann told Debbie they ought to be going.

Arnie: "So soon?"

"I've got a meeting after school," Mary Ann told him. "School newspaper. I'm girls' sports editor. And Deb's got practice."

"Big game Friday," from Debbie. "Ellwood City."

Arnie nodded. The Wolverines. He thought they had lost only once all year.

Debbie slid down from the table. "Thanks again, Mr. C. Really."

"Don't mention it, Deb."

"See you in a couple days."

"Bye, Mr. Castig," Mary Ann said.

"Bye, M.A."

Arnie watched the girls turn and hurry out of the library. And so that quickly---back into his life and out again. But at least it was in the bag now, he thought to himself. She was definitely going to get that scholarship.

He allowed his eyes to remain on the revolving door at the front of the library for several seconds after the girls had spun through it. Then he heard an overly-theatrical clearing of the throat. The old lady was back behind the circulation desk, and not happy.

"If I may say so, sir, you should be ashamed of yourself."

"For having eyes?"

"For using them as you just did."

"Aw, go swallow a toad."

Arnie had no idea where that came from, but the woman looked at him as if she had just taken his advice.

HE HAD JUST OPENED THE DOOR to a first floor room on his second round of the night when he heard the clatter outside. He stepped over to a window and separated the slats on the set of blinds. Looking out narrowly into the night, he saw nothing out of the ordinary, not at first. After a few seconds, though, accustoming himself to the deepening twilight, Arnie saw movement. There were people on the porch of the recently-remodeled Victorian house across the street that had been converted to lawyers' offices. Two people, Arnie thought, boys, older boys, colored. One of them wore a dark jacket and sat on the porch railing, his chest curled behind a pillar and his arms wrapped around it. The other boy, taller and broader than his mate and wearing a sweatshirt, sat with a swagger on the porch steps---not something easy to do, *sit* with a swagger. A cigarette in his mouth drooped almost at a perpendicular to the ground.

Arnie opened the blinds wider.

Next to the boy on the steps was a pile of rocks and he was throwing them at the mailbox in front of the house. Usually he missed, and Arnie heard the stone roll across the street, maybe as far as the opposite curb. Sometimes he hit his target; the result then was a pinging sound and a growing assortment of dents. The mailbox was perfectly shaped, Arnie recalled, and newly painted when he came to work today. Not anymore. The boys were committing a crime. It was not his responsibility, but property was being destroyed, and he could not let it keep happening.

Suddenly Sweatshirt looked over at the school. He said something to Dark Jacket and pointed to the opening in the blinds. Sweat Shirt picked up another of his rocks and stood. With an exaggerated windup, like a pitcher from baseball's olden days, he hurled the rock at Arnie. It fell far short, barely reaching the strip of weeds at the edge of the sidewalk---but so pointlessly angry did the gesture appear that Arnie felt himself flinching anyhow.

The boy threw a second rock, missing the school by even more. Dark Jacket dismounted from the porch railing and stood alongside his friend, cupping his hands to his mouth and shouting. The words carried better than the missiles. They were "Mind your own business, fuckface," followed by the extension of four middle fingers. And the same threatening laughter, Arnie thought, that he had heard last night.

He pulled his fingers from the blinds. Why had he let the punks see him for so long? He took off his glasses and looked at them, making sure the sharp edges of the slats hadn't damaged his new frames.

He decided to finish the second round, the blitz, then look out at the porch again, although this time from a different vantage point. Afterward, he would return to the locker room and, depending on what he saw, or didn't see, would either call the police, as he had been instructed to do when trouble loomed, or dine in peace.

Ten minutes later, in the room across from the administration office, he stood next to a window without blinds, allowing just a single eyeball to peek out through the glass. He thought the porch of the old Victorian was empty. He slid his other eyeball behind the pane. Confirmation: the boys were gone. The only sound Arnie heard was the rattling of pipes from the boiler room directly below. He maintained his position for a minute or so to see whether the boys would return, or maybe were there all along but had tucked themselves into the shadows. They had not. The coast was clear. He hadn't been paying attention to his heart, but he supposed it beat a little slower now.

When he got back to the locker room, he was without an appetite. The boys had upset him enough to throw him off his usual schedule. He would eat after the third round tonight instead of at halftime. Despite having been a football player once upon a time, he did not understand violence, in any form. It threw him off his game.

He sank into his usual spot on the sofa, a shallow indentation in the foam rubber, and unfolded an article about the Denver Broncos that he had slipped into his wallet. A preview of this week's game. He had carefully torn it out of the *Chronicle* today when the librarian had her back turned.

But no, he would save that. Instead, he picked up the crossword magazine, starting a new one. Three puzzles now left in "Middle Difficulty." Early next week, at the rate he was going, he would work his way to the tough ones.

He filled in one across . . .

Europe's neighbor. (4 letters)

"Asia."

And one down . . .

Dry, said of a desert (4 letters)

"Arid."
And then the light bulb in the lamp on the coffee table blew out.
"Aw, geez."
There was no overhead light in the room, no other source of illumination, no choice for Arnie but to tramp down the hallway and downstairs to the janitor's closet. He unlocked it, something he seldom had occasion to do, and looked for a package of bulbs. He couldn't find any, not on the shelves, inside buckets, or inside a large cardboard box full of mopheads. Nowhere. He could not find a single bulb. In this building that demanded hundreds of them.

"Shit. You're kidding me." What he *did* find was a pencil and piece of paper, and he left a note for the janitor. He taped it to the closet door, but just to be sure, he wrote another note to himself. In case the janitor forgot, he would bring his own bulb tomorrow. He put the note in his shirt pocket.

Back to the locker room.

It was not black outside yet, not completely, but dark enough so that he could no longer work on the crossword puzzle. "Damn it anyhow." He thought he was in a groove.

He sat on the sofa arm, mulling over his options. He could go up to one of the classrooms and turn on the lights and work on his puzzle at the teacher's desk. But he decided against it. What if one of the school officials happened to be driving by and saw a light when it was not supposed to be on? A slim chance, but why risk it?

He had tried to bring his radio to school when he first started the job, but reception at night was poor. A shame, because "Evening Serenade" was his favorite of all the WAMB programs, each night highlighting the music of one particular vocalist or band, with the disc jockey, Bernie Blyleven, telling stories about the person's life and career between songs. He even claimed to have met Vaughn Monroe once. Arnie didn't know whether to believe him or not, but ultimately it didn't matter. Maybe one day Stats Castig might brag to someone about a conversation he had not really had with Broadway Joe Namath. No harm done, and you could tell a lot about a person not just by whether or not he told the truth, but by what kind of lies he told, whom he told them to, and how often.

Vaughn Monroe. Now there was a name from the past. Arnie really liked Vaughn Monroe---so mellow, so effortless was he, as if doing little more than chatting with his listeners while this band happened to be playing in the background, hitting all the right notes but, for the most part, just keeping ol' Vaughn company. In that way he was like Der Bingle, Bing Crosby, but with a little more oomph.

Arnie's favorite of Monroe's songs was "There! I've Said It Again." Softly, he sang his own rendition.

> *I love you,*
> *There's nothing to hide;*
> *It's better*
> *Than hurting inside.*
> *I've loved you*
> *Since heaven knows when;*
> *There!*
> *I've said it again.*

That was when he heard the first scream.

Not until it had passed all the way through him, like the tremors of an earthquake, did he realize what it was. He had never heard such a piercing sound before; in fact, until this moment in his life the only screams he had heard were in the movies and on television. They were louder. But this was real.

He tried to dial the phone, but was too jangled to get his finger into the right holes in the darkness.

"Shit," he said, and gave up after reaching a number that did not answer. A police station always answered.

What he *could* do in the darkness was find his cap, and he shoved it too far down his head to the ears, giving him an unintended comic aspect. Nor did he need a light to find his jacket; he grabbed it from its nail and slipped it on without bothering to zip it up. In less than a minute he had pushed through the locker room door, leaving it open behind him, and started down the stairs leading to the basement.

Through the corridor and into the boiler room, where the sputtering motors seemed louder and more ominous than usual. He jogged toward the back door, but there was no window in it and there were no windows in the boiler room wall, so Arnie couldn't even imagine what awaited him outside: how many people were there, what they were doing, whether he could do anything about it. Maybe not even people at all; maybe an animal.

Another scream, a woman, he was sure of it. But as he threw open the door and climbed the basement steps to ground level, he couldn't see anything in front of him. And this time the sound seemed farther away. Or muffled, that was it. Somebody was holding something over the woman's mouth. He could not tell where she was, or even guess what was happening to her.

A male voice now, infuriated, from behind him: "Owww, you rotten cunt!" And then a kick delivered to some part of the woman's body, followed by a low, tortured moan.

Chico and Davey? No, they might have been sore losers, but they were still factory men at heart, and would never do something like this. But what? What was "this"?

Arnie got to the top of the steps, turned and started toward a pile of rotting lumber. On the far side of it, just their torsos showing in the watery glow of a caged yellow light bulb, were Dark Jacket and Sweatshirt. The woman, he assumed, lay on the gravel at their feet.

"Hey, you goddamn punks!" Arnie said and, slowly approaching the boys, he brought his whistle to his lips and blew into it as hard as he could. It was the first time his mouth had ever made contact with it, and he suddenly felt like a fool. A kid playing with a toy. What was the whistle supposed to do to help the woman? Would anybody hear it? If so, what would that person do? Calling the cops, Arnie thought, was a long shot.

"Well, if it ain't ol' fuckface!"

"You try tootin' that little piece a plastic again an' I'll rip it off your neck an' shove it up your ass."

It was, for the moment, a standoff. Walking against the back edge of the alley, away from the school, Arnie had reached an angle at which he could see the woman, wounded and terrified, lying between the two boys. She, too, was colored. And that, more than anything else, would make this the most important night in Arnie Castig's life.

84

HE GUESSED that she was in her late forties or early fifties, her hair dark but with several silver streaks. Her nylons were ripped, legs scraped and bleeding. She was holding onto her purse with both hands and had wound the strap around one of her arms. Dark Jacket had been pulling at it, one foot braced against the side of the woman's head, and as he tried to remove the purse from her desperate grasp, the strap had dug into her arm and rubbed away skin. More blood dripping into the gravel. Ignoring Arnie, he went back to work.

Sweatshirt, meanwhile, was standing over the woman, trying to keep her quiet by grinding one of his sneakers into her mouth. All of this, the entire scene, Arnie had registered in a maximum of three seconds.

"What the hell do you guys think you're doing?"

The two boys looked at each other, then back at Arnie. He could read the questions in their eyes. Was he a real policeman or just one of those rent-a-cops? Was he alone? Did he have a gun? Should they flank him, try to bring him down? Had he already called for help and, if so, how much time did they have?

After a few seconds, Arnie read their dawning awareness of the answers, saw it in the gradual relaxation of their shoulders and the slouch to their hips. He was by himself. He was unarmed. He was an old man, out of shape and out of his league. Hired on the cheap. Not having expected any trouble, he was not prepared for it. Sweatshirt allowed a smirk to spread across his lips, and to Arnie it was the unveiling of evil.

Still: "Get away from her," he said.

Dark Jacket glanced at his friend out of the corner of his eye and took the cue, showing his own smirk.

The woman wedged her head out from under Sweatshirt's shoe and wailed. The boy kicked her in the jaw; Arnie thought he could hear teeth crack.

"I warned you sons of bitches," he said, and took a few more steps toward them, blowing into the whistle again, this time louder and longer.

"Lloyd, stop 'im," from Dark Jacket.

Lloyd did not need to hear it again. He launched himself at Arnie, covering the distance between them like a long jumper, wrapping his arms around the old man in the uniform, swinging him around, and flinging him back into the pile of lumber. Arnie hit it with a thud. Lloyd leaped into him again and planted his shoulder in Arnie's ribs. Then the boy slammed his forearm under Arnie's throat and, with the other hand yanked the whistle from his mouth before he could empty any more air into it.

"Gimme that, fuckface!"

"Get your filthy hands off, you bastard!" Arnie tried to tear Lloyd's grip from the only means of protection he had, but to no avail; the punk's hand was like a pair of pliers, and Lloyd yanked on the shoelace so hard that it sliced into the back of Arnie's neck, cutting a groove into the skin. After a few seconds the lace broke, the impact causing Lloyd to lose his balance and fall over backward, landing on the colored woman and skittering off her.

"Cut 'im, Lloyd," Dark Jacket told him, "cut the lousy prick."

"I don't need no lousy blade fer him," Lloyd grinned, proudly holding up the whistle as he got to his feet. "Say goodbye, fuckface," and he threw the whistle as far as he could into the weeds behind the alley.

Angered beyond all reason or sense of self-preservation, Arnie could not think, could only react, and his reaction was to employ violence of his own. He dived at Lloyd head first, ramming him in the stomach, the bill of his cap leading the way. He knocked the wind out of his young foe, sending him onto the gravel again. Arnie had knocked the wind out of himself in the process as well, but he did not let up. He threw punches crazily, in an indiscriminate fury, one that caused him not only to fight like a more formidable opponent than he really was, but to ignore a sharp, black bolt of pain in his chest that should have reminded him of why he no longer worked in a steel mill. But he had a hundred pounds on his opponent, and a toughness honed on a football field and at American Bridge, and that ought to be worth something.

The woman screeched. "Helllp! Gawd A'mighty, he'p me, somebodeee!"

Arnie turned to the side to see Dark Jacket clamp his hand over her mouth.

She bit it.

He punched her in the eye.

She spit at him, and one of her teeth nicked his cheek.

"Danny," the other one called, "forget the bitch! Get this lardass offa me!"

Arnie and Lloyd began to tumble around on the ground in a single lump: legs wound around legs, chests smashed into chests, fists flailing---sometimes making contact, sometimes not; just as often the combatants punched the gravel beneath them, cutting their knuckles.

Danny hustled over to them, waiting for Arnie to end up on top of the configuration, and when he did Lloyd's buddy reared back and kicked him in the hip; he might have been trying to boot a field goal from the very limits of his range. Arnie's glasses flew off, but he was near-sighted and Lloyd could not have been nearer. He maneuvered himself under the boy again, seeking shelter from Danny's foot, but Lloyd quickly got the positions reversed, Arnie on top again, and in the clear for another kick. This one landed exactly where the first one had, exactly as hard; the pain was more than doubled.

Arnie could hold onto his adversary no longer. He fell backward across some loose planks, screaming inside but silent to the world. He was afraid he had nothing left.

Lloyd pulled out his switchblade.

"Need it after all, huh, punk?" Arnie panted.

"Make another move," Lloyd told him, "I mean you fuckin' move a fuckin' half a inch an' I'll cut that fat face of yours into a thousand pieces." He pushed a button on the side of the knife; the blade shot out of the handle, glinting faintly in the pale yellow light.

Arnie should have been frightened, more frightened now than at any time in his life since he had seen the sheave wheel falling. But he wasn't. He was, rather, relieved, and was honest enough with himself to welcome the feeling rather than be ashamed of it. The knife, he believed in that moment, was his exoneration, the tangible sign that he no longer had to keep up the fight. The odds against his winning, huge at the outset, had become impossible now that one of the young hoods was armed and ready. Few people would have blamed Arnie had he decided not to do battle with Lloyd in the first place. Now, with a piece of deadly sharp steel between them, no one would blame him. He sat in the alley with his knees up, bent to the left so that he could stroke his right hip, Danny's target. Meanwhile, his heart was beating so wildly that he could feel it in the back of his throat, like hiccups.

Then: "What's that smell?" Arnie had noticed it just as a breeze came up and blew it at him, and it was like nothing he had ever smelled before. It wasn't curiosity that made him ask about it; rather, he was afraid it might be a sign of danger, some new threat on this night that still remained threatening enough.

Lloyd and Danny seemed puzzled at first. Then Danny whispered something to his mate and the two of them giggled. *Giggled*, of all the things! Whatever the scent was, it blended into the stink from Valvoline on the other side of the boulevard. At least temporarily, the two odors had formed an unholy brew carried unwillingly by the innocence of the breeze.

Lloyd stopped giggling first. "Man, you know what you are? You the man from yesterday, fuckface. This ain't your time no more."

Arnie did not search for a meaning. Instead, he searched for his glasses, and saw them out of the corner of his eye, next to the woman's shoulder. He reached for them, picked them up, slipped them on. But one of the temples was broken and fell off; there was nothing he could do for now but put the piece in his pocket and let his lenses flop around his nose, demanding constant adjustments.

Lloyd and Danny broke into another fit of giggling: Arnie's cap down to his ears, his glasses jiggling with each movement of his head---he would have been vaudeville to them, if they had known what vaudeville was. Meanwhile, he took advantage of his improved vision to look carefully at his adversaries. The boys were staring out at the world through small oval clouds, the way someone's eyes appear after he has been up all night with a cold, and their pupils were so big that they took up almost the whole eyeball. The corners' of their eyes, all four of them, were red and moist---so moist, in fact, that they were leaking. It didn't seem possible to Arnie that a person could focus on the world through a set of peepers in that condition.

WHEN THE PUNKS regained control of themselves, they changed their plan of attack. No more inflicting pain on the old man; now it was humiliation.

Lloyd ripped the badge off Arnie's cap and threw it in the general direction of the whistle.

Danny pulled the cap off his head and pissed in it, a cloud of steam rising as the warm urine met the brisk night air and overflowed in vapor like the concoction of a mad scientist. Arnie turned away from the sight, the smell, the cap he had worn so proudly, so honorably, since the end of his days at American Bridge. He felt a tear glide down his cheek, and then another, wiping them quickly before the boys could see. But they did.

"Aw, lookee Dan," Lloyd said, "da big baby's cryin'."

"Don't cry, little boy," Danny chipped in, "yer mommy'll buy you a new hat."

And more giggles.

When Danny had emptied his bladder, he tugged off Arnie's jacket, meeting no resistance. He threw it on the woodpile, and poured some of the pee from the cap over it. Then he placed the cap upside-down in the alley like a dog's dish. The two boys were cackling with delight at their originality. But they were not done yet.

Lloyd ripped off Arnie's shirt and the night turned immediately frigid for him as the young hoodlum cut the garment into slivers with his switchblade.

Danny tugged off Arnie's belt, coiled it tightly, and left it in the cap to soak.

Lloyd reached into Arnie's pockets but nothing fell out except a few coins and a St. Christopher's medal.

"Hey," he said, "the cunt. Get the cunt's purse now."

The woman's chest was moving in and out, but not going very far in either direction. Danny didn't care, barely even looked at her. He was finally able to unwind the strap from her arm and began to dig through it for her wallet. "Got it," he said, "yeah, man!" He threw out an ID card, a photograph of two young children, some receipts. Then he found a credit card, and held it up to his partner.

"Forget that shit!" Lloyd demanded. "I don't know what to do with no credit card. You?"

Danny shook his head.

"So get the fuckin' money!"

Danny pulled out the cash, ripping the wallet's lining in the process. He started counting. "Five, six, seven, eight---fuckin' shit, man, that's it! Eight goddam bucks!"

"No way, man!"

"Chickenfeed, Lloyd!"

"Son of a *bitch*!" Except it came out "bish."

"You're a whore, lady," Danny shouted at her, "a lousy, no-good nigger whore!" Except what Danny said was "loushy" and "war."

Then they heard the siren, all three of them---maybe four; Arnie had no way of knowing whether the woman was still conscious. The two punks ran up through the woods and disappeared, leaving behind the shame and destruction they had inflicted---a woman whose pain was like nothing she had ever imagined and a man whose life would be changed in ways he could never have imagined.

THE ENTIRE NIGHT SHIFT of the Rochester Police Department, with the exception of the dispatcher and one man out sick tonight, got there before the ambulance did. Two cars, five men. They sealed off the alley, one end of it with their vehicles, the other with strips of crime scene tape secured to tree trunks. When the ambulance finally arrived, its siren piercing a night that had already had more than its share of grating noises, one of the police cars moved aside and the ambulance sped past it, stopping a few feet from the colored woman. Sgt. David Spadafore was in charge, and the moment he appeared Arnie started explaining why he hadn't called: the burned-out light bulb, the finger he couldn't control in the pitch-black locker room.

Spadafore patted him on the back. "Not to worry, pal," and explained that one of his patrol cars heard Arnie blow the siren as he was driving past the school, idly patrolling. "It was a fluke, a real fluke, but the timing couldn't've been better." Then, looking closely at Arnie: "'Course, it would've been nice if we'd got here a little earlier."

One of the other cops had found a blanket in the trunk of his car and covered Arnie with it. He nodded his gratitude and, after a few seconds, started shivering more slowly.

As the EMTs unfolded their stretcher, Spadafore and Arnie sized up the colored woman, whose legs had been twisted into angles that it seemed only a stick figure could achieve. One of the EMTs arranged them in a more dignified position, then felt the blood on her legs and in the corners of her mouth. It was dry, but the blood in her right ear was fresh and dripping down her neck. The EMT bandaged it, then gave her a quick once-over with his stethoscope. He raised his thumb at his partner, and they lifted her onto the stretcher and carried her into the ambulance. The woman was silent, bubbles of saliva dripping down her chin, but her eyes were open and she was watching.

"You'll be fine, lady," Arnie said, having no idea whether he was telling the truth, "don't worry. Everything going to be fine."

The doors closed on her. The St. Mary of the Mount Hospital in New Brighton was about ten minutes away. The men would get there in six.

"Thing is," Spadafore said, "I'm not so sure how fine *you're* gonna be, Stats. You oughtta be in that ambulance, too, you know."

"I'm okay, Dave, really. What they did to me, it's the kind of thing that's just going to make me sore. I'll get over it. The lady's the one who needs the help."

"Don't have to be either-or, you know. You could both get the help you need." As the ambulance blasted its siren, racing out of sight, Spadafore snapped his fingers at a third EMT, whom he had ordered to stay behind, and the man conducted as thorough an examination of Arnie as was possible on the scene. He grimaced every time the man tapped his hip, sucking in air, squeezing his eyes tightly shut. But the EMT said the injuries didn't seem to be serious, although a part of the body like the hip would heal slowly; Arnie would probably need crutches for a few days. Maybe a week, maybe a cane after that. As for the rest of his injuries, the EMT said they were superficial. He cleaned out the cuts with mercurochrome, applied gauze and extra-large band-aids. He folded open the blanket and taped Arnie's ribs, making him wince every time the tape looped around him. The EMT gave him some pain killers, and told him to call his doctor in the morning.

"Check his heart," Spadafore said.

"Come on, Dave, I---"

"Just shut the hell up, Stats. I'm runnin' the show here, an' you're doin' what I tell you." The attendant took his own stethoscope out of a small bag and applied it to Arnie's chest, front and back, shifting it around slowly to several locations.

"I'm freezing, man. Even the stethoscope's cold."

"Sorry," the EMT said, then covered him with the blanket again. He checked Arnie's pulse rate against the second hand of his watch.

"Seems okay to me," he said.

Yeah, but you're not exactly Ben Casey, he thought, referring to the famous TV doctor.

"I'm really serious, Stats," Spadafore said, "you got to see your M.D. in the morning. First thing, ya hear me?"

"I will, I will, don't worry about it."

"All right," and Rochester's Chief of Police pointed over his shoulder, telling the EMT he should take the back seat in the cruiser on the right. "We'll get you to the hospital again as quick as we can."

"I got work to do, y' know."

"You *been* workin', right here. This is where we needed you. So just pipe down an' we'll do the best we can, got it?"

"You ain't my boss," he said, and tramped back through the alley.

"Unemployed people don't have to worry about bosses," Spadafore said. "Just cool your tool, man."

The EMT muttered something unhappily but unintelligibly, then slid into the car as ordered. He lit up a cigarette, puffing away until, even with the back window partly open, he had enveloping himself so thoroughly in a cloud of smoke that, after a minute or so, he disappeared. It looked as if the back seat were stuffed with a bale of graying cotton.

The manhunt for Lloyd and Danny was a brief one. For some reason, neither had left the area, tried to hide, or even decided to behave inconspicuously. Rather, the two thieves were sitting on a curb on a side street of Rochester, less than two blocks from the school, and as a police car approached, they ignored it, continuing their game of rock, papers, scissors and laughing no matter who won. When the cop got out of his car, Danny stood up and mooned him. Lloyd found the sight so witty he wrapped his arms around his stomach to hold in the laughter.

The punks were handcuffed, shoved into the police car and driven back to the alley for Arnie to provide a positive ID. He did, but had to lower his eyes quickly. They had humiliated him as he had never been humiliated before. He did not want to see their faces any longer than necessary.

"Hey, fuckfash," Lloyd yelled, "ain'tcha glad t' see ush again?"

"Yeah, brotha. We like ol' friendth by now."

The cop in the front seat gunned the engine and the car threw up streams of gravel as the boys headed merrily off to the police station.

By this time, a handful of people had gathered to watch the doings behind old Abe Lincoln, and as the perpetrators departed, Spadafore addressed them. "Party's over now, folks. Time to get yourself home, let us finish up here. Come on now, everybody out. Trust me, you're not gonna miss anything, just a couple of cops on clean-up duty."

The small crowd dispersed, grumbling, all of them on foot, all glancing over their shoulders to make sure they really *weren't* missing anything. Some were headed home, others to their favorite watering holes. Finally, some excitement in the air, Rochester's sickenly-scented air, and they could do no more than mutter their speculations as they departed.

"Let's get outta here," Spadafore said to Arnie, "go around front while they finish cleaning up." He pointed to the lone police car remaining in the alley. "Hop in."

"Actually, Dave, I'd rather walk."

"Walk? You kiddin' me?"

"No, really, it'll be easier than bending over and getting in and out of the car."

Spadafore shrugged. "If you say so."

"Trust me."

Spadafore told a cop named Mike to drive the chief's car around to the main entrance of the school, and he and Arnie trailed slowly after it, saying little. Arnie was trying to stifle the pain as he limped, and might have been exerting so much energy in the process that he had little left for speaking.

"What a night, huh?" Spadafore said.

"Never thought I'd see the likes of it."

Although a few years older than Arnie, Sgt. David Spadafore appeared, at first glance, younger: his body trimmer, his carriage more erect, face less lined, although permanently reddened from after-hours liquor. But a closer look revealed that his hairline was beginning to recede and his jowls to thicken; as for his eyes, they had long since grown weary from the ennui and occasional violence of his job, although more of the former than the latter in a town like Rochester. His cheeks were pinched and his nose upturned; the cops who had known him longest sometimes called him "Bulldog."

Around front, Arnie sat on a cement bench that had been secured to the pavement with steel straps. Spadafore stood next to him, his shoulder against a flagpole that did not have a flag on it; idly, he fingered the ropes, occasionally snapping them against the pole. Behind them, the school was lit up for business as usual; one of the night school teachers carried a key to a side door in case of emergency and had let everyone in. But classes were almost over now; the last few stragglers were walking out of the building behind Arnie and Spadafore, a few looking over at them questioningly but having no idea what had happened. No one came to ask.

The police car pulled up to the curb, Mike at the wheel, and the smoke-enveloped EMT in back.

Arnie mentioned the colored woman.

"Really no way to know 'til they get her to the hospital, Stats."

"No, I guess not."

"Be a while before she enters any beauty contests, though."

Arnie would have chuckled, a gentle sound, but even that would have felt like a punch in the ribs.

The two men could hear the rumble of overnight trucks on the Ohio River Boulevard a few blocks away. The drivers were probably on their CBs, whiling away the hours talking to strangers they would never see, but who would accompany them through the darker stretches of their jobs. Looking downriver, Arnie could just make out the flaring stack of Findlay and Russell's by-products plant as it poured coke oven gas into the sky. The gas was a blue flame with an orange crown and a pinpoint in the distance. Such a clear night.

"Those punks," Arnie said, "You saw what I meant about their eyes."

"Couldn't hardly miss it."

"And the way they behaved, laughing like idiots. I mean, how can you be laughing when you just beat the shit out of somebody and got arrested?"

"You don't know?"

"Should I?"

Spadafore sighed. "Probably not," he said, "not really your style. Hell, not even your generation. Or mine, for that matter."

"What're you talking about, Dave?"

"They were stoned," he said. "Smoking marijuana, Stats."

"You're kidding."

"I'm sure of it."

"I didn't see any cigarettes."

"They probably smoked them before you came out, then threw 'em away when they saw the woman. It takes a while for the stuff to kick in. Then you can turn all kinds of goofy."

"So that was the smell back in the alley."

"They were probably takin' some other stuff too, if I hadda guess."

"Like what?"

"I don't know," Spadafore said. "A lot of these drugs I haven't even heard of. LSD, though. That's some really powerful shit. I heard of that."

"Yeah, me too." Arnie paused. "What's that stand for, though---LSD?

"You got me."

"Liquid sulfur dioxide, maybe?"

Spadafore shrugged. "As good a guess as any."

Arnie was frowning. "I know about these . . . what do they call them? Mind-altering substances, that's it. But I thought they were pretty much a big city thing. I didn't know you could get them around here."

Spadafore was shaking his head. "Things're changin', Statsy. It's like you wouldn't believe. Just the last couple years. Before that, well, you're right. You wanted dope, you might have to go all the way to the 'burg to get it. Maybe Youngstown. An' it used to be pretty much a private thing. You were lookin' to get high, you did it at home. Maybe even in your car. But never in public. These days it's out in the open. I mean, you can't hardly miss it. You can make your buy in bars, pool halls, restaurants. I even heard a coupla days ago you can get your hands on weed in some of the mills."

"Get outta here."

"Spinks-Wyler's supposed to be one of them. You believe that. The frigging' mill.

"But that could be dangerous, Dave. You're acting like Lloyd and Danny and operating heavy machinery, you could kill somebody."

"I didn't say guys were usin' it in the mills, Stats. I just said you could buy it there. 'Course maybe after you buy it you can't resist taking a few drags on the job, who knows. It's . . . it's all just different these days."

"I wonder how come."

"That's the million-dollar question."

Arnie tried to adjust his glasses comfortably on his nose, and that's when Spadafore noticed they were no longer whole. "That happen in the fight?"

"Yeah. I got the piece that fell off but I don't know when I'll have the time to get it fixed. Besides, it's not like I got money to burn, you know?"

"I hear ya, but for the time bein', a little tape'll fix ya right up."

"I got a roll at home," Arnie told him. "But these glasses were new. First new pair I bought in probably about ten or fifteen years. Son of a bitch."

A cop whom Arnie hadn't noticed before walked around the side of the building holding Arnie's cap as far away from him as he could at the end of a stick. "Whattaya want me to do with this chief?"

"Get a plastic bag outta my trunk. We'll keep it there for now."

"You want me to use the same bag we put the woman's wallet in?"

"Fuckin' moron," Spadafore whispered to Arnie. Then, raising his voice, "No," he said to the cop, "a different one. We're gonna throw the cap away as soon as we can, but right now we need it for evidence."

"Keep the shirt, too? It's like a bunch of rags."

"Put it in with the wallet, as long as it's not wet."

The cop started for the car and Spadafore said he was afraid the cap was ruined.

Arnie knew. But he would pay a rare visit to the office tomorrow to get another one. After a few seconds, he said, "I probably don't smell so good myself."

"Well, nobody'd mistake you for a rose garden, that's for sure."

"Probably won't even let me on the bus."

"Forget the bus, Stats. We'll take you home. We'll wrap you in a clean blanket and you take a hot bath before you go to bed. Nice, hot bath to soak those achin' muscles."

The cop with Arnie's hat was just opening Spadafore's trunk. "Hey, Lou."

He turned to his superior officer.

"The cap? I think ya better double-bag it."

"Gotcha, Bulldog," he said, and started looking for the bags.

For some reason, Arnie found himself thinking about the truckers and their CBs again. A funny thing, he thought: the notion of talking to people you'd never seen as if they were friends. He shrugged. Maybe they *did* run into each other once in a while. And even if they didn't, maybe it *was* possible to have a friend you never met. Like pen pals. Arnie thought about how lonely he'd be without Zook.

Then he glanced down at his watch. Crystal broken, strap mangled, stem missing. But still ticking. Nine-thirty. "Well I guess I better get my ass in gear." He needed both hands to push himself up off the bench.

"What're you talkin' about?"

"Gotta get back inside and make my last round. Enough of this sitting around out here, loafing."

"Hold on, Statsy. Christ, you're as crazy as those potheads we just arrested. No way you're going back to work tonight."

"I'm all right."

"All right? You're a walkin' advertisement for wheelchairs, that's what you are. An advertisement for *not* walkin'."

"I can do it, Dave, I swear. I just made it all the way from the alley up front here, didn't I? Besides, I can't let those two bums get the best of me. I gotta finish what I started."

"In that case, you're under arrest."

"What?"

"Smellin' like a cesspool in public, I don't know. I'll think of somethin'. Getcha a night in jail and maybe a hundred dollar fine. Now, you gonna come peaceful-like or you want the cuffs on you."

"Come on, Dave, you can't treat me---"

"This is Rochester. I can treat you any way I want. You either spend the night behind bars or at home in your own bed, on your own recognizance." He unfastened the handcuffs from his belt and jingled them at Arnie. "You think I don't mean it? Try me."

"But---"

"I know who to call about turnin' the lights off and makin' sure everything's secure. Don't worry about it." He paused as Arnie struggled for words. "Stats?

"Yeah?"

"Just shut the fuck up."

IN THE POLICE CAR driving back to Ambridge, Spadafore turned the volume down on his radio and tapped his hand on Arnie's thigh a few times. It was several more seconds before either spoke, though. Somehow both men sensed it wasn't a time for talking. Until . . .

"You really laid yourself on the line out there tonight, Stats. You didn't give a damn about yourself, all you were thinkin' about was someone else, an' you didn't even know her an' it was a colored lady besides. Really showed me somethin'," he said. "Showed me a whole lot." Spadafore put both hands on the wheel now.

"I was just doing my job," Arnie said. "That's all I was thinking about."

"You underestimate yourself, my friend. You're a brave man, and believe me, it's not the kind of thing I say lightly. I'm proud to have you on the beat in my town."

"You are?" Arnie's eyes showed wonder; he had never expected to hear anything like that.

"Wasn't for that damn heart of yours, Stats, I'd try to get you on the force, and that's no shit."

"You can't be serious."

Spadafore chuckled. "*You're* the one who can't be serious, my friend."

Brave. The top cop in all of Rochester had said he was brave. All these years of living, all his hard work, putting duty above all, never complaining about anything---and he had finally earned his stripes. And not in a steel mill. Not even in Ambridge. What a funny thing his life had turned out to be.

Not, not funny, not at all. Otherwise, why did he start crying now? He couldn't remember the last time he had cried---not just a few drops, like in the alley, but a stream of tears, washing down his face. That's what he felt now. Lloyd was right. He was a big baby, tears falling although he was long into his adult years. Too long.

Spadafore didn't say anything. He reached across Arnie, opened the glove compartment, and pulled out a few tissues, handing them over. Arnie took them, embarrassed, and began to wipe. On this night that had started out like every other, he had ended up losing control of himself twice in a single hour. And neither time because of pain. First there was Danny's emptying his cock as he did, an insult like none he had ever experienced before. Then came Spadafore's calling him brave, saying he would like to have him on the beat in Rochester, praise that was like the ribbons worn by soldiers.

He was dizzy with conflicting emotions. He glanced over at the Findlay & Russell blast furnace, but nothing really registered tonight. The flame didn't seem as high as it was before. Then again, he might not have been able to tell, might not even have been the same man he was before.

Wednesday,
September 29,
1965

THE BEAVER VALLEY OFFICE of Gibraltar Security Services, Inc. was located in Ambridge, on the second floor of a building whose first floor was Eugene's Excelsior Tavern & Fine Dining. As Arnie entered, the place was empty. The men who worked the graveyard shift at the mills had finished their drinking for the morning and gone home; it was too early yet for anyone else to have started; and those in search of a fine dining experience had never entered the joint, no matter what the time of day. Arnie had no idea where Eugene was.

"Eugene," he called. "Hey, 'Uge."

No answer.

A clock in the window next to the front door, with the words "Fort Pitt" above the face and "That's It!" below, ticked like a carpenter pounding nails. It showed four minutes to eleven.

It was not just the food at Eugene's that disqualified it as a venue for fine dining; no less was it the smell of stale beer. Over the course of more than twenty years, beer had been spilled on the bumper pool table and pinball machines in the back of the place, on the lamps along the wall that advertised brands of beer other than Fort Pitt, on the floor and on the bar, on the bartenders' aprons and on the shirts and pants and blouses and skirts of customers, and on stool tops and tabletops and the seats in booths. The residue of old beverage hung in the room like humidity on a steamy summer day; sometimes it was even visible, resembling dust motes in the air when the sun came through the windows at just the right angle.

Arnie pushed his way through the atmosphere, proceeding to the back of the Excelsior and through a doorway in the side wall. Then he turned to his left and stopped. Before him was a flight of stairs, eighteen steps, if he remembered correctly, and nothing out of the ordinary about them. Except today, when, in his present state of decrepitude he found the ascent as daunting a prospect as a cliff with a sheer face. He had not been able to make an appointment with his doctor until later this afternoon, but his present appointment could not be postponed. So he had no crutches, no cane, no assistance for the climb. But if the steps were Goliath, he was David, and everybody knew how *that* turned out.

He got started.

Because of the kicks he had taken to the hip last night, lifting his leg the height of each step was a strain; because of the fragility of his ribs, breathing in and out as deeply as his effort required was painful and enervating. And his head ached. And the cut on the back of his neck from the shoelace's vicious removal sizzled with each movement of his collar. His knee throbbed, probably from the wrestling match with Lloyd, and even his ankle was tender, although he had no memory of twisting it. In fact, the only thing about him that had improved since last night was the condition of his glasses, which were back in one piece against thanks to a strip of tape wound around the broken intersection, and who knew how long *that* would last.

"Only seventeen more, Arnie babe," he said after his first step, "you can do it, you can do it." He pulled himself up as best he could, both hands gripping the railing.

When he finally reached the summit and allowed himself a few seconds to recuperate, he found himself strangely elated. He leaned into the corner of the small landing and looked back at the height he had just scaled. Hell, he thought, if I can make it up those stairs there's no reason I can't go back to work tonight. He tried to remember whether any of the stairways at Abe Lincoln had as many as eighteen steps. He didn't think so. He allowed himself a smile, and was pleased to discover his mouth didn't hurt. At least there was that.

The lamp in the locker room. He would have to remember to bring a bulb with him tonight.

In his best spirits of the morning so far, Arnie rapped on one of two second floor doors. There was Gibraltar Security and there was a rest room for either sex. His knuckles landed squarely on the "c" in "Security" and knocked it loose; it fell to the floor in a flurry of tiny gold flakes.

"C'min'!" growled a voice from inside. "Butler's off today, gotta open the door y'self, not too much trouble.

It wasn't. Arnie did.

Matthew Mathias D'Imperio sat at his desk behind the only window in the room, holding the phone to his ear. His head was bobbing as if a puppet master were manipulating its strings and, turning the mouthpiece away from him, he quietly mouthed obscenities. And gestured, Italian style: tops of his fingers under his chin, then flipped out, palm up: Italian sign language for "fuck you."

Several times Matthew D'Imperio opened his mouth to say something to the person on the other end, but he could manage no more than an occasional phrase, something so short that Arnie had no idea what the conversation was about. Except that it wasn't good, and maybe the person for whom it wasn't good was Arnie. But that couldn't be. Couldn't possibly be. Could it?

"Right, right, got it, you betcha, clear's a bell," Matthew D'Imperio said at last, and slammed the phone into the cradle. "Aaaaugghhh! If that guy ain't the bigges' douchebag in the world, he 'least gotta be in the top five!" He leaned back in his plastic-wheeled chair with such force that it rolled into the window sill behind him, clanking off the radiator beneath it and ricocheting partway back toward the desk. "Ya take 'is brains, ya take that guy's brains an' ya put 'em under one of them microscopes so powerful they can even make out even atoms, ya *still* wouldn't be able t' see nothin'." He spit a toothpick onto the linoleum floor and pedaled his chair the rest of the way up to the desk.

"Hey, Mr. D'Imperio," Arnie said, since it seemed he might not have another chance to enter the conversation, "how's it going?"

Mister, he was to Arnie, even though nothing in the man's demeanor suggested a polite title was appropriate. Mister, even though he was the younger of the two men by a few years. But he was the boss, and in addition, such an intimidating presence that Arnie could not help but treat him with a deference that was not the same thing as respect. He was also the hairiest man Arnie had ever encountered, with his arms in particular being dark and bristly. When Matthew D'Imperio wore a short-sleeve, black T-shirt, as was the case today, a person could think he had instead donned a long-sleeve shirt of the same color. His suspenders, of the clip-on variety, were also black, but always a puzzle to Arnie. Every time he had seen his boss he wore suspenders, and every time he had seen him he was also wearing a belt.

"Siddown, Early," he said. "Early Arnie."

"No," was the reply. "Right on time, give or take a minute."

Arnie had already dropped into a captain's chair in front of Matthew D'Imperio's desk, across from a chrome rack upon which was a small selection of night watchman's shirts, pants and caps. On top of the rack was a box full of badges. Maybe that was the reason for this morning's visit; he had been summoned to get a new outfit; he could even use a new pair of pants. Well, maybe that was *one* of the reasons. He felt certain that his boss had already learned what had happened last night.

"I knew yer ol' man, Castig. I tol' ya that, din't I?"

"Yeah." Several times in fact.

"I was jus' a paper boy back then, had me the afternoon route. Yer dad, he was workin' days, an' I'd run inta him when he come home from the mill. Never stopped off fer a beer, always come back t' his wife an' boy. Good man, good man. Fam'ly man. Always had somethin' nice t' say t' me. Tol' me lotsa times I was good foreman material, he could tell even though I was just a kid. Yep, good man. How long he been dead now?"

"Thirty-eight years."

Arnie shifted positions in his chair, causing a squeak from somewhere. Matthew D'Imperio wasn't acting like a man about to offer congratulations for service above and beyond the call of duty, which was Arnie thought was another reason for his having received an early phone call from his boss.

Rosa was thinking bigger. She believed her husband deserved a plaque or a medal or a pay raise or maybe two of the preceding, if not all three. She thought there might even be some kind of public ceremony, with the mayors of Ambridge and Rochester and other dignitaries paying their respects.

Arnie had to grin, telling her she was going way too far.

But at least for the moment, a brief moment this morning over coffee and a piece of unbuttered toast, Arnie could not help imagining himself standing on a platform of some sort with an award in his hand and all kinds of people clapping and a band playing one of those Sousa marches, the kind of music that makes any accomplishment seem grander than it is.

And then, with a shake of the head, Arnie directed his grin inward, conceding that *he* was the one going too far.

"'Bout what happen' las' night," Matthew D'Imperio finally said.

"Yeah?" Okay, so he probably wouldn't get more than a handshake and an expression of gratitude. Maybe, just maybe, Gibraltar would throw in a few extra dollars a week. After all, he hadn't had a raise in the three years since he'd started. Or a trophy. They were usually cheap little things, but nice to look at once in a while. Did they make trophies with tiny, silver-colored security guards on top of them?

"'Fraid it's gunna cost ya yer job."

It was as if, expecting to be told that his recuperation from an illness had been complete, he had instead been told of a relapse; as if, expecting riches, he had learned of a stock market crash. So far away were the words he had just heard from what Arnie had prepared himself to hear that he pushed himself into the back of his chair, as if that would somehow force the room to slow its sudden spin. It didn't. He had never ridden the rides at West View, only danced; this must have been what the tilt-a-whirl and the rest of them felt like. He closed his eyes and yielded to the disorienting movement, unable to say anything at first, and then, after a few seconds, able to let them a few words straggle out. "What?" he said, and fell forward, his elbows landing on Matthew D'Imperio's desk. "I don't . . . I mean . . ."

"Yup, gunna hafta shitcan ya."

No less feebly: "But . . . Why? I don't . . ."

"Not yer fault, Castig. Gotta give the job t' a nigger."

"To . . . give my job to who?"

"Ya heard me, all right. Goddam jungle bunny, that's who."

Arnie wanted to ask why again---why a colored man was going to get his job, why there wasn't even a little medal for him if not the whole parade? But although his lips formed the word, he could not squeeze a sound through them.

Matthew D'Imperio spun around in his chair. Rising, he turned his back to Arnie and stared out the window at the American Bridge Company's Forge and Bend shop a few blocks away, its black walls streaked a dirty orange, as if someone had poured buckets of rust on them and they had baked in the sun. He folded his arms across his chest.

"It's a long story, Castig," his boss said, "but here goes. First off, there's this buncha niggers in Freedom call theirselves the Beaver Valley Colored People's Action Committee. Ya prob'ly never hearda them, but when I hired ya a couple years back, they 'bout shit a brick. Never tol' ya 'bout the situation, din't wanna get yer ticker in an uproar when ya was jus' gettin' started, but they was some kinda pissed off."

"What for? I---"

"Ya were the wrong color, asshole."

"But---"

"But nothin'," he said, facing Arnie again and beginning to curl his arm hairs. Arnie couldn't watch. "Yer *still* the wrong color, enda story. Now, the head Ubangi, name a Ronald Leander Washington---how's 'at fer a name, by the way. Ronald Leander Washington! Nigger names, they a hoot er what?"

It was a common enough word in the Valley. In whispered tones, behind their backs, even to their faces in an argument, every colored person was a nigger. But Arnie knew the pain the name caused, and was uncomfortable in the presence of those who used it. He was a dago, after all, a guinea, a wop.

He did not have any colored friends, did not even really know any coloreds except for a few in the clean-up crews at the mill. But he watched them play football on television, and between the lines a man was judged solely on the basis of ability. The play-by-play men always treated coloreds with the same respect as whites. Never even called them coloreds. You watched a whole football game on the tube, and you never had any idea what color a man was, unless maybe he took his helmet off.

Matt Snell, who caught a touchdown pass from Broadway Joe a few days ago, was a Negro. Dee Mackey, whose block kept a defender away from Joe long enough for him to air mail the ball to Snell---he was a Negro, too. And there were others, men who were Namath's friends and protectors, his aides and fellow warriors.

As for the Steelers, they had their own share---stars, many of them. Roy Jefferson and Jim "Cannonball" Butler on offense, and defensive stalwarts like Charlie Bradshaw and the great Brady Keys. They were men Arnie depended upon, men on his team. A different color from his own, true, but they were not niggers. And a man didn't have to play football, or any other sport, to be entitled to some dignity. He just had to be alive, and decent. For Arnie to hear the word was like hearing fingernails scrape on a blackboard. For him to hear it in the present context was even worse.

He leaned back in the chair again, still tilt-a-whirling.

"Anyhow, where was I?" Matthew D'Imperio continued. "Oh, yeah. So ol' Ronald Leander Washington, he calls me las' night, wakes me up, the S.O.B., then comes barrel-assin' into my office this mornin' an' says, an' this is jus' how he talks too, he says, 'I told you, suh, not to give this job to a incapacitated white man when it first became available. You ignored me, and now you see the wages of your prejudice. This time you will hire one of my people or there will be hell to pay, I assure you.'"

"Incapacitated?"

"Yeah, I don't know how the hell 'e knew, but he says there's so many able-bodied spear-chuckers out there that hirin' ya was like spittin' in their face." Matthew D'Imperio sneered like a cartoon villain. "I still remember what I tol' ol' Ronald Leander when I gave ya the job. I tol' 'im it's my business who works fer me an' if 'e din't like it 'e could go fuck hisself up the ass with a broomstick. That was, when, 1963, late '62? Well, lemme tell ya somethin'. Ya can't tell niggers go fuck 'emselves no more, an' ya wanna know why? I'll tell ya why. I'll give ya one name. Mr. L.B. Johnson, 'at's why. He signed 'at civil rights bill this summer an' white guys been droppin' like flies ever since. 'Course it was Kennedy's bill. He did it 'cause of all the goddamn Kennedys."

Arnie cleared his throat. There was nothing in it. "But can't you---?"

"I can't do nothin', Castig. Ronald Leander Washington says when he leaves my office this mornin' he's gonna call"---he had to refer to a piece of paper on his desk---"the Equal Employment Opportunity Commission an' the Fair Employment Practices Commission, an' you, my friend, the son of one a the finest men I ever knew, an' a pretty damn fine fella yerself, are up shit creek without a paddle. Yer tax dollars at work, creatin' them agencies."

Arnie couldn't remember ever seeing his boss light a cigarette, but he lit one now and raced through a few drags.

"It ain't up t' me what happens, ya understan'. It's up t' the main office in Pittsburgh. But I can tell ya what's gonna happen, don't take no genius. Soon as Ronald Leander Washington calls Mr. Wall-ace Sampson---he's the dickhead runs the company, guy I was talking to when you come in--- he's gunna knuckle under and then Ronald Leander Washington's gunna run the joint. He's gunna make an announcement, tell all the coons in the Valley yer ass is grass. So that's it, Castig, ya risked yer life las' night--- don't think I don't know it---an' now ya got less chance than a snowball in a blas' furnace of keepin' yer job." And then he sang: "My country 'tis a thee, sweet land a liberty . . ."

And then he sat, landing on his chair with enough impact to bounce it on the floor. He was already halfway through the cigarette.

"Jesus, yer jus' sitting there, Early. Ain't ya got nothin' t' say?"

Say? Arnie couldn't even swallow; his Adam's apple was glued to the wall of his throat.

"Ya ain't gonna have another heart attack on me now, are you?"

"My heart didn't have anything to do with what happened last night, Mr. D'Imperio."

"Look, ya know I'm on yer side, but don't try t' pull 'at crap on me."

"What do you mean, crap?"

"How long it take after ya heard the nigger broad scream 'til ya got yer ass outside?"

"How long?" Arnie repeated. "Well, I don't know. I mean---"

"Then I'll tell ya. Twice as long it take a guy carryin' 'bout thirty less pounds an' with a good ticker. 'At's how long!"

"But I---"

"An' if 'at guy's a nigger t' boot . . . Hellfire, them guys're greased lightnin'. Lookit the guy won all them gold medals in the Olympics las' year. Bob Hayes. Bullet Bob, they call 'im. Now he's a rookie fer the Cowboys. I'm talkin', this guy's so freakin' fast the Dallas Cowboys sign 'im up as a wide receiver even though he never played football in 'is life. They probably got a play, they tell 'im, okay Bullet, we snap the ball an' you jus' outrun everybody fer the goalpost. Meredith throws the ol' pigskin as far as he can and you catch the fucker. Touchdown, Dallas! Shit, man,

Bullet Bob's on the job las' night, he's inna alley 'fore the lady's head hits the groun' the firs' time."

Arnie needed time. He had never had the tectonic plates of his life shift beneath him like this. When he finally responded, he was disappointed in himself. The best he could so was, "I gave it a hundred-ten percent out there last night, Mr. D'Imperio."

And for the first time, a softening of his boss's voice. "I know ya did, Early. Believe me, I know what kinda man ya are, ol' Early Arnie. That's why I hired ya. Problem is, yer hunnert ten's another guy's fifty." He paused. "An' then there's the fact ya never *shoulda* been in the alley las' night. What the hell's the first thing I tol' ya t' do when there was trouble."

"The light bulb burned out in my room. You seem to know everything else about last night. Didn't anybody bother to tell you *that*? It was dark as midnight in there. I couldn't *see* the phone. I tried to call the cops but I couldn't get the numbers right and if I'd've waited any longer---"

"The spook lady woulda been dead. I know, I know. Hell, ya saved 'er life. Even the Beaver Valley Colored People's Asshole Committee knows that."

"They do? Well, then why---"

Matthew D'Imperio held up his hand. "If I'm lyin' I'm dyin'. But it don't matter t' them. Wouldn't matter t' Mr. L.B. Johnson, if he knew 'bout it. The fact is, an' this is the thing ya gotta get through yer head, this ain't got nothin' t' do with a man losin' 'is job. What this here situation is 'bout is politics, plain an' simple. An' powerful. Too powerful for little people like you an' me. Nex' time there's any kinda fuckup at Abe Lincoln, I'll be standin' in the unemployment line with ya, don't kid yerself." He mashed out his cigarette on the windowsill and it hissed for a second or two against chips of old paint.

Arnie nodded, not accepting his fate so much as rejecting further conversation; it was all too much for him, too bizarre, demoralizing. No band, no medal, no parade . . . no job! He could not think, could not make his mind work, and did not want to do it anyhow in his present company. He wanted to be done with Matthew D'Imperio, whether it was his fault or not. And it wasn't, he knew it wasn't.

"Do I go to work tonight?"

"'Less I call ya, tell ya different. Not that I can figure out why the hell ya'd wanna show up. I'll pay ya fer the whole week, no matter what. Even try t' give ya a little extra, but I was you, I'd leave fuckin' Wall-ace in the lurch, let 'im see what it's like not t' have anybody aroun'. Get the word out t' all the scumbags in Rochester, invite 'em inta Abe Lincoln fer their own personal riots."

"How long do you think it'll take the main office to find a new man?"

"Beats me. I had t' guess, though, I'd say our friend Mr. Washington already got one a his buddies in mind an' he's probably chompin' at the bit t' get started."

"You think maybe they'll need me to break the guy in? You know, show him the works?"

Matthew D'Imperio narrowed his eyes in wonder at the man before him. "Jesus Christ, Castig, you are some piece a work! These black bastards throw ya in the garbage can an' yer askin' me if they need help puttin' the lid on."

"It's not that," Arnie insisted. "It's not. It's just that . . . well . . ." What *was* it?

Matthew D'Imperio stood at his desk, bracing himself with elbows straight, both fists pressing into the blotter. It was as close as he had been to Arnie all morning. He slid his voice into a whisper, in case the walls had ears. "I'll tell ya somethin', but this gotta be jus' between you an' me."

Arnie didn't want to hear it, but to get up and leave now wouldn't have made any sense.

"I think L.B. Johnson got nigger blood somewhere in 'is family, an' not too far back, neither. Only way I can figure out what's goin' on in the country these days." He slid another cigarette out of a pack on the desk. "Ya know?"

THERE WAS A COLORED MAN sitting on the ledge of his stoop. Arnie had been walking slowly down Maple, the condition of his body not permitting a faster pace, but when he saw his visitor he downshifted even further, making his limp all the more pronounced; he was like a sailor on the deck of a ship in a storm, trying to find his balance.

He did not think he had ever seen a colored man at his house before, except for the rare deliveryman or repairman. But this person was not someone like that; he was too well-dressed to fix a faucet or drop off a package, and his posture was too rigid: a firm set to the chin, a rigidity to the neck and shoulder, a chest that puffed out with no apparent effort on his part, taxing the buttons on his shirt and coat. Something military about him. A drill sergeant in mufti. Probably used to be a linebacker.

Arnie took a deep breath---stopping when his ribs could handle no more expansion---and turned up his walk. The man removed his hat, a brown porkpie, and stood. He wore a black suit, a dark blue tie, and a white shirt with collar tabs that snapped together under the tie's knot. His face was square, compact, dominated by a pair of black, horn-rimmed glasses that were stained white around the earpieces from the saltiness of old sweat. He inclined his head as Arnie took the two steps up from the sidewalk to the stoop, revealing hair cut so short that lines of scalp showed through on top, like small rows of ominous herbs.

In the hand that did not hold the hat the man carried a briefcase, and no sooner did Arnie see it than he understood. It was just a coincidence that a colored man was here today, a long shot that happened to hit. The man's being here had nothing to do with what Matthew D'Imperio had told him this morning. The briefcase was where the colored man kept his magazines---what did they call them?---the *Watchtower*, that was it. The guy was a Jehovah's Witness, trying to pitch his wares and his faith; they always dressed nattily in white neighborhoods. Maybe everywhere. Showed up probably once a year.

"Mr. Castig," the man said.

"You know my name?"

The colored man, puzzled, could not help frowning. "Your wife said you went to see Mr. D'Imperio," the visitor continued. "That being the case, you know of my conversation with him earlier today. Perhaps you are just returning."

Okay, so he wasn't a Jehovah's Witness. Arnie nodded, knowing it all along.

"I hope you do not mind that I waited. Your wife was very kind. She said you would be back before long and had no objections to my waiting.

I hope you will do me the honor of shaking my hand, sir. My name is Ronald Leander Washington."

Arnie took Mr. Washington's hand, immediately regretting it, but holding on for several seconds before dropping it.

"There are a few things I wanted to talk to you about, if I may, a different perspective on this situation that I would like you to consider."

"Look, Mr. Washington, I'm not in the mood to---"

"But first I would like to ask how you are."

"How I *am*?"

"How you're feeling. Whether you're in pain. Was anything broken last night? Sgt. Spadafore said you took quite a beating. I don't imagine you've had time to see a doctor yet, but I will try not to delay you much longer."

"I don't get it," Arnie said, unsnapping the top few buttons of his jacket. "Why would you care?"

Ronald Leander Washington seemed genuinely puzzled. "Why wouldn't I? I know about you, Mr. Castig. I know you are considered by all who know you to be the most decent of men. Surely you don't think I wish you ill."

"Well, yeah, as I matter of fact I do. You cost me my goddamn job. At my age, maybe it's the last chance I'll ever have to get one. So I wouldn't exactly say you're doing me any favors."

Arnie sat on the stoop ledge, where Mr. Washington had stationed himself moments before. The latter backed up a few steps, leaning against a column of bricks that connected the stoop to the underside of the roof.

"The woman in the alley behind your school last night? The woman you struggled so nobly to rescue from the clutches of those sleazy young criminals?"

"Yeah?"

"She happens to be my sister."

Arnie picked up one of Rosa's flower pots. What was it Matthew D'Imperio had said? He didn't have a snowball's chance in a blast furnace to keep his job? Well, as he had this instant discovered, his odds were even less.

"And she believes, does my sister, as do I, that if you had not interceded on her behalf, both when you did and how you did, she might very well not be alive today. All because of eight measly dollars and a few coins."

"Is she going to be okay, your sister?"

"Well, sir, she most assuredly is not okay at the present. She has contusions, abrasions and broken bones. Her nose will have to be almost completely reconstructed and she will need extensive dental work. She is being tested this morning for a concussion. Perhaps I've forgotten a thing or two---Lord knows the good doctors at St. Mary's gave me such a list. Suffice it to say that she did not escape from her trials of last night nearly as well as you did. She is not walking down the street today." He pulled a precisely folded handkerchief from his breast pocket and dabbed at his forehead. "She has a long and painful period of recuperation ahead, but the doctors seem confident there is nothing wrong with her that time, and plenty of it, won't eventually heal. I saw her briefly this morning. She was not conscious for long. They tell me she is still in a state of shock. Nonetheless---and this is the kind of woman she is---she asked me to convey her most sincere appreciation for your, shall we say, your 'attempts' to be of assistance."

So his efforts were now reduced to attempts, were they? Ronald Leander Washington knew what Arnie would make of the word, and gave him a sorrowful moment for it to sink in. But the moment turned out to be an angry one. "I think if I saved her life, I did more than make 'attempts.'"

Now Ronald Leander Washington let the word sink in. "Yes, now that I think about it, sir, I think you are right. An apology is in order and you have it. In fact, as I was going to say, for my sister, and for me, as well as our entire family, and the entire membership of the Beaver Valley Colored People's Action Committee, I want to express my sincere gratitude."

Arnie shifted positions, trying angle himself so that his hip didn't throb. "You want to express your gratitude?"

"Most deeply, sir."

"By getting me *fired*? That's the way you say thank you to someone?" He slammed the flower pot back down on the ledge; the plastic cracked along the side.

As if he were beginning to undress, making himself at home, Ronald Leander Washington set his hat atop his briefcase on the only chair on the porch. He loosened his necktie, unsnapped the collar tabs, and unbuttoned the top button of his shirt. He began to pace, despite the porch's confines.

"Mr. Castig, there is a war going on inside me this morning---a war, I tell you. My feelings as an individual are at war with my feelings as a member of my race."

"I'm supposed to know what that means?"

"You see, as an individual, I am deeply indebted to you for what you did last night. No man is capable of more than his best, and I am certain you gave nothing less than your best. If I may speak candidly, I, as a colored man in this filthy, doomed part of the world, am not used to white people acting in such a manner.

"But there are larger issues here than merely your intentions and my reaction to them, larger issues than merely your sudden problem with employment. You are just one man, sir, and so am I, and what, I ask you, what is the one when the concerns of the many are involved? Not very much, I say, not very much at all. For this reason, the one must often make sacrifices for the many. Actually, I consider it a sacrifice not to be expressing my gratitude to you more fully, not to be *feeling* it more fully. But I am willing to make that sacrifice, Mr. Castig, and do you know why?"

Arnie drew a blank.

Ronald Leander Washington lowered his voice as two young white girls passed on the sidewalk. "Precisely because of those larger issues I mentioned. Those issues have to do with the place of the colored man in this country, and they are the most important thing in the world to me. So much so that whatever sacrifices a poor man like myself may be called upon to make are totally and absolutely irrelevant." He ran his hand pointlessly through his hair rows. "As is the sacrifice you are now being called upon to make."

"Mr. Washington?"

"Yes?"

"Is that supposed to make sense to me?"

"Sense?" Ronald Leander Washington stopped pacing, seemed to coil, readying to spring at Arnie. "You want sense, do you, Mr. Castig? Well, isn't that fortuitous, because so do I. Do you realize that colored people make up thirty-one percent of the population of Rochester, yet we comprise seventy-four percent of the unemployment rolls and sixty-eight percent of those arrested for crimes? Does that make sense to you?"

Stats. The man was throwing statistics at him. And his numbers were the winners. By default. Arnie knew nothing about the figures Mr. Washington was hitting him with now. Ronald "Stats" Washington. Jesus, could things *possibly* get any worse?

"Colored people are thirteen percent of the workforce in Rochester, but we make less than four percent of the income. Does *that* make sense?"

"Well, I don't know."

"You don't know?" His jaw muscles had tensed to the point of rippling, though whether from anger or resolve, Arnie couldn't tell.

"I never thought about it."

"Of course not. Why should you? For the system works so overwhelmingly in your favor, sir."

"What're you talking about?"

"I'm talking about the system that forbids a colored man from finding such meager employment as a night watchman while handing the job to a white man who does not meet the physical requirements of the position, and who does not even live in the same town where the job is located."

"I needed that job, Mr. Washington."

"So did a lot of colored people."

"What makes them deserve it more than me?"

"History," he said, and Arnie deflated.

The same two girls walked back again, perhaps having forgotten something. This time they looked at the odd pairing on the Castigs' stoop, and began to walk more quickly.

"I will spare you a lecture on the last three hundred years of injustice to the colored man in this country. I will simply tell you that when one of us takes over for you at the Abraham Lincoln Elementary School, it will be the most conspicuous achievement yet for my people in the Beaver Valley."

Arnie was getting lost. "How come? The job, it's not *that* big a deal. Like you said, meager."

"Oh, but for us it's more than that, Mr. Castig. You see, it is because of the job that you, more than anyone else I can think of, have been a symbol of what is so terribly wrong in this society of ours. You are not just a white man, Mr. Castig, you are---and forgive me, please, I wish there were some other way to say this---you are a damaged white man, and as

113

such you mocked the colored people of Rochester every day you walked through those halls and turned the key in that time clock of yours. Now, at last, this symbol will be destroyed."

"Destroyed?" Arnie did not feel he had heard Ronald Leander Washington's words so much as been slapped in the face by them, as if they were a blow to his body like the ones he had suffered in the alley last night. His fingers curled reflexively into fists. "You want to destroy the man who saved your sister's life?"

"Not the man, the symbol."

"I'm not a symbol."

"But you are. A symbol of prejudice."

"I'm not prejudiced."

"You got your job *because* of prejudice."

"I got my job 'cause an old friend of the family did me a favor, that's all."

"Your favor sir," Ronald Leander Washington said, "was our injustice." He retreated back to the ledge of the stoop, sitting on it with his back to Arnie and legs outstretched. Still, Arnie could hear the sound of his breaths. "Do you have any children, sir?"

"No."

"Any other dependents, besides Mrs. Castig?"

"What the hell is it to you?"

"I am merely trying to make a point."

"Which is?"

Ronald Leander Washington turned back to Arnie. "Which is that when you lose your job, only two people will be affected, you and your wife. That's all. And in the long run, you probably won't be affected at all. Let us be honest here. You'll receive unemployment compensation for a while, maybe that's even more money than they paid you for being a night watchman. Then you'll get another job. Maybe *that* will pay you more money. You have lived in this town all your life, you have friends, people who respect you, and one of them will find you a position of some sort."

"So," Arnie said, "how many people's it gonna help, me getting axed?

"Well, on the most basic level, it will help four or five individuals---the man who gets your job, his wife and kids, taking an average-sized family."

Stats again. This getting trounced at his own game was killing him.

"But much more important is the effect it will have on the colored community of Rochester as a whole. Even the entire Valley. You see, it will set an example, especially for the young people. The man who replaces you will be the first colored man in the entire law enforcement profession in Rochester. It's not exactly chief of police, I realize that, not even patrolman, but it's a start. It's the kind of start I envisioned far too long ago, sir, when I was looking for office space for the B.V.C.P.A.C. By all rights we should have settled in Rochester. There were more choices, nicer places, easier access. But I chose a third-floor walk-up in Freedom, and do you know why? I could not resist. I wanted the word 'Freedom' in our return addresses when we sent out mail. I wanted our own address to be 'Freedom.' I wanted people to make the connection between 'Freedom' and the dreams we are trying so hard to turn into reality. For we are abolitionists, you see, every bit as much as the people who gave the town its name more than a century ago."

Arnie paused, looking off at nothing in particular. The guy sure could talk. After a few seconds he said, "I'm definitely gonna lose my job?"

"Yes, sir."

"And a colored fella will take over?"

"Yes, sir."

"You know who?"

"That will be up to Gibraltar. Tomorrow, Mr. Wallace Sampson will interview a couple of men that my group has suggested."

"And I thought I was a hero," Arnie said, digging a finger into the soil of the flower pot he had just cracked. "Funny how a guy can get confused like that, huh, Mr. Washington? Think he's a hero when what he really is is out of work."

Ronald Leander Washington grabbed the handle of his briefcase, swinging it a time or two. "You are a man with a strong sense of duty, wouldn't you say, Mr. Castig?"

"Yeah, I would.

"Well, I suggest to you, sir, that you are now faced with a different kind of duty."

"And what's that?"

"Being a big enough man to step aside and turn your duties over to someone else, someone who can handle them with equal dedication but more ability. Someone who can blaze a trail into a new era for the colored man in the Beaver Valley, a trail that will one day be followed by many, many others. It's as a white man named Bob Dylan sang in one of his songs last year, Mr. Castig. 'Oh, the times, they are a-changin'.'"

And with that, Ronald Leander Washington slipped on his hat and repeated his good wishes for Arnie, that his wounds would heal promptly and thoroughly, and that he would find a new position in the workplace as soon as possible. Then, with a tap of the porkpie brim, he took his leave of the Castig stoop, walking briskly down Maple Street without turning around. Arnie watched him until he disappeared, then made the sign of the cross without even thinking about it, and went inside to confront the wrath of Rosa.

"*YOU MUSTA BOUGHT* lot of magazines from him," she said. "You been out there talking for long time." She was standing at the sink with her back to him.

"What?"

"Magazines. Books. Whatever that Negro man selling."

"Oh," he said. "Yeah, right." It seemed so long ago, the notion that Ronald Leander Washington was a Jehovah's Witness, that he had come to the Castig residence to peddle salvation rather than to deny it. Arnie latched onto the refrigerator door, but did not open it. He needed a beer, but didn't want Rosa see him drinking so early in the day.

She began to run hot water over the top of a Mason jar full of peaches that she had put up in the summer. She turned off the faucet, tapped the lid on the countertop and unscrewed it. "So, you buy any?"

"Huh?"

"What? All of a sudden you can't hear. I ask you if you buy any---"

"He wasn't selling magazines, Ro."

"What he want, then?"

Arnie took off his glasses, rubbed the bridge of his nose, then put them back on. He hoped he could get his glasses fixed, rather than having to buy a new pair.

Rosa turned and looked at him. "Something wrong?"

"Yeah," he told her, "that's for sure. Something's wrong."

116

"What?"

"Well, I'm not sure you'll believe it."

"Arnie, you tell me." She thumped the jar on the counter. "What that man want? What Mr. D'Imperio want? What kind of thing going on here? We not going to get as much as we expect?"

Should he break it to her gently. No, he decided, news like this could not be broken gently. No matter how long he beat around the bush, there would still come a moment of truth, a moment when he would have to reveal his unemployment and it would sink into his wife like a dagger. One second he would be a hero, the next a bum; there was not enough time to ease her from one perception of him to the other. Everybody thought he was a man of duty, after all. His wife was his duty now. "We're not getting anything, Ro," Arnie said, "except fired. That's what happened. I got fired."

"You *what?*" It was barely above a whisper, so stunned was she. She stood perfectly still, unable to move.

"I'm out of work, finished, retired, on the scrap heap. They cancelled the parade."

"This is some kind of joke, right?"

"Look at me, Ro. You see a man who's laughing?"

"I . . . I don't understand." She untied her apron, pulled it over her head and held it, and worked it into a ball. She still was not facing him. "*You* understand?"

"No," he said. "Well, I'm getting there."

"How can they fire you?"

"They got to give my job to someone else?"

"Who?"

"A colored guy."

"What colored guy?"

"Any colored guy."

"Man on the stoop?"

"No, not him."

"Who, then?"

"They don't know. Just . . . somebody."

She turned to face him, confusion giving way to anger. "Who these people called they?"

"Matthew D'Imperio. Gibraltar. The Beaver Valley Colored People's Association, everybody in the whole world with dark skin. Even some people with light skin, like President Johnson and this singer who says things are changing."

"Arnie, what kind of stuff you talking? You scare me." She threw her apron onto the kitchen table. "You really don't have your job no more?"

He shook his head.

"But what you do wrong? You saved that woman's life. And you have bad heart! You could have died. You were hero, big hero. And they *fire* you?"

"Aw right," Arnie said, still hanging onto the refrigerator, still trying to get up the nerve for a brew. "Here's the story. Listen up close. I'm not gonna repeat it or try to make sense of it. Okay? There's these colored folks in the Valley, a group of them, so they're official. They got their headquarters in Freedom. When I got hired at Abraham Lincoln, they were really ticked off 'cause here I am a white guy with a heart problem getting a job when there's all kinds of colored guys that don't have heart problems but Matthew D'Imperio never delivered papers to *their* houses when he was a kid. And you know him, he hates coloreds anyhow.

"So what happened was, this particular group of coloreds from Freedom, they been waiting for me to screw up ever since I got hired so they could make an official complaint. To the government, I guess, I'm not sure. What they were hoping is that I'd get fired and one of their own kind would take over. And that's what happened last night."

"But what you do to---"

"I know, I know, what'd I do to screw up. I saved that woman's life. Yeah, right. Well, maybe. But they said if the night watchman would've been someone in better shape than me, he could've got to her quicker and then maybe she wouldn't've been beaten up so bad. She's really suffering now. So," he said, "I did good but somebody else could've done better. I guess that's the whole thing in a nutshell."

"But how they know someone else get there quicker?"

Arnie snorted, a sound that annoyed even him. "It's not hard to figure, Ro." He tapped his stomach. "I got a lot to carry around with me. Besides, I'm the wrong color."

She needed to gather her thoughts. She wasn't used to assembling so many facts so quickly, herding them into her brain, arranging them in the right order. "Who was man on porch?"

"The brother of the lady."

"What lady?"

"The lady that got the shit kicked out of her."

"Why he come to see you?"

"'Cause he's also the head guy of the group of coloreds I told you about, the one that made the complaint against me."

"Wait a minute," she said, "jus' wait a minute." There was a large bowl next to the Mason jar on the counter. She poured the peaches into it and rinsed out the jar. More facts to gather and assemble, hear and arrange. "This man, you save his sister's life an' then he goes to people at your company an' complains an' so he gets you fired?" She hissed the words, like an escape valve letting off steam to avoid an explosion. Or prepare for one.

"Uh, yeah."

"What'sa matter with him? What kinda no good lousy man would do something like that?"

"He's not a louse. He said there's larger issues here."

"There's what?"

"Larger issues."

"Larger than what? This is crazy, make no sense. I never heard nothing confuse me like this before in my life. The Negro man on the porch, he should be shamed of himself. So should all the rest of his coloreds. They should put them all in jail."

"What else? Oh, yeah. He said, let me see, he said I was a symbol that all the colored people in Rochester---and maybe Freedom, too; I don't know---and even other places, have been wanting to destroy ever since my first day on the job and now they did so everybody's feeling all hunky-dory."

"They want to *destroy* you?" She was almost gasping in her indignation.

"Not me. The symbol."

"What you trying to tell me?"

"It's pretty complicated stuff."

"But it can't happen, this kinda thing," she said. "it just can't. There should be law against this."

119

"The thing is, Ro, I think there's laws *for* it today."

She plopped down in a chair at the kitchen table. "What we gonna do? Where we get the money to live. No way we can live on what you get from American Bridge for disability."

"Well, you know there's always Social Security."

"By that time we be broke."

"No, we won't. I'll find another job."

"Uh!"

"I will. I got the Abe Lincoln job, didn't I?"

"You was lucky."

"Well, luck won't have anything to do with it this time. This time it'll be a question of determination and I've got it and that means I won't give up until I find something. I'll bust my hump, Ro."

"We never shoulda bought this house. Cost too much money. I tol' you. We still pay the mortgage, got to pay it for six more years."

"And I told *you*, for Christ's sake, I'll---"

"Arnie." She reached for his hand, the one that wasn't clamped to the refrigerator, and spoke her harsh words as gently as she could. "Look at yourself. You old man, you way too heavy, you got a weak heart, you only graduate from high school, an' you don't care for much of anything except football an' in the summer baseball. What kind job you gonna get?"

"A desk job," he said, surprising himself with the speed, if not the astuteness, of his reply. "I'll sit on my duff all day like the big-shot executives do. That ought to be easy enough for me."

She dropped his hand. "Whatta you gonna be, chairman of the board?"

"Dispatcher, maybe," he improvised, "for the cab company or something like that. Yeah, that'd be perfect. I'd be great at it. Who knows this town better than I do, Ro? Name a single person who's got a map of Ambridge in his head like me. I know every street, every store, practically every house. No cabbie'd ever get lost with me on the phone, giving him directions when he needed them. And meanwhile I'll sign up for unemployment. See, there's nothing to sweat for at least six months. So just take it easy."

"Maybe nobody *need* a dispatcher. Maybe *we* the ones gonna take a cab an' we gonna take it to the poorhouse."

"You're not making this any easier, Ro."

"An' you are?"

Arnie's head snapped back slightly. "What the hell's that supposed to mean?"

"Something I don't understand here."

"What?"

Arnie could wait no longer. He finally opened the refrigerator door and took out a brew.

Rosa didn't care. She removed a box of cellophane wrap from a drawer next to the sink and ripped off a piece. She covered the bowl of peaches with it, smoothing down the edges around the side.

Arnie held the bottle of Iron City against his cheek and waited for her.

"Remember when you lose your job at the mill," she said, "how mad you was at that doctor, the one who told you couldn't go back to work?

"I wasn't *that* mad. He was doing what he had to do.'"

"You was mad at so many people. The people at the mill who lef' that slippery stuff on the ground an' the man at Sol's who was gonna give you job in his store to sell sports equipment and then change his mind. Remember? Even Mr. D'Imperio, when you found out how much he was gonna pay you."

"Okay, I was mad. So what?"

"You not mad now, not really." She spoke in a normal tone of voice, yet in its way it was the loudest of accusations. "How's come?"

He found a bottle opener in the drawer next to the refrigerator and snapped open his beverage, swigging noisily, then wiping his lips with his sleeve. "I been through too much to be mad right now," he said, "I'm just kind of numb. And besides . . ."

"Beside what?"

"Well, I think I'm starting to understand what's going on here. You know, those larger issues?"

"So these people that take your job, this job you do better than anybody else could ever do, you on *their* side now?"

"I didn't say I was on their side, goddammit! You want me to get mad, I'll get mad. Just say something like that to me. Just tell me I *want* to have my life go to hell in a handbasket like this."

"But you say now you understand these terrible people."

121

"What I understand is that they're *not* terrible people. They're trying to take care of their own and their own've had it rough for a long time. A real long time." He emptied more Iron City into him.

"And so now they give their rough time to you, when you do nothing to deserve it. And that's all right with you."

"Don't put words in my mouth, Ro."

"Then make sense when you put own words in your mouth."

Another gulp. The bottle would not last long. It went down so easily so early in the day. He began to walk out of the kitchen. "I've got to make a phone call. I'd appreciate it if you didn't listen in. You mind going upstairs."

Arnie could not remember the last time she glared like that, focusing such anger at him. He could not meet her eyes. After a few seconds, she left in relief.

He went to the living room and picked up the receiver. A few minutes later, Arnie called her from the bottom of the stairs. She appeared at the top, but it was shadowy and he could not tell whether she had been crying or whether she was still angry. What a foolish thing to think. *Of course* she was still angry.

"I'm going out for a walk."

"Where you go?"

"I don't know. I just got some time to kill before I go to work and . . . aw, I guess I don't really feel like walking after all. I'm just going to sit on the stoop, maybe read a magazine."

"You go to work today then?"

"Today and tomorrow."

"You should stay home. Tell them go to hell."

"Maybe you should stop giving me so much advice."

She remained in the upstairs shadows, her voice cold, without inflection. "So just two more days you work?"

"Well, they got nobody else to do the job tonight, and tomorrow the new guy starts."

"How come you gotta be there when the new guy starts?"

"How come you've got to ask me so many questions, Ro? It's my life, for chrissake!"

"Your life same as my life, Arnie. Husband and wife, you know, in case you forget. An' that means you got no right talk to me like that."

And he knew it. He didn't tell her he knew it, but he did. His voice mellowed and it wasn't an effort. "Like I said, the new guy starts tomorrow---"

"Colored person."

"---and I'm gonna show him the ropes. If you want to do the job really good, there's more to it than just walking through the building and looking around. I'm the only who knows what he's doing."

"Who's idea to show him ropes. Yours, right? You just called Mr. D'Imperio an' tell him you wanna do it. Like little beggar boy."

"I don't *need* to be a beggar boy, Miss Rosa Yacovoni! I get paid for the rest of the week whether I work or not."

"Maybe we should have parade for *that*."

"Maybe I *should* be begging, though. Yeah, okay, Ro, I'll beg. I need someone to be on my side here. You be on my side, okay? Can't you please be on my side? I mean, who else have I got?"

"How I'm suppose to be on your side when you act like crazy person? Maybe you not acting. Maybe you *really* crazy person. No. No, I tell you what you are. You a traitor. You like a traitor to yourself. I don't know what's happen to you."

"Well, let me tell you something" he virtually spat the words, all mellowness gone, "you got no right to talk to *me* like *that*. I'm the one who's going through all this shit, not you. You're just cleaning the goddamn house! I'm the one who's out there in the world, and if you think it's hard to understand from in here, you should be out there with me, trying to figure out all these changes that're going on."

As she started walking down the stairs, her footsteps sounding like the thud of marching boots, Arnie moved out of her way, back into the living room, into a different veil of shadows. But it hardly mattered. She did not want to see him right now any more than he wanted to see her. He heard her crying from the kitchen closet as she slipped on her coat, but could also hear her fighting the emotion, trying to swallow the sound. Her footsteps kept thudding, this time circling him to the front door, where she just stood, not opening it, not even moving.

Arnie's own tears were dry, silent, and quickly gone, meaning there had probably never been any in the first place. He was still a steel man, after all. He had sobbed enough in the past twenty-four hours.

Rosa opened the door and slammed it so hard behind her that the whole frame of the house seemed to shake.

"UP NEXT, LADIES AND GENTLEMEN," said Gino Casperi, the afternoon disc jockey on WAMB, "we've got a little something for you from Mr. Bob Crosby and the Bobcats."

"Oh, yeah," Arnie said. "Bing's little brother."

"Now, a few years ago, actually all the way back in 1958, Miss Connie Francis, who is really a *femmina* named Concetta Rosa Maria Franconero---did you know that?"

"Of course I knew it," said Arnie. "Play the music, Gino."

"At any rate, Miss Connie Francis had a smash hit, number one on all the charts, called 'Who's Sorry Now?' And I liked it, I really did. But there was something about it, just a little bit too much of a beat for me; it was a little too mechanical."

Hmmm, Arnie thought, now that you mention it . . .

"At any rate, for your listening pleasure this afternoon, we just happen to have a different version of 'Who's Sorry Now.' It's by Bob Crosby and the Bobcats, recorded live at the Starland Ballroom in Newark, New Jersey on April 26th, 1947."

Who's sorry now?
Who's sorry now?
Who's heart is achin'
For breakin' each vow?

Arnie did not sing along. Instead, he remembered the night he and Rosa danced to the song and afterward had their picture taken by the official West View Park photographer. He had not seen it for years but, somehow, could close his eyes and envision it in the cheap frame he bought: Rosa with her hair thick and curly, tumbling down to her shoulders, her lips moist, breasts large and hips full---so much did she look like a woman who could bear child after child, and so much did she want to.

As for Arnie, he was almost unrecognizable in his white dinner jacket with the red carnation in the lapel. No wrinkles, no worries, the future seeming assured for him and his bride-to-be; the war might be over, but the mills were still hiring, still needing men to man the machines for the consumer society, as it would be called.

The photo was in Arnie's dresser drawer now, after all these years. Face down under his socks. But he never looked at it; he never wanted to see it again, and not just because it would show how much the Castigs had aged. It was more sinister than that, an indication that life had become displeased with them for their various failures and decided to rush them along, hurry them through their days until they reached the one that would be their last. Life needed the space for more promising people. Arnie knew it didn't make sense. He also knew it was true.

He blamed himself. If only he could have figured out a way to keep looking as young as he did in the picture, to have hung onto that person and his prospects, then Rosa could have hung on, too. She would still have been long-haired and beautiful, not a wrinkle to be seen, not a sorry thought in her head. Maybe somehow she would even have managed to give birth. Instead, in the name of love, Arnie had dragged his wife through the years on what now seemed a mission to oblivion. He had dragged her through time. "I'm sorry, Ro. I'm sorry. I didn't mean it. I didn't know what would happen."

Maybe he *was* crazy.

You had your way,
Now you must pay;
I'm glad that you're sorry now.

When the song was over, Gino Casperi introduced a commercial and Arnie started to get ready for his next-to-last day in the Abe Lincoln corridors. He washed his face and shaved with a blade he would have to change soon. He sprayed on some deodorant. Then he limped back into the bedroom as Mel Torme began to sing "Heart and Soul."

125

He turned the radio off. He had not heard a word about the new WAMB. If he remembered correctly, it started tomorrow. It couldn't be worse than anything that had happened today.

This morning, Matthew D'Imperio had said he'd have someone leave a new cap and shirt for him at the school. Even a new pair of pants, since he didn't have time to take his old pants to the cleaner. All that for just two days. Like a going-away present. Arnie would dress for duty in the locker room.

Meanwhile, he slipped into some casual clothes. It was as he finished that he remember he had missed his doctor's appointment.

"Not meant to be, I guess."

It was harder for him to walk down a flight of stairs than it was to walk up. When he got to the kitchen, he found that Rosa had not made him a meal before she ran away. "No surprise, I guess," and he rooted through the refrigerator to assemble his own lunch. He made himself a ham sandwich and tossed it into a paper bag with an unpeeled carrot and half an apple, the inside already browning.

He took a few aspirins and set out against the pain. Yeah, maybe he was a crazy person, or had turned into one, but he had dragged himself through the years in addition to Rosa, and never before had he felt such a strain in the effort.

FATHER DANIEL SCHACT of St. Veronica's Roman Catholic Church in Ambridge was the chaplain for the Beaver Valley Colored People's Action Committee. He took to the altar every day when the church was empty and prayed for the success of the group. He also went to the Committee's monthly meetings, getting them started with the invocation and bringing them to a close with the benediction.

The silence that followed, after he told Arnie the news, was Arnie's acknowledgment that this streak he was on might never end; he was in a slump, maybe the worst of his life, and there was no way of knowing what would snap him out of it.

Once before, while running an errand, Father Daniel had seen Arnie at the bus stop, ready to make his daily excursion to Rochester. He had waved at him from across the street and continued about his business.

This time it was no accident; the priest was waiting for Arnie; like Rosa at the hospital, he had woven rosary beads through his fingers. Arnie turned away for the moment; his bus was several blocks away.

"I don't get it," he said at last. "You're not colored."

"A lot of people in the B.V.C.P.A.C. aren't colored. There are plenty of us white folks who want justice for the coloreds, too. And, of course, the more white people in the group, the more it represents society as a whole, and so the more powerful it is."

Arnie swallowed once or twice. Something to do. "What do you want me to say, Father?"

"I don't know," he said. "I guess what I want is for you to understand why I decided to join the group. And we're friends, you and I, so I wanted you to hear it from me, not somebody else."

"Well, if you want me to understand, you better hurry."

"I know, your bus is coming and you're probably sick of talking about last night. And maybe we're not even friends anymore. Maybe that's the way you feel. You feel like I've turned against you. Nothing could be further from the truth, Arnie, I swear it to you. But . . ."

"Yeah?"

He straightened a tangle in his beads. "The thing is, I know you. You know the justice of what's going on here."

"You think so?"

"I wouldn't be here if I didn't. If I honestly believed that our relationship would never be the same again, I'd consider it one of the worst personal tragedies of my life. I wouldn't have had the courage to face you today."

Arnie opened and closed his lunch bag, as if confirming that everything was still there. Something else to do. "I know you didn't turn on me, Father. You didn't have any idea what was going to happen. Still, it's hard knowing, well, knowing about you and Mr. Washington's people. That you're on his side."

"It's not a matter of sides, Arnie. If it were, I believe there's a part of you, maybe a small part but at least a part, that's on Mr. Washington's side, too. At any rate, I believe it's my responsibility to tell you that I agree with the decision to give your job to a colored. If it were up to me, I'd have done the same thing. It's a matter of principle. The problem is that you're the victim, and that makes it personal. *You!* Of all the people in the world. I'd never have wanted it to turn out like this. No matter how you're feeling now, I will always be there for you. Whenever you want me. I can't tell you how much I respect you for all you've been through and the way you've comported yourself."

Arnie had never heard the word before, but it wasn't hard to figure out the meaning because of the words around it.

"I know that Mr. Washington wants a colored man to take over your shift so that he can set an example. Well, in a different way, *you're* setting an example too, and it's just as important. You're the very definition of a good Christian man, Arnie, even more than people who sit in the pews and *don't* talk about football games during my sermon."

Arnie knew he should smile, and even wanted to. But he couldn't manage it.

"There's a bus a block away. I guess it's yours." Father Daniel said.

"Yeah. For tonight and tomorrow, at least. I don't know if I'll need one after that."

"I know a lot of people around town, Arnie. When you're ready to talk about a new job, maybe I can help."

"I'm ready now."

"Come and see me, then. Say, next Monday. I'll be in all day. You don't need an appointment; just drop in whenever you feel like it. We'll talk about it. Meanwhile, may the good Lord be with you, my son. May he recognize your achievements and your decency and reward them as they deserve to be rewarded. Always remember that He is a benevolent Lord. If you have faith, you will see that He is as proud to know you as I am. In the name of the Father, the Son, and the Holy Ghost, amen."

The bus came to a softly screeching stop beside the two men, the light just having turned red.

"Did you write that?" Arnie said.

"No. I wanted to say something from the heart. That's what came out."

"It was pretty good."

"Not if it doesn't mean something to you."

The bus doors opened.

"Thanks for coming, Father."

"Like I said, I wanted to tell you myself. It's the kind of thing that friends owe each other."

Arnie nodded. "I appreciate it."

"Who do the Jets play this week?"

"C'mon, Stats," said Gus, the driver. "I ain't got all day."

"The Broncos," Arnie said as took the first step into the bus, sighing so deeply it sounded as if he were saying "Ahhh" to a doctor. The pain shot through his whole body, top to bottom. "Well, I guess I'll see you before kickoff." He leaned out the bus door, holding on with one hand; Father Daniel stepped forward. The two men shook hands.

"Stats, damn ya!"

Father Daniel watched as Arnie wobbled down the aisle to his usual seat. He slid into it and saw the priest still standing there. It was the strangest thing, to find out that the man you thought was your friend . . . well, he really *was* your friend, but at the same time he was playing for the other guys. He remembered having seen a movie once starring Glenn Ford and some slinky woman. It was in black-and-white, lots of shadows. Like with Rosa and him today. The story was a complicated one, about Cold War counter-espionage. He wondered whether this qualified. Was the priest really a double agent?

The light finally turned green. Gus shifted noisily from neutral into low and the bus began crawling down Merchant Street. Arnie looked back once more at the priest and saw him continuing to stand on a public sidewalk, already attracting attention with a black cassock covering him from neck to shoetop---and now attracting even more by making the sign of the cross in a cloud of exhaust fumes. Arnie knew, of course, that Father Daniel meant it as a gesture of ongoing friendship, but at first had a different reaction. "Jesus Christ, Rev," he whispered to no one, "it's not *that* bad. You don't have to give me the last rites!"

Thursday,
September 30,
1965

HE TURNED ON THE RADIO. Just a reflex. It was barely after nine, less than a minute since the news had begun, and Arnie had just awakened.

". . . a spokesman for American Bridge saying he was disappointed his company's bid was not accepted. He said he thought the bid was a fair one, and pointed out that the company has had a great deal of experience in building offshore oil-drilling platforms, where the Japanese company, Sakamura, had had none at all."

He could hear Rosa in the kitchen, although he could not tell what she was doing, nor how upset she was about doing it.

The phone rang.

"Turning now to news from overseas . . ."

He put on his glasses, squeezing the tape at the broken hinge.

". . . the war in Vietnam continues at what is being described at a moderate pace. There were no major battles today, although an American pilot shot down over North Vietnam is the one-hundredth pilot to have been lost since the air war began."

"Arnie," Rosa yelled upstairs, "is for you. Telephone."

He turned off the radio and hobbled down the stairs, pushing his hands into the walls on both sides for balance. Watching him descend, Rosa could not help but look at him more tenderly than she had yesterday

"You got to see doctor today," she said, handing him the phone.

"Yeah, you're right, I'll call him again." To the phone: "Hello."

Rosa whispered, "Is Mr. D'Imperio?"

"Hey, Early, how's it goin'?"

130

"Oh." He nodded at his wife. "Going great, Mr. D'Imperio. What do you think?"

That was all she needed to know. She did not want to hear her husband talk to this man who used to be her husband's ally. She quickly turned off the burners on the stove and climbed upstairs, closing the bedroom door behind her.

"Coupla the night school people said you was really in bad shape las' night."

"Yeah," Arnie said, "it hurt pretty much, I gotta admit it."

"I tol' ya not t' go. Ya shoulda been lyin' in a hospital bed."

"I made my rounds. And I don't feel any worse this morning. That's all that matters."

"Well, I got good news for ya," and Arnie braced himself, although he couldn't imagine what else could go wrong.

"I'm listening."

"You don't have to show up tonight, help the jigaboo figure out what's what. The people at Gibraltar, they tol' me just type up a sheeta instructions fer the new guy. So that's what I'm doin'."

"It's all right," Arnie said, "I don't mind."

"I don't think ya understand, Castig. I'm *tellin'* ya not t' go. That's a order, got it?"

"A piece of paper's not the same thing as having a human being there beside you. Questions are bound to come up. I mean, you've only been inside the building once or twice, what do *you* know? There's a lot of stuff you can't write down because you got to be able to see it and show somebody. No offense, Mr. D'Imperio. What I'm saying is the new guy deserves to have a chance to get started on the right foot."

Arnie could hear anger in the two or three seconds of silence before Matthew D'Imperio spoke again. "Ya *still* don't understand, Castig. What ya do is, ya keep yer fat ass outta that building tonight, got it? Gibraltar decided they ain't gonna pay fer two people makin' the rounds. Aw right? So there ain't no reason in the world fer ya t' show up."

"Yes, there is. There's *my* reason."

More silence, but this time Matthew D'Imperio was settling down. "We got us a nigger. Moses Michael Dunbar, another one of those dumbshit

131

names. Anyhow, it's *his* job now. He's stoppin' by on 'is way t' work t' pick up the instructions. When 'e gets 'is uniform, y' know? End of story."

Arnie paused. "Is it okay if I make a suggestion?"

"Ya jus' don't give up, do ya?"

"One suggestion, that's all."

"What?"

"When you finish writing the instructions," Arnie said, "rip them up into little pieces and shove them up your own fat ass! Then when the colored man comes by, tell me I'll meet him there about quarter to five," and Arnie slammed the phone into the cradle.

The phone rang again a few seconds later. He picked it up, dropped it down again.

He had read, a few weeks earlier, about a running back for the Steelers named Clarence Howard: six-one, 215 pounds, a six-year veteran out of Texas Christian University. His career in the National Football League had been mediocre at best. His biggest accomplishment had simply been hanging onto a roster spot for so long.

But this year his luck ran out. Jim "Cannonball" Butler, a fourteenth round draft pick who played his college ball at a little place named Edward Waters, had won the fourth and last of the backfield spots. Howard was through. But it didn't really hit him, he said, until the equipment manager came up to him the last week of training camp and told him to clean out his locker. Those were the man's exact words, Howard said: "Clarence, clean out your locker."

And that was another reason for Arnie to go to his old building tonight. He had left a lot of his possessions there: his crossword puzzle magazine, some pencils, an old pair of sneakers. Nothing important, but they were his, and they didn't belong in the school any longer. "Castig, clean out the locker room."

AFTER AN ARGUMENT with Rosa about suing the federal government for discrimination---it seems Vinnie had a friend who had a brother whose son just got his law degree, and he was looking to start his career with a bang---Arnie went back upstairs and Rosa resumed her duties in the kitchen. Two ships passing in the morning. Arnie turned the radio on again and, seconds later, would lose his coordinates in time and place.

As he brushed his teeth, he listened to an announcer, someone he had never heard before, boasting about the latest bargain at a local hardware store, Seal-Mor Weather Strip and Caulking Cord, a ninety-foot roll for only a dollar twenty-nine. "Now's the time to do it," the announcer said, "because winter is right around the corner and what ya gotta do is, ya gotta stop dem bad old leaks."

"Huh?"

Then his radio station changed as suddenly and unexpectedly as the rest of his world had changed. A different announcer came on the air, someone with a maniacally amped-up decibel level, and blasted his vocal cords into the microphone so violently that Arnie thought his radio might crack under the strain.

"ALLLL RIGHTY, GUYS AN' GALS, HERE I IS AGAIN1 THE SCREEEEMAH, SCREAMIN' JAY ANTONOPOULIS, COMIN' ATCHA ON YOUR RAY-DEE-O MACHINE!"

"Screamin' Jay Antowhatsis?" Arnie said, and looked at the radio to make sure it was still set to 1420 am. It was.

"YES INDEEDY-DOODY1" the voice went on, "IT'S SCREAMIN' JAY ON THE VERY FIRST DAY OF THE NEW, I SAY *BRAND* NEW, WAMB AN' THAT SPELLS WAMB AN' IT RHYMES WITH LAMB AND A WAMB-A-LAMB-A-DING-DONG T' *YOU!*"

Arnie wanted to turn the volume down, but for the moment was afraid even to touch the radio.

"AN' NOW, BACK TO THE COUNTDOWN FOR THE NUMBAH TWO-WENNY NINE SONG IN THE U-NI-VERSE THIS WEEK. HERE THEY ARE, EVERYONE, THE BARBARIANS WITH 'ARE YOU A BOY OR ARE YOU A GIRL?'"

"Am I *what??*"

"CAN YOU DIG IT, GOOD CHILLUN!!!"

First a drumbeat that could have drowned out a jackhammer. Then a tinny guitar rushing in behind, the guitarist trying to rip the strings off his instrument rather than pluck out a melody. Then came the lyrics, sung by a man who sounded as if his throat had been massaged with a rough-grade of sandpaper.

> *Oh, are you a boy*
> *Or are you a girl?*
> *With your long blonde hair*
> *You look like a girl;*
> *You may be a boy---*
> *Hey!---*
> *But you look like a girl.*

Arnie tried to get his eyes to focus on something, anything in the room, but they kept flitting around, would not settle onto anything, certainly not the radio. It, too, had turned against him. Even the familiar wasn't familiar anymore.

> *You're either a girl*
> *Or you come from Liverpool,*
> *Yeah, Liverpool . . .*

Was it just a coincidence that so many untalented musicians had been assembled at one time in one place for one song? A joke? Unlikely, Arnie thought, although he didn't really know anything about the recording business. But what, then, was going on here? What was the reason for a song like this? And the big question---why was WAMB, which had always been such an oasis of auditory civilization, playing it?

> *You can dog like a female monkey, but you swim like a stone,*
> *Yeah, a rolling stone.*

"Arnie." Rosa had come back upstairs and was standing in the doorway, leaning into the frame to brace herself. "What you doing?"

"What am *I* doing?"

"Why you not listen to WAMB."

"This *is* WAMB, Ro."

"Can't be. You make some kind of mistake."

"How could I make a mistake? I never touched the radio. Hell, the announcer even said it was WAMB."

"*Our* WAMB?"

"Used to be," Arnie said. "It's somebody else's now."

"But I don't get it."

"You think *I* do?"

"Turn it off," she said. "It hurts my ears."

Arnie reached behind the dresser and yanked the plug out of the wall by the cord, causing a small flurry of sparks in the outlet and choking off the Barbarians in mid-measure.

He was familiar with this kind of music, of course---although maybe nothing quite this extreme---and he understood the reference to Liverpool, whence came the girly-haired Beatles, and he knew who the Rolling Stones were. He had seen both groups on the Ed Sullivan television show and marveled at the response from the teenagers in the audience, one set of shouts drowning out the other, and the volume rising to a point that Arnie didn't think the human ear was meant to accommodate. But maybe the Beatles and Rolling Stones could actually sing. Who could tell? It was almost impossible to hear them. Even Vaughn Monroe wouldn't have sounded good if he had tried to drown out an audience of bellowing teenagers.

But Vaughn Monroe, it seemed, had lost his job at WAMB as surely as Arnie was no longer employed in Rochester.

"What's going on?" Rosa asked. "Why is everything like this all of a sudden?"

"Well," he said, "I figured there were probably radio stations that played this stuff, maybe in a big city, like Pittsburgh."

"But why they have one here?"

"I don't know."

"And why they take *our* radio station away?"

"I don't know."

"It was ours, Arnie. It was part of our life." Rosa was taking it hard. "Why they not have two stations, one like this we could ignore and one like we used to have?"

"Maybe this is just some kind of special program," Arnie said, reaching. "You know, like they have 'Polkafest' on Saturday afternoons and religious music on Sunday mornings."

"And this is special program for people got no brains."

"I'll give the station a call after breakfast, find out what's what. Don't worry, I'll get to the bottom of this."

"I know you try your best."

With adversity comes reconciliation.

BUT THE RECEPTIONIST at the All-New WAMB was receiving so many calls by the time Arnie tried to get through that she had stopped answering the phone and instead begun working on her nails with an emery board, touching up here and there with a small jar of green polish. She was supposed to keep track of the calls, find out how many were in favor of the new format and how many hated it. But *everybody* hated it. What difference did it make what the actual number was? She would just make up the figures pro and con when the station manager wanted to see her tally.

It was a few minutes after noon when she thought she heard a knock at the door. "Come in," she shouted, "if somebody's there."

She had to shout because there were speakers in all four corners of the lobby of the All-New WAMB and music was roaring through them, the air seeming to vibrate in the wake of the records---so much noise, so confined a space.

> *In this dirty old part of the city*
> *Where the sun refuse to shine*
> *People tell me there ain't no use*
> *In tryin'.*

Even the lyrics, Arnie thought as he opened door with one hand, didn't make sense. They were cruel, pointless; they barely rhymed and in some cases didn't rhyme at all. And they were not about love. Songs were supposed to be about love, but this so-called music was about hair length, slums, and who-knew-what-the-hell-else; it was almost impossible to understand what the singers were saying. Probably a good thing, he decided.

And imagine trying to dance to this crap! You'd fall on your butt, maybe even break your ankle. If Arnie tried to dance to it, he'd end up in traction.

In the hand that did not open the door, he held a small packet of information for first time applicants from the Ambridge office of the Pennsylvania Department of Employment Security, which he had just visited to declare himself a candidate for benefits.

Arnie limped to the receptionist's desk.

"Can I help you, sir?" she said, not bothering to look up at him from under a banner that read "THE ALL-NEW WAMB." She seemed to be at a crucial point in the greening of one of her nails.

Arnie leaned over the desk, wanting to get as close as possible to her ears before attempting speech. She angled her body to the side, so that he would not bump the polish brush.

Watch my daddy in bed a-dyin',
Watch his hair been turnin' gray,
He been workin' an' slavin' his life away.

"I wasn't sure if anybody was knocking or knock," the receptionist told him. "I never heard anybody knock before."

"No wonder," Arnie said, but she did not seem to get it.

With the continuing distractions of phone-ringing, fingernail-filing, song-screaming, and introductions to more song screaming---"ARE YOU RED-EYE FOR MISTAH FREDDY 'BOOM-BOOM' CANNON? YOU BETTER BE, GUYS AN' GALS, 'CAUSE HE'S COMIN' ATCHA RIGHT NOW WITH THE SMASH HIT, 'ACTION'"---with all of this going on, it took Arnie several minutes to relate the purpose of his visit to the receptionist, and be ushered out of the lobby and into the office of John Groom, Station Manager. That was what it said on the door.

Groom was sitting behind his desk, feet up on the blotter, riffling through some papers. A polite young man, he stood to greet his visitor.

"Thank you for seeing me like this," Arnie said.

"Well, I want you to understand, Mr.---Castig did you say?--- I want you to know you usually wouldn't be able to just walk into a radio station like this and get yourself a meeting from the man who's running the show, especially on his first day at work. Without even making an appointment."

"Well," from Arnie, "like, I said, I appreciate it, but---"

"Have a seat."

He did, and Groom slid behind his desk.

"The thing is, though, we're going to be doing things different on the All-New WAMB, especially the first few days. We realize we're shaking things up here in the Valley and we've got a lot of listeners who are confused, to say the least."

"Pissed off, I'd say."

"That, too. So today, tomorrow and Saturday, my door is going to be open for any members of the community who have concerns about what's going down here, and who're willing to take the time to come and see us. That's a pretty different way to do business, let me tell you."

"Well, I won't take up much of your time," Arnie said, "but I was wondering when the big bands're gonna be on again."

Groom shook his head. "I'm sorry to break it to you, my friend, but the big bands died twenty years ago. All we're doing here at the All-New WAMB is burying them. It's long overdue, let me tell you."

He was a slender young person, clean and bright-eyed, who seemed to have been given a haircut by the old-fashioned soup bowl method. But the bowl was several sizes too big. A punch bowl, maybe. His ears were covered and hair spilled so far down the back of his neck that his collar was invisible. It was similar, Arnie thought, to the way the new groups from England were wearing their hair. Never before, though, had he seen so much hair in person.

Nor had he ever seen such a suit, although Arnie wasn't really sure it *was* a suit, because the jacket and pants were slightly different shades of beige. He had never seen lapels like Groom's before; they flared out toward his shoulders like the tail fins of a '63 Chevy Impala. And he had never seen trouser cuffs like Groom's; they were so wide at the bottom that they almost covered his shoes. Arnie felt his head shaking, trying to understand.

There was about the station manager an air of perpetual perspiration, of energy too energetically deployed. He was snapping his fingers to the beat of the music, but it played much more softly in his office than it had in the lobby. Still, "Boom-Boom" kept on booming.

> *If all day long*
> *You been wantin' to dance,*
> *All night long*
> *You're gonna get your chance . . .*

"Here," Groom said, "let's get rid of this so it's easier to talk," and he turned off the radio speaker in his office.

"Thank you."

"Let me explain things so you know just what's what. Maybe you can spread the word to your friends, save me some trouble. It's all math, pure arithmetic. *And* demographics."

"Demographics?"

"Just hang with me a sec and I'll explain." Groom picked up the phone and asked Dotty the receptionist what the latest count was.

As he waited for her to make up some numbers, Arnie looked around at Groom's small office. There was little to see: a framed Bachelor of Science degree in business from Mankato State College, Mankato, Minnesota, 1961, and a blow-up of a photograph showing Groom posing toothily between a man whose autograph identified him as Sonny and a woman similarly identified as Cher. Groom was obviously overjoyed to be with them; they, on the other hand, wore long, shaggy clothes and long, shaggy expressions, seeming to want to be anyplace other than where they were. According to a small sign above the frame, the picture had been taken at a party in honor of a television show called *Shindig*.

"Be right with you," Groom said. "Dotty's giving me an up-to-the-second score."

Arnie nodded.

Old, coffee-ringed issues of *Variety*, *Billboard*, and *Cashbox*, publications of which Arnie had never heard, were stacked on a small table next to his chair. The current issues lay open across Groom's desk. A small pile of 45 rpm records leaned out of the "In" basket on one corner of the desk and in the "Out" basket on the opposite corner was a small stack of papers.

Groom hung up and reported to Arnie. "Okay, Mr. Cassidy. Fifty-one people called before Dotty stopped answering the phone," the station manager reported to Arnie. "Forty-eight thought we're the worst thing they ever heard on the radio in their lives."

Arnie pointed to himself. "Make it forty-nine out of fifty-two. I got a busy signal. See, that proves people don't want to listen to the music you're playing."

"On the contrary. What it proves is that certain *kinds* of people don't want to listen. And, nothing personal, but in a purely business sense, those are the kinds of people we don't want to listen to us."

"You mean, like me?"

"Well, yes, frankly, like you."

"What's the right kind of people?"

"Young," Groom said. "We want listeners so young they still put their teeth under their pillows at night and look for quarters when they get up in the morning. So young their mamas still dress them for school and their dads ride them around piggyback." He chuckled, enjoyed himself. "I'm exaggerating, of course, but not by much. You see, people in your age bracket and at your income level are, by and large---"

"Wait a minute now, just hold your horses. I met you, what, two or three minutes ago? And I haven't told you a thing about me except I hate the music you're playing. What makes you think you know how much money I make?"

"Well, I don't know how much *you* make exactly, but I do have the data for people of your age and background in this part of western Pennsylvania, the median figures in income and savings and spending, and you folks've got it pretty tough. That means you just aren't the demographic advertisers are looking for today. So if our audience is full of big band freaks, even if there were twice as many of you as there are, there's no way we can attract the sponsors who pay the big bucks, and that means we can't make this station into the kind of paying proposition it ought to be."

"So this demographics thing you're talking about---"

"It means attracting the right audience for the right product. The right product in the music business is the British invasion, the kind of rock and roll that started in England, like the Beatles and Stones and Herman's Hermits and all of them, and it's sweeping America now like wildfire. The

140

people who like it most are teenagers, kids in their early twenties. They're the ones we've got to deliver for our sponsors."

Arnie still held the packet from the unemployment office in his hand, beginning to sweat through it now. As inconspicuously as possible, he folded it and shoved it into the back pocket of his pants. He said, "Are you telling me that the kids have more money than *we* do?"

"Well, discretionary money, yes."

"Discretionary money?"

"It's kind of complicated, Mr. Castle. When you get right down to it, it has a lot to do with the steel industry."

"How the hell do you figure that?"

"Things just aren't booming around here the way they used to. And it's going to get worse, a lot worse. The Valley is steel country, as you well know, and a couple months ago United Wrought Iron cut back to two shifts a day. Merrick Tool & Dye is probably going down to one shift before the end of the year. Did you know that?

"Yeah, sure, everybody does. But those are just---"

"And Fairbanks, I assume you heard about them, too. They're thinking about shutting down all together, selling their facilities to a company that wants to use them as storage space."

"But this is just temporary, Mr. Groom," Arnie said, "a little slowdown. Sometimes the orders drop off a bit, then they go right back up again. It happens all the time. Besides, these companies you're talking about, they're just specialty shops."

"You think American Bridge is a specialty shop?"

Arnie snorted. "Well, of course not, but AB's not---"

"I don't know the names of all the mills, but did you know that, as of next month, American Bridge is going to start running two shifts a day instead of three at some of their mills?"

Arnie stopped. There was nothing to do with a statement so dramatic other than deny it. "I don't believe you."

Groom pulled the papers from his "Out" box and started thumbing through them. "I've got the research here somewhere. Let's see, where the hell--- Oh, nuts, I'll never find it with you sitting there waiting, but it's true. Take my word for it, Mr.---What was it again?"

"Castig."

"Mr. Castig. Sorry But I'll tell you this. If you don't take my word for it now, remember what I told you when you're reading the papers next month, or the month after. Before this year's over, things're going to be a lot different here in mill country. And this is just the beginning."

"So how's this gonna help kids get more money to buy your sponsors' products?"

"You're getting ahead of me here. Now, let's say it takes a decade or more for the steel industry to die. And make no mistake, it's gonna die, at least around here."

"No," Arnie said, "No, that can't happen! Steel's who we are in the Valley."

"It's who you *were*, I'm sorry to say. More and more people're going to get laid off but it'll be gradual. In the meantime, folks like you, say, you'll hang onto your jobs. You've probably got seniority. But you've also got pay cuts coming, can't be helped. The thing is, though, there won't be any cuts in your house payments, your car payments, your insurance payments. Then there's food and clothing you've got to buy, you've got utility bills and water---by the time you fork over everything you owe for all your monthly expenses, there's three and a half percent of your gross, on average, left over. Gross now, not net. So you go out to dinner once a month, take in a movie a month, and if there's anything left, and there probably won't be, you put it in the bank. No impulse buying at all."

"Impulse buying?"

"It means buying something for the fun of it, not because it's a necessity. You buy it because it's an impulse."

"Why would anybody do that?"

Groom could not imagine how to answer a question like that. "Kids can do it, see? They impulse buy like crazy. Maybe they don't have as much money as you; they only have part-time jobs after school or, if they've not in school, they work at fast food restaurants or as stockboys in supermarkets. A few of them get allowances, but mostly they're at the bottom of the ladder. But---and here's the key thing---they live at home with their parents. It doesn't cost them a penny. *All* their money is disposable, I'm talking one hundred percent. Okay, not a hundred; maybe they kick in some money for the mortgage. Still, they've got enough left to buy the products we want them to buy. And as they grow older and become better off financially, well, then, they'll be hooked on our sounds, grooving to the music they can only get from us."

"But that doesn't---"

"And so they're depending on us to find out what the hippest new products are."

"The what?"

"And another thing. I'll give you an example of a different kind of impulse buying. People in your demographic---"

"Old people," Arnie said.

"Right, you're catching on. You people, see, you're set in your ways. You're not going to hear about a new brand of toothpaste and stop using the brand you've been using for thirty years. You're not going to experiment with a different kind of antacid or lipstick or chewing gum. But kids, they're just getting into the consumer market. They don't have any habits yet, no product loyalty. They're open to new ideas, new goods and services. And they don't want to do the same old thing their parents did. They want their own drinks and snacks and hair cream and breath mints. So here it is, the big chance for the companies who make this stuff. There's a new consumer base in the country now with its own brand of music, and that makes them susceptible to their own brands of everything else. Zit cream, for cryin' out loud! There's a product that's *only* for kids. Clearasil's going to be the richest company in the world someday, and it's not going to get there by advertising on a big band station. You got any pimples, Mr. Castig? Do you give a shit? I didn't think so. There's hundreds of millions of dollars to be made here, and hundreds of millions to be lost for the manufacturers who don't know how to play the game. Right now, right this very minute, this is transition time, time to change all the rules."

"But how can you forget about the rest of us, all the people who like your station the way it was? It's not fair."

"Why not look at it the other way? What about all the people who didn't like the station the way it was, who hated it because the music we played was recorded before they were born. Is *that* fair?"

"But I thought the score was 48 to three."

"The scoreboard just got turned on, my friend. *Of course* people are going to be against us at first. They're the ones who are used to the old product. Besides, the kids are in school now. But wait 'til they get home and the word starts to spread about what WAMB has turned into. No more trying to pick up the Pittsburgh stations at night and getting an earful of static. No sir, now they've got their own station in their own hometown. The numbers're going to turn around dramatically, I promise you."

Arnie could never remember getting his ass kicked as much as he had in the past two days. Stats, huh? It wasn't bad enough that Ronald Leander Washington made a laughingstock of his nickname. Now this kid who was probably a boy but looked like a girl was doing it.

"One last thing, Mr. Castig. You've got to admit I've given you a lot of time and as good an explanation as possible. But I've got to get back to work."

Arnie *did* have to admit it. He hadn't expected to find out as much as he had about the All-New WAMB. It went by so quickly that he couldn't pick up all of it, but he was starting to think that he was not only the wrong demographic for the music, he was probably the wrong demographic for life. This morning, demographic was a word he had never heard before. Now he knew it was an enemy he would never be able to defeat.

"First, though, here's the thing I wanted tell you. This is a little dicey to get into, but, what can I say, the truth is the truth, and people who care as much as you do deserve to know."

"Go ahead."

"You take the people who were big fans of Helen O'Connell, Ray Eberle, June Christie---oh yes, I know who they all were; believe me, I know the music business, "A" side and "B"---but those people have all passed away. I mean the singers *and* their fans. I'm sorry to say it, I really am, but you folks won't be around that much longer---you're dying off, to put it bluntly---and then who do we get to listen to our shows? Our demographic now's in the low sixties. The *sixties*, you believe it? You're running out of time and that means *we're* running out of time. So, in a sense, the music we're starting to play today on the station is an investment, one that's going to bring us a lot of new listeners, and a lot of cash flow--- not immediately, maybe---but every year for the next half-century at least we're going to grow and grow and grow. We're the new American Bridge around here!" he said, pounding his fist on his desk and laughing. "Do you understand where I'm coming from?"

Arnie didn't know about the "coming from" part, but he *did* understand. He was old, he'd be dead soon, he'd matter even less then than he did now.

Groom popped up out of his chair. Arnie started struggling out of his a second later.

"Look," the younger man said, giving Arnie a tap on the shoulder as he steered him to the door, "I know how much you like the old music. I know how much your whole demographic likes it. So buy the records. Play them for yourself at home. Be your own deejay. You can listen to whatever you want, whenever you want. Simple solution, am I right?"

Not if you can't afford a record player, Mr. Groom. Not if you can't even afford to buy any records right now. Don't your statistics tell you *that*?

Groom opened the door to the lobby, into the eye of the new music's storm.

Wooly Bullee, Wooly Bullee,
Wooly Bully, Wooly Bully, Wooly Bully.

"I wish you all the best, I really do," Groom said. He handed Arnie a business card. "You give me a call once things settle down a little if there's anything I can help you with. Good seeing you, it really was. And listen, you stay with us, you give us a chance, I'll bet you find a few songs even *you* like after a while."

They all wished him the best, all the people who were making his life unrecognizable from what he had known before. Groom went back into his office and Arnie tossed his card into the waste basket in the lobby.

He said goodbye to Dottie, but she didn't hear him. He walked out the door of the All-New WAMB and banged it shut. The timing was perfect. The door closed with a boom just as the drummer on the record pounded his instrument with the sticks, thus converting Arnie's small moment of rage into nothing more than one more beat in one more song that he would never listen to again.

DEAR MR. D'IMPERIO,

Here is my uniform, or what's left of it, and also my time clock and my spare cards. I suppose you know what happened to my cap the other night and the cops probably threw it away

145

by now at the police station. The shirt is all ripped up because of the kid's knife since he sliced it up but I'm returning it anyhow just so you can see what happened. Not that anybody cares. The pants are OK, I guess, although they don't look so hot. The time clock works just fine and I'm enclosing my keys.

I hope the new guy will turn out good for you. I'll do my best with him tonight. I'll even have him take notes.

Thank you for all you did to try to help me keep my job.

Sincerely,
Arnie Castig

He put the note on top of the shopping bag that contained the remnants of career number two in his life, and set it just inside the front door. He would deliver it to Gibraltar late this afternoon, when Matthew D'Imperio had locked up for the day and Arnie would not have to see him. He would leave the bag outside the door.

Then maybe he would have a beverage or two at Eugene's. Arnie didn't drink very much, a few beers here or there, on special occasions, good or bad. But today he might want some company. Rosa had gone to stay with Vinnie this morning and told him she wasn't sure when she'd be home. He had the flu, she said, and it depended on when he got better. He was a bachelor and lived alone. Somebody had to take care of him. That was the story, at least.

Then again, Arnie might not want any company.

Now what?

He walked around the house for a few minutes with his hands in his pockets, looking at the place as if he had never seen it before, wondering what it had to offer him by way of diversion. He remembered somebody having said to him once that when you retired, or didn't have a job for some other reason, what you did was, you killed time until time killed you. It was a grim thought and Arnie was not a grim man, but the expression seemed appropriate now.

Demographic. Impulse buying. Discretionary money. He tried to shake the words out of his head but they hung on stubbornly.

There was always the chance that Zook could come through for him. Zook said he had an idea, he knew somebody who might want to hire him. He said that, if everything went right, Arnie would be working again as early as next week. He would give his buddy a call, so Arnie looked at the phone. And when he got hungry he looked at the refrigerator and when he got tired he looked at the sofa, where he would stretch out when he wanted a nap.

Except for sports, he did not like to watch television. So he had no idea what it offered at this time of day when he would usually be on his way to Rochester. He had bought the *Post-Gazette* this morning to check the final statistics for the Pirates. Roberto Clemente, the right fielder with a cannon for an arm, had had another great year, batting .329 with 10 homers and 65 RBIs. Left fielder Willie Stargell, the Pirates' lone power hitter, only hit .272, but had knocked 27 balls out of the park and drove in 107 runs. And center fielder Bill Virdon, a better defensive player than an offensive force, stroked 4 home runs and knocked in 24, pretty feeble figures even for a leadoff hitter. But his average wasn't awful: .279. All in all, though, not a bad performance from the outfielders.

Now he found the paper on the kitchen table, and was not even sure where the television listings would be. After a lot of page-flipping, he saw them on the page behind the comics, and checked his options.

> Ch. 2. *To Tell the Truth*---game.
> Ch. 4. *Queen for A Day*---game.
> Ch. 11. *Edge of Night*—drama.
> Ch. 13. *The Wonderful World of Zebras*---nature.

What the hell could be so wonderful about zebras?

He had never heard of any of the programs, but *To Tell the Truth* sounded the most interesting. He sank himself into the sofa and watched as three distinguished-looking gentlemen, all with gray hair and long mustaches, claimed to be the original Chef Boy-ar-dee, after whom a popular line of macaroni products and sauces had been named and whose face appeared on all the cans and boxes. Of course, no real Italian cook, including Rosa Castig, would resort to such swill, but most people weren't as discriminating.

After the three men introduced themselves with the same words, they sat at a desk, where they faced four panelists, apparently celebrities; it was their job, through the questions they asked, to separate the two imposters from the real Chef Boy-ar-dee.

The first panelist asked the second contestant if he had been born in Italy.

The man said yes, in Palermo.

The first panelist got another turn. He asked the third contestant what rigatoni was.

He said it was a form of pasta that took the shape of short, hollow tubes.

Arnie had a question of his own.

Who gives a shit?

The first panelist started to ask the first contestant something, but then the doorbell rang.

He would have some company after all. But who?

He decided to remain ignorant of the real Chef Boy-ar-dee's identity, turning off the television and limping to the front door. He couldn't think of anybody who'd be visiting him now. Zook was working; he would meet with Father Daniel about a job next week; and Rosa, who wouldn't have rung the bell anyhow, was still at Vinnie's. Other than that . . . well, there were so few people in his life.

He had forgotten about his majorette.

He had forgotten about the chocolate.

He had forgotten that this was delivery day.

He opened the door and there she was, beaming her rays at him yet again. "Hi, Mr. C., how are you?"

"Debbie!" It was as if he had already had a few drinks at Eugene's, so light-headed and woozy did he feel upon seeing her, so unreasonably elated, and so quickly. And no wonder, considering what had happened to his life since he last saw her.

"I got the goodies," she said, her arms wrapped around a large cardboard box. HERSHEY'S PLAIN JUMBOS, it said on the side, and then below it, INSTITUTIONAL SALES ONLY.

"Great," Arnie said, "that's great," except that, not having remembered about Debbie's visit today, he had not set aside any money to pay for his booty. "C'mon in. Geez, it's nice to see you. Can I give you a hand?"

"No, that's all right."

"I don't know, it looks like a heck of a load."

"I've got it sort of balanced," she said, prancing into the living room ahead of him. "Besides," and she dropped the box onto the sofa, "Whoooo! I'm all done with the heaviest part of the load now. Thanks to you."

"Gosh, I hope you didn't have to walk too far with all that."

"No, my mom dropped me off right in front of your house. So there was nothing to it. And guess what, Mr. Castig."

"What?"

"You happen to be looking at---*ta-da!*---the top salesman of chocolate bars in the entire Ambridge Senior High School Varsity Marching Band." And she struck a pose for him, the typical, heart-thumping majorette pose: one arm folded as if she had her baton under it, the other arm up in the air; one leg off the rug, the other folded at the knee.

"No! Really? Were you really the top?"

She shook her head yes, holding up her index finger. "Numero uno."

"Wow," said Arnie, "that's terrific." He grabbed one of her hands in both of his and pumped it a few times. It was, he thought, the best news he had gotten all week, which, he had just enough sense to realize, said more about the week than it did the news itself.

"I know," said Debbie, "and I owe it all to you, because guess how many more bars I sold than the girl who came in second."

"How many?"

Pause for effect. Again she held up fingers. This time it was two.

"No."

"Yes."

"Holy smokers, you won because of the order I got from my friend Zook?"

She nodded. Please, *please* tell him I said thank you. I really mean it. Maybe you could give me his address and I'll write him a thank-you note."

"That's really nice of you. I'll do it. He'll think it's really great.

"Oh, and guess what my mom says."

"What?"

She laughed. "She says when I get my movie passes, I ought to take you as my guest. She's kidding of course, but that'll give you an idea how much she appreciates what you did, too."

"What movie are you going to see, have you decided?"

"Maybe *Doctor Zhivago*. Except it's in Pittsburgh now. I'm not sure whether it'll play in Ambridge or not."

He nodded. He didn't like medical movies anyhow.

"So, if you'll just fork over the money for the original twelve bars, we'll be all set."

"Oh, yeah. That's right. What do I owe you now?"

"That'll be eighteen dollars."

Arnie blinked rapidly as he repeated the sum. "Eighteen dollars."

"I have change if you only have a twenty."

"No, no, that's all right. I've got the money. It's just waiting for you. You stay here, don't go anywhere. I'll see you again in a minute," and he backpedaled his way into the kitchen."

"Geez, Mr. Castig, you look like you're hurting real bad. Are you okay?"

"Oh, I . . . I had a little accident the other day. Wasn't paying attention to where I was going. It's nothing serious."

"I hope not," she said.

"Anyhow, I'll be right with you."

"Did you see a doctor?"

Everybody wanted to know. "I'm going to. Real soon," and he disappeared into the kitchen.

On the back of the stove was a set of red plastic canisters. Rosa kept her "rainy day money," as she called it, in one of them, as part of a filing system whose logic she, and she alone, understood. Sugar was in *Flour*, flour in *Coffee*, and spare keys, safety pins, paper clips, coins and bills were in *Tea*.

Out of Debbie's sight now, Arnie emptied his pockets onto the stovetop, spreading out the contents: four dollar bills, a quarter, two pennies and a nickel. $4.32. He brushed aside the silver; call it four. He pried the lid off the tea canister, hoping to find the remaining fourteen, knowing Rosa did not always keep that much on hand.

He pulled out a small roll of currency, the bills folded over twice and secured by a rubber band. He slid it off and counted: five, fifteen, sixteen, seventeen, eighteen, nineteen. And, for good measure, another five-spot. "Thank you, Jesus in Heaven and all the angels," he whispered, and removed the ten and a five, replacing them one of his own singles, more for the sake of his conscience than anything else. So he had three dollars left from his pocket and fifteen he had borrowed from the rainy day stash. Hell, he thought, why not? It's been raining harder on me lately than anyone else. Before he put the lid back on the *Tea* canister, he tossed his thirty-two cents in, more conscience salving. Although actually, he considered the money he had given back, a meager amount though it was, a down payment on the loan. He did not know how he would explain the missing money to Rosa, but swore to himself now as he would swear to her later that he would return the fourteen dollars when he received either an unemployment check or his next paycheck, whichever came first.

"Here you are," he said, returning to the living room and handing her the money as he rejoined her on the sofa. She sat on one side of the candy box; he was on the other.

"Oh, wow," she said, thumbing through the bills. "Thanks a lot, Mr. C."

"My pleasure."

She stuffed the money into her jacket pocket, then began to dispense the Hershey's plain jumbos, taking them out of the box and arranging them in rows on the coffee table.

"Can I help you?"

"Oh, that's okay. I've got my own system here."

The bars were long, thick slabs of chocolate wrapped in silver foil with red-and-white paper sleeves, on which was the slogan: *"I'm A Bridger Booster!"*

"See what I mean about how big they are?"

"You got that right," Arnie said. "They're like ingot molds. practically."

"What's that?"

"Oh, just something from the steel mills."

She kept unloading bars onto the table: four rows of three bars each, and then two bars across the top of the pile "Boy, getting rid of these babies is going to make it a lot easier to carry the box the rest of the way."

"I thought your mom was driving you around."

"No, she had some errands to run. I told her I'd be okay after I dumped the load at your place, though."

Just as there had not been as much of Debbie to see Tuesday at the library as there was last Sunday, there was not as much of her to see today as there had been on Tuesday. She had not taken off her jacket and her skirt came down to her knees with an orange fringe tickling the tops of her calves. A pair of orange socks rose almost to the bottom of the fringe, and she wore a pair of shiny black penny loafers into which she had not inserted nickels.

She looked at the chocolate bars on the table, quickly counting them again, and when satisfied that the number was indeed fourteen, said, "Well, I guess that's it. I better be going now. It'll be dark soon."

"Already?"

"I've got a lot more deliveries to make yet. This was my first stop. Plus there's tons of homework waiting for me."

"Can't you stay just a little longer, a few minutes, maybe."

"What for?"

Good question. Arnie hadn't been expecting anything so direct. "Well, there was something . . . I mean, see . . . well, ever since you stopped by the other day I been thinking about what it's like to be a majorette and, you know, and I was just wondering how you got to be so good at twirling a baton."

"You were thinking about *that*?"

In retrospect, it would seem to Arnie the moment when Debbie first found something unusual about his interest in her. It was a small moment, no more than a second or two, but it did not seem to fit with the others, and Arnie sensed it just as she did.

"How I got to be so good?"

"Yeah," he said, "spinnin' the ol' wand, you know. We didn't have majorettes back in my days, but I always thought it was a really neat thing and I wanted to know more about it. If it's okay with you. I mean, it seems like it's really hard work."

For a moment, she didn't say anything.

"I never met anybody I could ask before, see? And I've been watching majorettes ever since they started."

"Well," she said, "I guess the main thing is you need to start practicing when you're really young."

"Sure, that makes sense. Just like the athletes. How old were *you*?"

"Six. Or maybe five and a half."

"Holy smokers, that sure is young, all right. Six years old. Or less. You must've been about the same height as the baton back then." He tried to coax a smile out of her, but could not manage it. He thought it was a clever thing to say, but she seemed suddenly on guard, no matter what he said.

"Could you actually twirl a baton when you were six?"

"Mostly I just dropped it. But it seemed like such a cool thing to do that I kept picking it up and trying again. Sometimes, especially when I was older, I did it so many times my hands even got bloody. And in the summer I'd get so sweaty that even when I caught the baton it slipped out of my hand. I remember crying when that happened. It seemed so unfair."

"Oh, man, that's amazing. You really gave it everything you had."

"My mother was a majorette in high school and she's the one who taught me." She was speaking faster now. "She showed me how to work your fingers and wrists so you can get the baton to flip around the way it's supposed to."

"And what happens next, once you get the basic twirling down?"

"Then you start to work on some of the trickier stuff, like your figure eights and crossovers and when you get good enough at those you start in on our cartwheels and reverses and things like that and I really think it's time for me to be going now, Mr. Castig."

She reached for the box.

He grabbed his side of it, held it in place.

"Not yet."

If the small moment had occurred a minute or so ago, when he expressed too much interest in baton-twirling, this was the large moment. It was not the words so much, although they were bad enough; it was the urgency with which he spoke them, the kind of urgency that made a command out of an invitation, which was all he had intended. She had caught him by surprise, sneaking in her goodbye like that and, not being ready for it, he had responded in the most inappropriate manner possible. This was the moment that *really* didn't fit with the others, the turning point, the precise instant at which the momentum of their relationship, superficial though it was, shifted too far ever to shift back again. Debbie's wariness would now distance her from her benefactor at the same time that his attempts, ever more desperate, to put her at ease would make him seem even more of a threat, more eager to hold her against her will.

153

And you say you realized this at the time? one of the shrinks at Western Psych would later ask him.

Pretty much, Arnie would say.

Then why didn't you change your mind and tell her she could go?

I didn't want her to go.

Why not?

She was the only thing I had to look forward to then.

But you'd already lost her by now. She didn't want to stay any longer.

I could try, he said, I could try. I'm not the type who gives up.

"What I mean," Arnie said to Debbie, "is, well, I just wonder if you realize how special it is---what you do, I mean. It's really not the kind of thing you should take for granted. You're about the best a person can be if she's a girl and if she's your age, all decked out in fancy clothes and with all that skill you've got. And you get to march across the field at halftime when people are all fired up from the game and then they see you out there and they get even more fired up. And there's this terrific music playing and you're just like the whole center of attention. That's why I say it's so special, it really is. Me, I think I told you, I played football in high school but I was only a lineman, a tackle, just one of the guys in the crowd. Even my parents had a hard time picking me out when they came to the games.

"You, though," and even he had begun to wonder how much longer he could go on with this, "nobody could miss you. Nobody could miss the majorettes, each one of you. And I'll bet all the girls in school, like M.A., I'll bet they all envy you and all the boys want to go out on dates with you and it's the kind of thing so few people get to experience in this world. That's why I want to know more about what you do. That's all. See? Understand?"

Nothing from her.

"Deb?"

She quietly said, "I just have a lot more houses to stop at. I have to go. Please."

"I know," Arnie said. "I'll make you a deal. Just tell me your goal, that's all, just that one thing. Tell me, of all the tricks a majorette can do, which one would you like to do the most? Sort of like the majorettes' equivalent of running back a kickoff for a touchdown or hitting a home run in the bottom of the ninth. You know?"

Her fingernails were long and she had begun to nibble at them, not biting them off but folding them back at the top. "Well, there's one thing I want to do that I can't do yet. I keep trying, but---"

"What?"

She sighed at him. "Three turn-arounds on my aerial."

Arnie thought he knew what that meant. You spin around in three circles on the ground while your baton is in the air and then you catch it. He said, "You ever come close?"

"I did two and a half a couple times, but just when I was practicing. Never in public, like a game or a parade.

"Maybe if you threw the baton up higher, you'd have more time for the other half a spin. You ever think of that?"

"It doesn't work that way."

"No? Hmmm, I wonder why."

"If you throw the baton up too high, you might have more time to turn around but it's a lot harder to catch when it comes down. It comes down really hard."

"So then you need to spin around a little faster, I guess."

"Not really. If you spin too fast you'll lose your balance."

He was quiet for a moment, thoughtful, not the least bit threatening. "It's really a fine line, I guess, isn't it?"

She stood. "I have to go."

"Sure," Arnie said. "I know, I'm sorry."

He tried to stand up just as quickly as she had done, but his entire body rebelled. His pain was obvious; she didn't ask about it. "But I'm really glad I know these things. I mean, I know all about football; now, thanks to you, I know more about the halftime shows, too."

She picked up her box and started for the door, not glancing behind her.

"Do you have any brothers or sisters?"

"A sister."

"Older or younger?

She kept walking, trying to keep her pace even, not panic. "Younger."

"Is she gonna be a majorette when she grows up, too?"

"I don't know. She might. She practices a little but she's only eleven."

"Is she good, though? Got some potential?"

155

Arnie opened the door, then Debbie pushed the screen door with her shoulder and slipped out. She was nodding: yes, her sister had potential. She walked quickly across the stoop, down to the sidewalk.

"Thanks again, Mr. Castig." There was no gratitude in her voice, only relief. "I really appreciate what you did for me. I'll never forget it."

Arnie watched as that silky hair of hers shook from side to side and those perfectly molded legs of hers, covered by her skirt and her long socks, carried her away from him, a few doors down to old man Mijatov's place. He was such a miser (Stingy old man. Five letters.) Arnie couldn't believe he had bought anything.

After a few seconds, Sam Mijatov opened the door and greeted Debbie. She reached into her box and handed him a bar. As far as Arnie knew at that moment, it was the last time he would ever see her again in his life.

Friday,
October 1,
1965

HE WASN'T THINKING. He woke up foggier than usual, and forgetting that the old WAMB was now the All-New-WAMB, turned on the radio. It did not respond. He tapped it. Nothing. Tapped it harder. Still nothing, not even a hum. Then he looked down and saw that it was unplugged, which solved one mystery but raised another; he did not remember why it was unplugged. He pushed the prongs into the outlet and in an instant his memory returned. "SCREAMIN' JAY, CATS AN' KITTENS," came a roar in full-throated, ear-piercing splendor, "RAISIN' A RUCKUS IN THE BEAVAH VALLEEEE!"

That was it. Arnie decided he could take no more. He yanked out the plug again, picked up the radio in both hands and, thinking back quickly and fondly on the years of pleasure it had given him, bid it farewell. He lifted it over his head and threw it against the opposite wall, the plastic case making contact just below a crucifix that hung over the head of the bed, then crashing off the wall into a hundred pieces of plastic and tubes and coiled metal---nuts and springs that flew out at all angles, ricocheted off pieces of furniture and skipped across the wood floor and the area rugs that covered parts of it.

Arnie stared at the point of initial impact. The radio had taken a pyramid-shaped chunk of plaster out of the wall and a small cloud of dust hovered around it, slowly descending to the bedspread. "Mess with me, baby!" he said, and then called out to his wife. "Rosa! Hey, Ro, c'mon up. I fixed the radio."

But then he remembered she was not home. Just as well, he thought; she would probably not appreciate his creativity. Before she came home---whenever *that* was---he would have a chance to clean off the bed and maybe vacuum the plaster powder on the floor, and then go to the hardware store and get some spackle and paint and try to fix the wall, hoping Rosa wouldn't notice his outburst. But she would. She always noticed the results of his sloppy handiwork at home, and she would lose her temper yet again. So much shit had been hitting the fan at 422 Maple these days that it was amazing the fan still spun around.

He picked up one of the largest pieces of plaster still remaining and slipped it into his pants pocket, hoping to come as close as he could to matching the color. Oh, yeah. He'd need a paint brush. And also one of those tools that were sort of like spatulas and were used for applying the spackle and making it smooth.

He guessed he could write a check.

Maybe, he was beginning to think, silencing the All-New, Etc. as he did wasn't worth the trouble after all. Nobody ever cracked a wall with an on/off switch.

THE REST OF THE DAY passed slowly for Arnie and in small units: breakfast, lunch, dinner and, in between, random snatches of television shows, glances at the help-wanted ads in yesterday's editions of the *Beaver Valley Times* and the *Pittsburgh Press*, a half-hearted attempt at the *Times* crossword puzzle, and a short nap. No doctor's appointment, no stop at the hardware store; he could not have said why about either. At least he finally called the doctor, making an appointment for first-thing Monday; he would go to the hardware store tomorrow.

And there were even smaller increments of time: the moments spent in passage from one room of his house to another and from a sitting position to a standing position and from standing to lying down and then, after a while, getting back up again. He looked at his watch a lot, more than he could ever remember looking at it before in a few hours, wondering how long his various activities were taking, wondering how long it would be before they added up to a complete wakeful day. Time seemed to be moving so slowly that he kept bringing his watch up to his ear to make sure the second hand was ticking. It was. It just didn't feel like it.

He called Vinnie's house twice. Once the line was busy. Once it didn't answer. Fuck you, Rosa---but since the house was empty he did not bother to say the words aloud.

Late in the afternoon he called Zook at home. No answer there, either. So he tried him at Spee-Dee and found him folding an extra load of diapers because one of the men hadn't showed up today.

"Statsy babe. Hey-hey, what's up?"

"I was thinking maybe I'd go to the game with you tonight. What do you think?"

"Great, that'd be terrif, man! It's funny, I'm so used t' you workin' nights that I never gave it a thought."

"Well, no more of that, you know."

"I'm thinkin', and it seems t' me that we ain't been t' a game together since the cows come home."

"Well, I'm kind of feeling a little sick," he said, to give himself an out, in case he changed his mind, "like I might be coming down with something. But maybe getting some fresh air will be just what I need."

"Like yer gettin' some kinda disease?"

"Sort of. But some fresh air might be just what I need."

Zook agreed, "Yeah, that could be just the ticket. But listen, Stats, I got me a little problem here. I'm workin' late tonight 'cause one of the other guys had t' go to a funeral. I ain't sure what time I'm gonna get off, so we might miss the start of the game. You good with 'at?"

"Sure, whenever you can get here's fine."

"Be ready 'bout quarter t' eight. I'll probably be a little later, but maybe not. We'll play 'er safe, though, okay?"

"I'll be ready, Zook," and the two of them said goodbye and Arnie said, "What the hell am I doing?" He didn't feel like seeing a football game tonight. He didn't feel like being in a crowd, some of whom would probably know he had lost his job to a colored guy. It had been bad enough going through the whole story for Zook. If people were talking about him or feeling sorry for him, he'd feel it tonight, feel it like the prickles in the air just before a thunderstorm.

But at least it was the start of a football weekend, and maybe that would be the best therapy for him. Yeah, tonight it would be a high school game in person and he'd just ignore everybody there except Zook. Then tomorrow he would watch a few college games on the tube, and Sunday he would watch the pros, probably the Steelers, if you considered those palookas professional. Of course, if by some miracle, the Jets and Broncos were on in Pittsburgh, he'd glue his eyes to Joey again. No reason that his second start as a pro shouldn't be better than the first, especially because Denver just didn't match up to Buffalo. Yeah, he said to himself again, it didn't sound like such a bad weekend after all.

Then on Monday he would get serious, put his life back in order again. And he meant it! First he would finally get around to seeing a doctor. If nothing else, he needed to get the bandage changed on his ribs; it was starting to get dirty, and he wanted the doctor to take it off for a few minutes so he could scratch his chest. He was afraid that maybe he was starting to get a rash.

From there he would pick up the supplies he needed at the hardware store and fix the wall. Then he would get to work finding a job. He would start with the cab companies. There were two of them in town, each of which probably had a dispatcher on duty for three shifts. Six chances. Make that nine. He knew Rochester well enough so that he could work there and Dave Spadafore would be happy to put in a word for him. Actually, eight. Rochester was a small town and probably would not have anyone working overnight.

Oh, and he would fill out the forms for unemployment compensation and stick them in the mail. Couldn't forget those. In the afternoon, he would go talk to Father Daniel, and on the way home he'd pick up the papers, local and Pittsburgh; he would study the "Help Wanteds" and circle some companies to call first thing Tuesday morning.

Arnie wondered what kind of luck Clarence Howard was having. Ol' Clarence, he wasn't *that* bad. If he had any kind of offensive line in front of him . . .

While he was thinking about what to do after checking the want-ads, he hid the fourteen chocolate bars in various places around the house so Rosa wouldn't find them. If she came home, that is. He stashed four of them in a boot in the hall closet, wrapped four more in a dishtowel and stuffed them into an old paint can in the basement, a can that he had once used to store things like nails and screws and brackets. As for Zook's pair of bars, Arnie left them on the table in the hall closet; he would give them to his friend tonight.

So that meant four bars left. Arnie wouldn't have to hide them. He was planning on giving them as a gift. He found an old shoe box in the bedroom closet, brought it down to the living room, and wrapped the remaining bars in old newspaper before placing them carefully into the container; he did not want them bouncing against one another and breaking when the package was handled at the post office. He found a blank sheet of paper in the kitchen, one of the pieces Rosa used to make her shopping lists. Next to it was a pen. He took a few seconds to come up with just the right words, or as close to them as he could, and sitting at the table, facing the sink and listening to the faucet's sporadic drip, began to write.

Dear Mr. Washington,

It has never been easy for me to set my thoughts down on paper. On a day like this I am not even sure what my thoughts are because they are all mixed up with each other, but I guess I do know what some of them are and they are that I hope your sister is feeling better and keeps improving every day. I am sending her the enclosed chocolate bars as a present. I hope you will give them to her. You can have one too if you want because I want you to know there are no hard feelings. That is another one of the thoughts I have been having, and I kind of thought that if you and your sister have got the blues today, maybe a nice bite of something sweet might make you feel better.

I think Mike Dunbar, he told me it was okay to call him Mike, is going to do a pretty good job.

Sincerely yours,
Arnie Castig

He folded the note and put it into the box, then scotch-taped the lid onto it as securely as he could. He called information for Rochester and got the address for Ronald L. Washington, writing it darkly and thickly on the lid. It was too late to go to the Post Office today---something else for his list of errands on Monday. Or tomorrow. Yeah, he decided, he'd mail the chocolate Saturday morning; the college games started about the same time as the Post Office closed. In the meantime, Arnie decided to slip the box under the bed, out of sight. Just in case.

And then it hit him. The disc jockeys from the old WAMB were out of work now, too. What if *they* were thinking about being cab dispatchers? They might not know Ambridge as well as he did, but they probably knew it well enough to do the job---and they had those great voices from all their years on the radio. They would be naturals behind the mike in the dispatch office. Not only that, but they were famous, and it would be good publicity for a cab company to have one of them as its voice. Arnie, on the other hand, was a nobody, even in a place as small as Ambridge, a place where he had lived all his life.

Well, no sense complaining. He would give the job hunt everything he had; there was nothing more a person could do than that.

DUSK APPROACHED and found him lying on his back on the living room floor, beached and alone. He had laced his fingers behind his head and his feet rested on the coffee table. It was a Friday night in autumn, and that meant high school football in the Beaver Valley. He was thinking about Joe Namath, the times he had seen him in person. October of 1960, five years ago, had been the next to last, and the Beaver Falls Tigers, undefeated that fall and the eventual Class AA champions of the WPIAL, Western Pennsylvania Interscholastic Athletic League, beat a better-than-average Ambridge team 19-6. Joe threw for all three Tiger scores that night, the balls winging their way to the receivers with the spin tight and the release perfectly timed, each of the passes with a trajectory like a rainbow. There was an art to throwing a football like that, an instinct that transcended mere skill; it was as if the ball itself knew where to go and how to get there, with no human agency behind it.

The first pass, as Arnie recalled, was the most impressive, covering a distance of more than forty yards and featuring a nifty run by halfback Karlin "Butch" Ryan after the grab. Altogether the play netted sixty-seven yards and left the Bridger defensive backs, an adequate bunch if not even better, questioning the gods. The game was played in Ambridge but even so, many of the hometown fans, Arnie among them, cheered the excellence of the visitors' execution.

Outside, Arnie heard a vehicle of some sort, its engine rattling, pull up in front of his house. The driver beeped the horn to the tune of "Shave and a haircut, two bits."

Zook. The Spee-Dee van. The Bridgers and the Wolverines.

"Shit on a stick."

He looked at his watch and saw that kickoff was but a few minutes away. They would miss the start of the game. But as far as Arnie was concerned, they could miss the *whole* game. He had changed his mind about going. He had changed his mind back and forth at least half a dozen times, but now that the moment of departure had arrived, he was certain. He didn't want to see a high school football game; he didn't even want to see his best friend. And, more than anything else, he didn't want his best friend or anyone else to see *him*.

Besides, he had invented a reason to be annoyed with Zook, deciding he was out of line for making fun at him the other day about the majorette and the chocolate bars. He did not get "suckered" by her. He did not want to take her to the sock hop. Yes, she was a "looker," but that was not the only reason he made his purchase from her.

Another beep of the horn, a single blast this time, a long one. I'm sick, Zook. The house is dark, Zook. Maybe I'm taking a nap, Zook. I'll give you your candy some other time.

"Hey-hey, Statsy babe," Zook yelled. "C'mon, we gotta get a move on!"

Arnie felt guilty. He knew how much his friend was looking forward to the pair of them watching the game.

"Stat-seeee!"

It was his wrists that made Broadway Joe such an exceptional quarterback. Oh sure, he had the great instincts and the quickness, the footwork and the coordination, and he had probably put in more than his share of time on the practice field as a kid. But the key to his success at throwing the football was his wrists---the powerful snap, the quick release; without them he was just like any other quarterback you could name, capable of the big play from time to time but never of the transcendent experience.

And that made Arnie think about the last time he had seen Joe in person. It was a basketball game, though, not a football game: Beaver Falls at Ambridge, January, 1961, and the two teams were running through their warmup drills before the game: a few minutes of layups, a few minutes of three-man weaves. Then they broke off for individual shooting, and that was when Joe put on the most amazing exhibition Arnie had ever seen on a basketball court.

"Hey, ya get sick again er what?" Arnie could tell that Zook had gotten out of the truck and was standing on the sidewalk. A few seconds later, his cough seemed even closer. "Rosie take ya t' the hospital er what!"

What Joe did was, he had the manager toss him balls and he moved so far away from the hoop that he was almost on the Bridgers' side of the court. In fact, two or three times he even had his foot on the line. He began hoisting one-hand push shots. Just to be able to raise the ball from that far out was a feat, but Joe was not only getting the distance, he was getting the accuracy, dropping one shot after another cleanly through the hoop, nothing but net, time after time. And---the really amazing thing---he was doing it all without leaving his feet and barely even getting up on his toes! It had nothing to do with strength It was all in those extraordinary wrists of his: his hand on the ball with the fingers splayed, and then, after a downward thrust of the wrists so quick you could barely see it, the ball launched into a looping but unerring orbit, its destination so far away that mere mortals could not have reached it even with a basketball on a catapult. Some of the Ambridge players noticed what Joe was doing and stopped their own warm-ups to watch. They could not conceal their awe. Neither could Arnie.

Flick. Whoosh. Swish.

Flick. Whoosh. Swish.

Flick. Whoosh. *Touchdown*!

"Aw, what the heck," Arnie said, and changed his mind; he would go with Zook to watch the Bridgers play the Wolverines after all.

He got up and hurried across the living room to the front window, hoping that Zook hadn't driven off yet. But it was too late; the van was gone. "Damn, Zee, you're supposed to be my friend. You couldn't've given me another minute? Thirty seconds?" But it did not matter. Zook always sat in the same seat in Bridger stadium; Arnie would find him there. But if he did not get his ass in gear, he would miss the entire first half.

IT HAD BEEN YEARS since Arnie had walked through the business district of Ambridge at night, and he saw signs of disrepair he had never noticed before. Ziggy's Distributors, for instance, with its neon proclamation of COLD BEER, was the only store in the entire block between Sixth and Seventh on Merchant whose electric sign had all of its letters functioning.

Next door to Ziggy's: P ince Bar and rill.

A few door ahead: Thom son & hompson Auto Bod nd Service.

Across the street: Edd e's Starlight L unge.

On the corner of Seventh and Merchant, Arnie waited for the light to change, idly noting its progress. Red. Yellow. Nothing. No green. The green had burned out and not been replaced, was merely a void beneath its predecessors.

In the next block were more dead bulbs, at a florist's shop and a sporting goods store, at a realtor's office and a plumbing wholesaler. Even the marquee of the State Theater, whose letters were plastic, not electric, seemed a display in a foreign tongue.

> B nY lake s MISSin
> CarO Lynl Y
> La renc Oli er

He had heard of the movie. It was a mystery. Except the way it showed up on the marquee, it was like a crossword puzzle. It took Arnie only a few seconds to fill in the letters. "Medium Difficulty," at most.

He found himself wondering: Was this the movie Debbie would see with her free passes, the one her mother had jokingly suggested she take Arnie to see. Who would she really go with? Her friend M.A.? Did she have a boyfriend, a football player? Arnie pictured himself in high school, dreaming that he could have appealed to a girl like Debbie, that she would have been willing to wait for him after a post-game shower and then gone out on a date with him. Unlikely, he thought. But possible; Rosa, after all, had been pretty, and she had waited for him.

But Rosa had been such a shy girl, a different kind of pretty from Debbie. She was quieter, less sure of herself, and it showed in her face, her posture. Besides, back in those days it was more important than it was today for a nice Italian girl to find a nice Italian boy. In 1965, anybody could date anybody, like Joe Namath and that actress with the big schnoz.

Arnie stopped at Eighth Street, next to Stavros R ligious Sup plies.

He was becoming disoriented, as if he were sinking into the flu that he never had in the first place. He felt as if he were trying to get his footing on one of those shifting floors of a haunted house at a carnival. How did his hometown get to look like this so worn out, so old? He thought of the Japs taking over American steel, and having no need of places like Ambridge, Aliquippa, Beaver Falls, Rochester, Freedom and the rest of the Valley anymore. The towns had spread out from the banks of the Ohio *because* of the Ohio, because at the turn of the twentieth century, there was no better way to transport steel than on the hard, rippled muscles of a barge. Steel on steel.

But since then enormous trucks had been built. So had airplanes that could soar in flight even though weighed down with cargo from American Bridge. The trucks were more flexible means of transportation, the planes faster. The rivers, once America's industrial lifeline, didn't matter anymore. In the summer there were far more motorboats than barges on the water.

If the Japs really did take over the steel industry because of their newly-developed efficiencies, and because the American factories couldn't afford to install expensive new equipment themselves---if this happened, then the mill towns in the Valley would continue to decay the way Ambridge was decaying now. They would indeed be the ghost towns of the twenty-first century. And the mills? Maybe it was true, as John Groom had told him, that the slump they were in was one from which they would never emerge. Athletes always did . . . but industries? This was something new for Arnie to consider.

His ribs hurt, his hip hurt, his knee hurt. It wasn't exactly a cold night, but a cold breeze blew up from the river every so often, and made him ache all the more. He pulled up the collar of his trench coat. He should have worn something heavier. He should have seen a doctor. But the truth was something he had never felt before in his life. He didn't care. He simply did not care enough about himself. Look at his poundage, the bulge of his waist. He did he ever let something like that happen?

He crossed Merchant and turned up Eighth toward Duss, where the stadium took up the entire block behind the back end of the American Bridge Beam Shop, and from which contrails of exhaust drifted up and over the football field. It was a reassuring sight.

But as for the game, it was probably midway through in the first quarter by now, maybe near the end. If Arnie could possibly walk faster, he would. He could not quite hear the crowd yet, but was beginning to sense the excitement of sport reaching out to him, a kind of rumbling at his feet. Maybe the home team had the ball. Maybe it was driving for a score. There was nothing like a football game to get your mind off your troubles. Well, depends on how many troubles you had and how bad they were.

He remembered the last time he had been downtown at night, a Saturday years ago when they put up the Christmas lights on Merchant Street. He and Rosa had sat on a bench and watched. And he remembered the strange thing he had noticed when the men turned the lights on for a test. He had expected them to brighten the town. Instead, the town made the lights look grimy, or at least dim. The little specks of color, of red and blue and green and orange that were hanging on their wires from light pole to light pole, and the tiny illuminated wreaths atop each pole, were simply overmatched by a dreariness so pervasive that it muted the attempts of electricity of brighten the surroundings.

It was like the effect that Zook had when he put on his pristine uniform.

Or maybe dreariness wasn't really the right word. Maybe the Christmas lights simply couldn't compete with the smokestack emissions that were a constant presence in the air. People in Ambridge called the grit that settled over their community "black sugar," and it was a necessary evil. Or to look at it more optimistically, as most people in town were prone to do, an unfortunate blessing. Some days---not every day but occasionally, depending on what the mills were churning out and how the winds were blowing---black sugar was insidious. It sneaked through the sealed windows of houses onto living room tables, through locked doors onto freshly vacuumed carpets. Wash your car and leave it in the driveway and a couple of hours later you could write your name on the hood with your finger. If you were exercising outside and perspired heavily, the sweat would soak the black sugar and it would drip down your forehead into your eyes; they would burn as if soap were in them.

By and large, the men and women of Ambridge were pro-black sugar. The former made it and the latter cleaned it up without complaint. Black sugar meant high production, good wages, the kind of life that generations abroad could only dream of. But now what? Was his town on the way to cleanliness, of all things?

"What the hell's going on?" he said, and hundreds of people cheered.

He glanced up at the Beam Shop and could see the row of domed exhaust fans on the roof, sprouting every ten yards or so like the huge mushrooms of an especially dank forest. Around the fans the lights of the stadium cast dingy halos. He looked at his watch. Definitely the second quarter, he decided, which meant that the guy who took tickets at the west gate had probably deserted his post for a few toddies at the taproom across the street. If Arnie was lucky, he would be able to get into the game for free.

IT WAS HALFTIME, and the majorettes led the band onto the field, with shiny white boots hugging their calves like a second skin. They stepped so high and so briskly that the pleats of their skirts never had a chance to settle on the tops of their thighs; the folds of fabric snapped up with every footstep as if magnetically repelled by flesh---and the flesh, Arnie thought, had a glow to it.

Some of the people in the crowd clapped as the girls appeared. Some of them cheered. Only a few did not pay attention at all, having already left their seats to go to the concession stands or bathrooms or simply to move about, stretch their legs, rub their asses after sitting for two quarters on splintered wood bleachers.

Zook, apparently, was one of them. Arnie looked around and did not see him in his usual seat. He decided to wait for him on the cinder track that surrounded the field, leaning up against the fence that separated the track from the field. Zook would be back soon, and in the meantime Arnie would listen to the band and watch the majorettes.

Epilogue

The Future

Sunday,
January 12,
1969

THE AMERICAN FOOTBALL LEAGUE did not go out of business, as Father Daniel Schact had predicted in the autumn of 1965. To the contrary, it had prospered. Television ratings increased from season to season, as did attendance at the various venues. And NBC, the network that broadcast the A.F.L. games, kept renewing its contract and paying larger and larger sums of money each time for the privilege, meaning that sponsors, eager to appeal to the ever-growing audiences, paid increasing sums of money to the network. NBC wanted to reach a different audience than did the old, established N.F.L. It wanted to reach young adults, men who drove flashy cars, drank beer, did their own repairs around the house, shaved their faces with both blades and electric, and slapped on manly-scented cologne afterward. NBC did not want an Ex-Lax-dependent viewership.

To attract this younger audience, the A.F.L. established a different set of rules from those of the N.F.L., and the result was a more action-packed, wide-open game. Quarterbacks were given more freedom to pass; receivers could not be thrown off stride by defenders before the ball arrived; and offensive linemen were able to manhandle their defensive counterparts in such a way that they could more easily clear paths for the running backs to rack up long gains.

What the A.F.L. was doing was exactly the same thing that the All-New WAMB had been doing, changing its product to attract its own particular demographic, people who wouldn't drop dead as soon as everybody else. Although, of course, the football teams weren't changing their style of play nearly as much as the radio station.

The most important step in the growth of the A.F.L. was its being recognized by the previously dismissive National Football League, which had always been *the* league when it came to football. The two organizations agreed to merge in 1970 and, before that, to play an annual end-of-the-season game between the teams with the best records in each league, the winner to be considered the best football team in the world. It was the World Series of the sport. The game was originally called the A.F.L.-N.F.L. Championship, but that was too awkward. An event of such magnitude demanded a name of magnitude as well, something attention-grabbing, memorable, pretentious. Starting in 1969, the game would be known as the Super Bowl, and the name would be followed by Roman numerals to distinguish one year's event from its predecessor. All that was missing was a chariot race at halftime, but eventually there would be halftime performances that made chariot races look like wheel chair outings on the grounds of a sanitarium.

As expected, the new competition started out a mismatch. In 1967, the Green Bay Packers of the N.F.L. crushed the Kansas City Chiefs of the A.F.L., 35-10, the game not even as close as the score indicated. The following year, Green Bay was again the old league's representative and it defeated the Oakland Raiders, 33-14. A few points closer for the A.F.L., but still a lopsided affair. There was no doubt in those first two years which of the leagues played the better brand of football. And as far as most fans were concerned, an even more one-sided outcome seemed on the horizon for the next confrontation.

On January 12, 1969, the N.F.L.'s Baltimore Colts would take the field against the New York Jets, the first of the games to be called a Super Bowl but still known as Super Bowl III. On the surface, though, there seemed nothing super about it. It was Cassius Clay versus a featherweight, the Boston Celtics against a bunch of kids from the local playground, the New York Yankees against the Little League All-Stars---on that order of injustice. The Colts were favored to beat the New Yorkers by nineteen points if you wanted to bet the spread, or seven-to-one if your preference was to take the two teams evenly and go with the odds. Never had a championship game, in any sport, seemed such a mismatch. Not even the Pack had been the bettors' choice by numbers like that. Phil McIntyre, writing in the *Pittsburgh Press,* said that he thought it would be a better game if the Jets stayed home and the Colts simply scrimmaged with their second-stringers.

Zook, though, was among the few people in the Western hemisphere who thought the Jets had a chance. Or, more accurately, he *had* been among them until he read something in the *Beaver Valley Times* several days before the game that left him deeply troubled. It was a prediction by Joe Namath that the Jets would come out on top. "I guarantee we'll win," the quarterback had supposedly said to a reporter. "Guarantee it." And when several other journalists pressed him on the matter, Joe repeated the boast and swore he was not kidding.

Zook ripped the article out of the paper and, the Excelsior having gone out of business, he brought it with him that night to a barroom on Duss Avenue called the Caviar. He was furious. "Christ on a cross!" he said to Arnie after ordering an Iron City draft to match that of his friend, "is this guy some kinda lunatic?"

"C'mon, Zook," Arnie said, "it doesn't mean anything. It's just Joey being Joey."

"It's Joey bein' a asshole, ya ask me. I mean, believin' yer team's gonna win's okay, Statsy. Hell, ya gotta believe in yerself in this world if yer gonna get anywheres, 'specially if yer an athlete. But ya can't say somethin' like that, not with a buncha newsmen jus' waitin' t' tell the whole wide world. Ya sound like a idiot! If nothin' else, it's a jinx, an' jinxes're real in sports. They might not be real in other partsa life, but once ya step between the lines, everything's different. Joe's *gotta* realize that."

"But that's his style, Zee. Hell, it's more than that, it's one of the reasons he's a winner, that kind of brashness and confidence."

"There's a difference between bein' cocky and bein' outta yer friggin' gourd! Y' imagine how pissed off the Colts are, hearin' 'at. They prob'ly got the article hangin' on their locker room wall. 'Stead of beatin' the Jets by fifty now, they'll whip 'em by a hunnert!"

Arnie shrugged and took a thoughtful sip of his brew. "Maybe Joe knows something. You ever think of that?"

"Whattaya mean, knows somethin'? What's 'e gonna know?"

"It could be the Jets were looking at the films and they saw some kind of weakness they can exploit, some kinda play they can run that they know the Colts can't stop."

"Oh, right, sure. The Jets found this weakness 'at every other team in the whole damn National Football League missed all year long. The Pack missed it las' week an' the Browns an' the Lions---an' the Colts were thirteen an' one in the regular season! An' now this rumdum team from the A.F.L. comes along an' *they're* the ones figure it out? *They're* the ones gonna knock the Colts off? Whattaya, tellin' me fairy tales er somethin'?"

"It's possible."

"It's dogshit."

After another ten minutes or so of argument, they ordered one more draft apiece. Arnie told Zook it would be his last, that Rosa would be waiting up for him, and she had turned into a drill sergeant where her husband's health was concerned. He even had a curfew.

THE PAST THREE YEARS had not been good ones for Arnie, but neither had they been as bad as he had initially feared. No criminal charges were filed against him for the attack on the majorette---so obvious was it that he had lost his mind for the moment and so spotless had his record been before that. Besides not having caused Debbie Savukas any physical harm, nor having issued a threat either violent or sexual in nature, Arnie did not seem to have broken any law, other than one of the catch-alls like disorderly conduct or being a public nuisance.

And he did not, as he had feared, become an outcast in his hometown. Occasionally people would point at him or snicker as he passed on the street, and on rare occasions someone would make a comment so hurtful that he feared he would never be able to put Debbie Savukas behind him. After one such comment, made in Rosa's presence, she told him they had no choice but to move to a new town where nobody knew their names.

But these were the exceptions. Most of the time, far from needing to exile himself from Ambridge, Arnie found himself something of a celebrity. As the story of the events leading up to that horrible Friday night became known, especially the part about his having risked his life one day and gotten fired for his trouble the next, people found their hearts going out to Arnie. And, the reverse side of the coin: To a certain extent, the Washington family and Moses Michael Dunbar III gradually became outcasts in Freedom and Rochester.

Furthermore, as the pace of the steel industry's decline increased, even more people began to sympathize with Arnie. It did not quite make sense, but he came to be a symbol of the decline, as previously he had been charged with symbolizing racism. Simpson Wrought Iron Works had closed its doors in the preceding summer---no more wrought iron, no more shifts; and it was the largest of the heavy industries yet to go out of business in the Valley. Most American Bridge and Russell & Findlay operations were down to one shift a day, and although nobody seemed certain whether or not the Japs were actually behind it, it *was* certain that no traces of recovery were visible. More and more, steel was beginning to mean foreign steel. The American product was no longer an athlete in his prime having a run of bad luck; it was an athlete too old to compete anymore, opening up positions for one newcomer after another.

To some people in the Valley, primarily hate-mongering, lip-twitching, saliva-leaking bigots, Arnie had become yet another kind of symbol---not the beneficiary of racism but the victim. If these people had been organized, as was the case of the Ku Klux Klan in pockets of the South and Midwest, Arnie could have been elected president. Or Grand Kleagle or whatever the hell the chief was called. He would, of course, have turned down the position with disgust.

When Ronald Leander Washington dropped him a note of condolence a few days after his arrest, a note that also thanked him for the chocolate (which Rosa had mailed at her husband's insistence), Arnie wrote back the next day to swear that he was not a racist. If he had lost his job to a white man, he said, he would have been just as upset. Then he erased that line and said that he would have been *more* upset if a white man had succeeded him. As Mr. Washington had pointed point, the young Dunbar fellow would be an example for others of his race, would give them hope. If Arnie *had* to lose his job---and he made it clear that he was still not convinced of the fact---he wanted some good to come out of it for others. And he believed that it would.

The letter brought an even warmer reply from Ronald Leander Washington, to which his sister added a postscript. She was out of the hospital now and feeling much better, she told him. She expressed her gratitude to Arnie not only for his efforts on her behalf but for his attitude toward subsequent events. She called him "a fine, decent man," and said

175

she hoped he would be able to find another job soon. Not to mention the peace of mind he so richly deserved. She was praying for him. A nice sentiment, Arnie thought, but he had long harbored doubts about the efficacy of prayer. Rosa had worn out her set of rosary beads after his accident at American Bridge, and he still lost his job.

That, however, was the end of communication between the two families. Arnie never saw Ronald Leander Washington again after that day on his stoop, and never heard another word from either him or his sister after the last letter. But he thought he had begun to notice a few more colored people in places he had not seen them before, in jobs in which he was surprised to see them---behind counters in stores, in ticket booths at theaters, in reception rooms at businesses. Was he imagining things? Or was there a new reality in the steel towns, one for which the Beaver Valley Colored People's Action Committee deserved at least some of the credit? He hoped it was the latter, for if some of the credit went to the B.V.C.P.A.C., that meant some of the credit went to Stats Castig. He might not have had a parade in his honor, but maybe he would be a footnote in history books.

IN THE LATE WINTER OF 1966, after nine Wednesday visits to the Ambridge office of the Pennsylvania Department of Employment Services, and after having healed from the attack in the alley to the point that he was back to his normal limp, Arnie found his new line of work. It was not a desk job, as he had envisioned, although he did have to spend a certain amount of time each day seated, keeping records up to date and making a few phone calls. Nor was it a managerial position like that of Matthew D'Imperio, which he also sought. Neither did he become a dispatcher for one of the cab companies. He still did not make much money, although more than he did at Gibraltar. Not enough, though, for him to own a car, to indulge in any impulse buying. But occasionally he thought he could afford to splurge, and instead of taking Rosa out for dinner on her birthday, he bought her---both of them, actually---a record player and three big band discs. He figured they could afford to add to their collection at least once a month. There could be an old WAMB after all, and they could be it. The brand new WCASTIG.

But after having owned the record player for five months, and although Arnie and Rosa listened to the music several nights a week while doing the dishes, they had yet to dance. That had been, and remained, the past.

Arnie's new position did have its advantages, though, the biggest of which was its ease on his heart. He worked regular daytime hours now, and one less of them each day than Gibraltar had demanded. As for his commute, it was a matter of blocks, which he could walk, rather than miles. And none of his co-workers---yes, he even had co-workers, the presence of actual human beings with whom to share during the day--- ever talked about the right demographic. In fact, in their line of work, the demographic would never change. There was also, in this third job of his life, virtually no chance that he would be set upon by scarily eyeballed young toughs some day in the street.

Thanks in large part to a recommendation from Zook---actually, dozens of recommendations starting the week after he had lost his job and continuing almost daily afterward---Arnie was hired by the Spee-Dee Diaper Service.

Job title: soil counter.

The process begins with the drivers unloading bags of dirty diapers from their trucks---small bags, one or two per household, not very heavy; the names of the families are attached to the bags by plastic clips. Then the bags are stacked onto hand trucks and wheeled into the counting room, a large, mostly empty space, with an oversized table in the middle.

Enter the soil counter. Arnie empties the bags by hand on the table and counts the diapers in each, the scent reminding him of the Valvoline refinery in Rochester, the putrid odor made all the more intolerable for its being combined with a foul sweetness. As he struggles olfactorily, he fills out tickets for the women in the front office recording the number of diapers per bag, so that the same number can be shipped out in the next delivery.

Yet he finds, in time, that the smell is not so offensive, after all. When Arnie is done with one hand truck full of bags, he sweeps the diapers off the table into a large, wheeled cart with canvas sides. Once the cart is full, he rolls it down the hall, past the loading dock and into the washing room. He leaves the cart next to one of the many washing machines of industrial size and strength, then returns with an empty cart to the counting room, where scores more of bulging bags await him.

Which is his cue to repeat the process.

Following which he repeats it again . . .

. . . and again . . .

. . . and again.

After each return to the counting room, he washes his hands up to the elbows, then rinses off the soap and washes again. The soap, provided by Spee-Dee, is Lik-O-San Merima, chosen especially for its pleasant scent. Which disappears gradually as he goes back to the table and unpacks the next load of bags.

With about half an hour left in the day, Arnie starts on his paperwork, noting the intakes and outputs of each Spee-Dee truck on its shift. This he does until the clock allows him to punch the same time card he had punched in the morning.

For his labors, Arnie makes $1.17 an hour more than he had made as a security guard. Even with the shorter work day, though, he comes out ahead; he has done the math.

But before he starts on the paperwork, he cleans up one final time. He scrubs his arms not with Lik-O-San Merima, though, but with Lava and a brush whose bristles are stiff enough to scrape the barnacles off a boat. The process is painful, but the reason for the pain brings about a kind of contentment Arnie has not known since he was a young man at American Bridge. For he has spent his day with diapers, and diapers mean children and children mean a child of his own, one he can imagine, a boy who is the budding football player he has so wanted to bring into the world, the boy about whom he dreamed long before he and Rosa had gotten their life-altering news.

He reminisces---if it is possible to reminisce about something that was never more than a fantasy to begin with---about his son, about the two of them tossing a miniature football around in their miniature front yard. The boy is just out of diapers, so small a creature that, if Arnie ever gave him a regulation-sized football, he would have to throw it underhanded, with both hands. He would giggle at his efforts, at his inaccuracy, and Arnie would smile back at him, encouraging him but never showing impatience.

Eventually they would move up to the regulation ball and move out to the street, there always being so little traffic on Maple that it is almost as safe as a playground. How many times had Arnie told Rosa about his dream, some form of it? She always listened without comment. She must have thought he was criticizing her, continuing to dwell on what was wrong with her body. But she let her man talk; it was, she must have decided at some level of consciousness, the least she could do.

At any rate, the Castig boy has big hands, and grips a football with just one of them now. With a snap of the wrist he throws a pass covering the distance from one phone pole to the next. Then, a year or two later, from one phone pole to the second pole in the distance. After that, just before he is old enough to play for the junior high team, he and his father work on routes; his father runs posts, sidelines, down-and-outs. The more his son masters his skills, the more time Arnie needs between passes to catch his breath. But what a glorious way to be winded, he thinks, being such an important part of your son's rapidly-increasing maturity as an athlete.

By the time Arnie's son gets to high school, he is a tough, young fellow, a steeltown boy, but always polite, always considerate to others, no matter whether those others are his peers, his elders, his juniors, his teachers or the janitors. He is a gentleman, because he has an advantage that eludes many of the boys in town. He has a father, a real father, a man who loves him more than he loves spending an hour or two after work downing boilermakers at the local tavern, more than he loves going bowling with his buddies on weekends.

How proud Arnie is at the results of such loving attention, sitting in the stands at summer's end, watching the youngster who bears both his name and the imprint of his training as he riddles opposing defenses with passes so precise it is as if their paths are machine-tooled. It doesn't make any difference who is on the receiving end; what matters is only that Ryan Castig has thrown the ball. Ryan. Arnie has always liked the sound of it, liked the way it goes with Castig. He has never gotten around to telling Rosa that that will be his name, but he is determined not to take no for an answer. Stats and Ryan. Could there possibly be a greater thrill than to keep the statistics for your own boy!

IN THE DAYS following her husband's insanity---that was the only word Rosa could think of to describe Arnie's behavior at the

Ambridge-Ellwood City game in 1965---it seemed as if they would never become connubial again. Even cordial. Or even roommates; after she got bored hiding out in the kitchen, she virtually moved in with Vinnie. She withdrew from him almost completely, would not even see him on visiting day at Western Psych. Only Father Daniel and Zook called on their friend, but the conversation was an unaccustomed strain. Such good friends they were, but they could not talk about football for more than a few minutes; it seemed too inconsequential. Nor could they discuss Arnie's recovery--- too embarrassing; or Moses Michael Dunbar III's progress---too touchy a subject between Arnie and the priest. And then there was the ambience, a further assault on communication: the woman who screamed every so often for no apparent reason, the man with the drooling chin who always dropped in on Arnie and his guests to slurp a greeting, and the other man who ran through the halls swatting non-existence mice with a broom. Who would have guessed that the three friends from Ambridge would ever find themselves in such a place--too nervous to talk as they were used to talking and, in Zook's case, too frightened, certain that one day the loonies would organize and attack. How could the pathways of simple men's lives become so appallingly twisted?

Father Daniel went to see Rosa one day to ask her to pray for her husband's recuperation. That's all, just to say a few prayers every day. She told him no. He said he knew for a fact that even Ronald Leander Washington and his sister were praying for Arnie; the least Rosa could do was join them. She glared at her priest and told him, in so many words, that her intention, then, was to do *less* than the least. She said Father Daniel could pray for Arnie if he liked. So could the Archbishop of Pittsburgh. So could the entire College of Cardinals and even the Pope, if they didn't have anything better to do. She would abstain, thank you.

It was one of Arnie's shrinks who finally got through to Rosa, that and the passage of time with its attendant blunting of memory and dampening of ire. The shrink told Rosa that what her husband had done was not a reflection on his feelings toward her. Debbie Savukas simply happened to be the person upon whom, for a variety of reasons, he had chosen to inflict the jumble of emotions that had been building inside him. Actually, the shrink said, "chosen" was the wrong word, as it suggested a conscious choice, carefully reasoned. It was not that at all. Debbie just happened to be there at the time when Arnie reached the breaking point. No, it was more than that: Inadvertently, she gave him the final push toward the breaking point, representing, as she did, solutions that would never be achieved, a kind of life that it was too late to live.

Rosa asked the shrink what the hell *that* meant.

The shrink changed his approach. If Arnie's wife refused to stand by him in this hour of great need, how was he to hope that anyone else would ever do so? How, in other words, was he ever to gain the confidence he needed to recover? Surely, the gentleman summarized, Arnie had not done anything so despicable as to have forfeited the opportunity to put the past behind him and start anew. Not after but a single episode. All right, he conceded, a single, *highly visible* episode, but still . . .

The first time the shrink said this to Rosa she told him to go croak.

But the more she thought about it, the more sense it all began to make. It was not fair to either Arnie or Rosa to throw away all the years they had spent together because of a single night when they were apart. After all, he had not committed adultery, had not robbed a grocery store, had not caused an automobile accident while under the influence. There was really no name for what he had done.

Of course, in the aftermath of the Ambridge-Ellwood City game, she would rather her husband had behaved differently---had punched Ronald Leander Washington in the mouth or smashed a stack of records at the All-New WAMB. But she came to believe that his timidity in the face of abuse was in truth a certain dignity. If he had given into the violence that he certainly felt somewhere within, he would not have saved his job or his music, but only made his grievances more unbearable. And pointless. He knew, in other words, when he was beaten.

Sometime between Christmas and the end of the insanity year, Rosa's thinking began visibly to turn. Slowly, gradually, she and her husband resumed the activities of their life together B.D., Before Debbie. They began shopping as a couple again on weekends and shared breakfast and dinner when Arnie went to work for Spee-Dee. They also shared the chores of the household, including sex, although its frequency dropped from bi-monthly to once every three weeks to once a month. Also once a month, they went to the fish fry at the American Legion to raise money for those who had fought in World War II and the Korean War. They watched

181

more television than they used to, such shows as *Daniel Boone*, *It Takes A Thief*, and Arnie favorite, *Mission: Impossible*. For the Castigs, a special occasion was something as commonplace as listening to their record player or inviting Zook over to watch the Jets in their first Super Bowl.

AS FOR ARNIE'S VICTIM, the young lady who had called on him one day, in all innocence, simply to raise money for a school project, she had been badly shaken by his desire to hold her, just hold her, and had to be helped from the field by her fellow majorettes, spending the second half of the Ambridge-Ellwood City game lying on a bench in the locker room, sipping Coke syrup as if it were patent medicine.

But Debbie was a girl of cheerful disposition and sound character---and her recovery was almost instantaneous. After the game, she went out for a snack with a few of her best friends. She was not one hundred percent herself, understandably, but she was there; that was the important thing, she was out in the company of others. She kept a date with the quarterback of the Bridgers on Saturday night to see *Bunny Lake Is Missing*, and in school two days later was cracking jokes about that "far-out half-time show on Friday," and "how wifty a person can get when they eat too much chocolate too quickly."

She graduated the next spring as a member of the National Honor Society and went to Edinboro State College, where she majored in elementary education and made the Dean's List both semesters of her freshman year.

Arnie did not know any of this. He never talked to Debbie again after they so clumsily embraced at the football game, and in fact he never saw her again in person. If he had lived long enough, however, he would have learned something that would have both surprised and disappointed him. In the *Beaver Valley Times*, early in the 1970s, there was a photo of Debbie on the "Hometown News" page, flashing dispirited peace signs with both hands. But her face was different from the one Arnie would have remembered---drawn, stringy-haired, even wrinkled slightly around the edges of her eyes and lips; and the story beneath it was one that Arnie could never have guessed would be written about *his* majorette.

According to the *Times*, Deborah Lynn Savukas, AHS Class of '66, had a new job. She had just been promoted to assistant manager of the furniture department at Bargain Barn, a discount store in a small shopping center in the hills behind Aliquippa, overlooking the coal-black flatland where Russell & Findlay's Basic Mills had once stood. The story went on to say that Debbie had attended Edinboro State College in Edinboro, Pennsylvania, but, for reasons unspecified, had left school after a single year and been employed by Bargain Barn ever since, working her way up from stock girl and part-time cashier. She had never been married but had two children, each with a different father.

What would Arnie have thought had he known? Maybe that she was not the kind of girl he had thought she was all along. Maybe that he, Arnie, had been responsible for her demise, his untamed embrace having triggered some kind of self-destructive mechanism that lies within all of us, mostly dormant. Or maybe that, no matter how much love a mother has for her child, no matter how much time she spends teaching her little girl the mechanics of baton twirling, there is no guarantee that all will work out for the best in the end.

THE FIRST QUARTER of Super Bowl III was scoreless but, as far as Arnie and Zook were concerned, it produced a couple of encouraging signs. One of them was Matt Snell's running off tackle and bulldozing into Colts' safety Rich Volk, hitting him so hard that Volk was knocked unconscious; he had to be carried from the field on a stretcher and did not return. Maybe the Colts weren't so tough after all.

The second sign, near the end of the quarter, was a pass from Baltimore's backup signal-caller Earl Morrall that was just an inch or two behind its intended target. Had it been caught, it would have been a touchdown; instead, Jets' cornerback Randy Beverley stepped in front of receiver Tom Mitchell at the last instant and picked off the throw. The Colts' first-string quarterback and future Hall-of-Famer Johnny Unitas was injured and had been out for most of the season. He sat on the bench in full uniform, restless and eager for action. Morrall had gotten the great U's team to the Super Bowl, but he wasn't playing like it so far.

Between quarters, Rosa made her first appearance in the living room with a bowl of homemade meatballs and a larger bowl of salad with parmesan cheese. She set them on the coffee table, then returned to the kitchen.

"Rosie," Zook said, "what the hell ya doin' out there? Come on in here an' watch with the game with us. Could be some hist'ry happenin'."

"I'm gonna watch," she said, returning to put paper plates and plastic utensils on the coffee table in front of the two men. "You don't worry, *mangia*."

In the second quarter, Joe completed three passes in a row and, three running plays later, the Jets were on the Colts' four.

"Easy does it, Stats," Zook advised, scratching his arms although they didn't itch.

"Got to stay cool, Zee, just stay cool." Arnie was almost afraid to look.

But cool they were, with Joe handing the ball to Snell who ran a simple power sweep around the left side, with tight end Pete Lammons and tackle Art Herman leading the way---and to the astonishment of 75,337 people in Miami's Orange Bowl and another sixty million watching the game on television all over the world, the New York Jets had put the ball in the end zone first.

"Aw riiiight!"

"Yeah, baby, yeah!"

Rosa had set up a chair in the kitchen doorway and put down her crocheting just in time to look up and see Snell cross the goal line. "That's good," she said, "go Beaver Valley!"

Jim Turner kicked the extra point. 7-0.

"You believe this, Zook?"

"Shhh, don't put the whammy on nothin'. We got more 'n half the game t' go."

"Oh, boy," Arnie said, "boy oh boy."

Rosa smiled, happy that the men were happy if never certain why. When the Jets kicked off, she returned to her needlework.

But with *exactly* half the game to go, the score remained 7-0. The Colts were driving as halftime approached, and Arnie and Zook were sitting on the ends of the sofa cushions. But the Jets intercepted Morrall again and the greatest football team in the world was held to a scoreless first half by the universal underdogs.

Zook went out to the kitchen for a glass of water and, trying to get his mind off the game for a few minutes, asked Rosa what she was crocheting.

"Vase of flowers," she told him.

"What kinda flowers."

"I don't know. I pretty much make them up as I go along."

"I guess you ain't usin' a pattern, then."

"Never use no pattern."

"My mother always used to use one," Zook said, and it occurred Rosa in that moment that, in all the years she had known Zook, she had never heard him mention a parent or sibling before. He might have been an orphan for all she knew.

"So," she said, "your team gonna win?"

Zook did not reply verbally. Instead, he showed her crossed fingers on each hand.

As for Arnie, he had spent the halftime show watching the Florida A&M Marching Band and the girls who led the way for them. Their precision was eerily perfect, as if drawn by hand and animated. Arnie hummed along with them, but tunelessly; he did not recognize the songs they played. Zook resumed his position next to him, hoping he did not have majorettes on his mind. Rosa paid no attention to them.

THE SECOND HALF began with yet another Baltimore mistake. Running back Tom Matte fumbled a handoff from Morrall on the first play from scrimmage and the Jets recovered on the Colts' 34. Three running plays advanced the ball only five yards, but Turner came in for a field goal and sent the ball winging through the uprights.

10-0, Jets.

"It's possible," Arnie said.

Zook had to concede. "Colts gotta get two scores now. So, yeah, possible. But long ways from definite yet, Statsy."

"Long way."

Still, Zook coughed a few times in his excitement, pounding his chest with his fist until he stopped. His coughing had gotten worse over the years, and Arnie knew that, since he didn't smoke anymore, there was no point in worrying about him; there was nothing else he could do. But he worried anyhow.

The Baltimore offense returned to the field following the kickoff, but something was different, and the two men from Ambridge caught it before the TV announcers. The cameraman caught it before the announcers too, and zoomed in on the legendary number 19 in white. Earl Morrall had been exiled to the bench. The old pro, perhaps the greatest quarterback the game had ever known, Johnny Unitas, was going to give it a go.

"Holy shit!" said Zook.

"Johnny U," Arnie said.

The legendary Unitas, back from oblivion. He had been virtually crippled by a knee injury that had kept him on the sideline for twelve games of the regular season, and there were those who said he could not possibly see any more action this season. In fact, that his career might even be over.

But a few days ago, Unitas---whom the bone-headed Steelers had once cut because he wasn't good enough!---had pronounced himself fit to play. He was not yet a hundred percent, he told reporters, but close enough to help his team win the Super Bowl. The announcement made headlines in sports sections all over the country. It also raised the odds against the Jets.

But strangely enough, after getting over the initial shock of seeing Unitas on the field, Arnie and Zook were placid, unfazed.

"So the question is," Arnie said, "is Unitas at 85 percent better than Morrall at a hundred percent?"

"Yeah," from Zook. "An' who says he's even 85 percent? Prob'ly he's even less. When athletes're injured, they always exaggerate how they're recoverin', y' know that, Statsy."

"I also know that, even if Unitas *is* a hundred percent, you still got the rust factor to take into account. I mean, he's gotta be rusty, doesn't he? He hasn't played practically all season."

"Gotta be. Absolutely gotta be. Ya ask me, the Colts're desperate. They're really 'fraid now they're gonna lose this thing."

Rosa almost asked who this Johnny Unitas was, but since she didn't care, simply continued with her crocheting.

The Colts first series with Unitas at the helm was a bust. It consisted of a three-yard run, a one-yard run, an incomplete pass and a shanked punt.

Unitas was worse than rusty; he was uncoordinated. His ball-handling was sloppy and the one pass he threw could not have been caught if the receiver were another foot taller. And by the time Johnny U got his hands on the ball again, the Colts were even deeper in the hole. Joe had directed the Jets into easy field goal range and Turned booted another three-pointer, this one from the 37.

Jets 13, Colts 0. It was not just an upset in the making; it was the greatest miracle since loaves of bread had been turned into fishes.

"Hist'ry," Zook said again.

"You believe Joey was a rookie, what, three years ago?'

"So your team, she's gonna win?"

"Rosa, don't say that," her husband scolded, "not yet. You just don't do things like that. It's bad luck."

But that was ritual Arnie spoke, not true belief. It was from the same school of ritual as a baseball pitcher's jumping over the foul line as he runs from the dugout to the mound, or a basketball player's dribbling a prescribed number of times before shooting his free throws; the pitcher is afraid of a bad inning, the hoopster of a missed shot, the fan of a blown game. Arnie's gut told him that the Jets were going to win, and when the third quarter ended and he looked at Zook, he saw the same expression on his friend's face. As the commercial break began, without either man signaling the other, the two friends approached each other for a brief embrace.

Rosa looked up and grinned at them. They were such infants, these men with their games, in particular, this man she had married and the man around whom he had always been so comfortable for so long.

After a few seconds, Zook disengaged, and, as if he had been holding his friend upright rather than just hugging him, Arnie fell in a heap to the floor.

He lay on his back and moaned softly, lacking the energy to convey his pain as his as deeply as he felt it. He wrapped both arms around his chest. He knew, as soon as he felt the pangs, that he was in the midst of his third and most severe heart attack in a little more than six years. With his arms as they were, he looked as if he were trying to hold his heart in place, afraid that if he didn't it would drop to his waist.

Rosa let out a wail.

Zook was suddenly as still as a statue.

Arnie's legs shook for a few seconds and stopped. His face whitened. He unwrapped his chest; his fingers curled into fists and then slowly opened. His heart was beating its last few beats and it would never start again.

But maybe it would. Maybe, Zook dared to think, the Jets' impending victory had been so much for him that he fainted. But a further look, and a quick one, was all Zook needed to know the truth, and, without thinking, he backed up a couple of steps against the wall opposite the television, unwilling to accept what he saw, to grant it his nearness.

He was no longer aware of the TV. The appliance sat in its usual place, demanding attention that normally would have been its due. Not today, though, not now. Now it was just pictures unseen, sounds unheeded.

"Rosie," Zook gasped.

But she already knew. She stood slowly and stepped over to her husband even more slowly. Silent now, the single wail having emptied her. she showed neither surprise nor alarm; it was as if she had been expecting this all along. And, of course, she had, ever since the accident at American Bridge. Maybe even before that. She looked down at her love---not feeling for a pulse or a heartbeat, just looking. She turned to Zook, everything in slow motion with her now, and saw that he had slid down the wall into a sitting position. She stared at him, but he could not meet her gaze, and did not understand what she was trying to communicate. Did she mean to share with him the sympathy of their mutual loss, or her disgust at the behavior that had ended her husband's life? Or was it something else altogether?

As for Zook, staring back, his eyes pleaded with her, a plea it was not within her power to answer.

"I call ambulance," and Rosa shuffled to the phone and dialed the operator. She gave the necessary information, choking out the words, then sat at the foot of the stairs and covered her face with her hands. But she was not crying, and had not cried yet.

"Rosie." This time Zook's voice was hoarse. "He ain't . . . gone, is 'e?" and he provided his own answer with a sobbing that was new to him, and came from as deeply inside as he could be reached.

THE JETS WOULD SCORE AGAIN that afternoon, Turner adding a third field goal, and the Colts would avoid a shutout, with fullback Jerry Hill taking a handoff from Unitas and plunging one yard for a touchdown late in the fourth quarter. But it was too late. When the Jets got the ball back, they kept it on the ground, forcing the Colts to use up all their time-outs. Then, as bookies from one end of America to the other stropped their razors, rolled up their sleeves and prepared to slit their wrists, the young field general from Beaver Falls, Pennsylvania, ran out the clock on the greatest upset in the history of professional football, perhaps in all of professional sports.

On television, a close-up of the scoreboard looked like the biggest mistake anyone had ever made with numbers:

"New York 16, Baltimore 7."

And then the shot that would capture forever in the minds of football fans the outcome of the game, the picture they would remember for the rest of their days, Broadway Joe Namath running off the field, wildly gleeful fans chasing him, trying to smother him en masse, as he headed for the locker room with his helmet off and his index finger wiggling back and forth in the air. We're number one, he was signaling, we're number one—*we* are, and he had known it all along.

But the two men from Ambridge, perhaps the biggest Jets' fans outside of New York, were unable to join the celebration. One was dead; the other, who might even have smiled at the outcome of the game, wasn't even aware of it at the time.

Neither man had so much as looked at the meatballs and salad.

THERE WERE VIEWINGS of the deceased on Monday and Tuesday evenings at the Fitzgerald and Syka Funeral Home, and Rosa was amazed by how many people attended, especially the number of old friends from American Bridge who came to pay their respects. After all this time. Even a few of the sandblast slobs were there. It was as if the AB labor force were a family, long separated in some ways but never apart in others. Crisis brought them together. Crisis changed the priorities.

Several of the night school people, the ones who bothered speaking to Arnie, drove to one of the viewings from all over the Valley. The first night, Matthew D'Imperio was there and said a few words to Rosa in extraordinarily tender tones, which were both surprising and unwelcome. She turned her back on him before he could finish, and thought the worse of herself for doing so. But when she decided to apologize, she saw that he was engaged with others. For those attending a funeral, it can be something of a reunion.

Several people from the Spee-Dee Laundry introduced themselves to the widow, telling her how much her husband had come to mean to them in so short a time. He was polite, gracious, never angry at their frequent mistakes. Another surprise for Rosa was that only one of the Spee-Dee employees, a woman who folded diapers after they dried, knew Arnie was a football fan. That was her husband for you, she supposed; when he was on the job he was all business. And to other people, it was their interests that he talked about, not his own. It made her proud. So many men and women milled around Arnie's coffin, so many men and women had liked him. She didn't even know.

On Tuesday, Ronald Leander Washington came to the funeral home with his wife and three young children, two boys and a girl, dressed in their finest, somber-colored attire, with expressions to match. Another colored man was with them, probably Moses Michael Dunbar III. Looked at by themselves, they made an impressive group, nicely-tailored, the most dignified people at Fitzgerald & Syka as far as both appearance and mien were concerned. But they were displaying courage more than good sense.

People made eye contact with them and as quickly looked away. They pointed, whispered. Good Christians all, they fought back their impulses and did not say nigger in a funeral home, but the few whispers that were audible, reaching the Washingtons, all spoke the same words, referring to Ronald Leander as the colored man who had stripped Arnie of his job and started his descent into the coffin.

So be it. Ronald Leander Washington couldn't have cared less what other people thought. My family and I are entitled to grieve the passing of this extraordinary man, he might have been thinking, and if you honkies don't like it, you can just go ahead and demonstrate your bigotry instead of your regard for the deceased.

He, too, tried to talk to Rosa, who allowed him a few lines of praise and then gave him her back as she had Matthew D'Imperio. In Mr. Washington's case, she did not think she owed an apology.

And, of course, members of her own family were there, not nearly as many as there used to be, so many having passed away themselves. Vinnie was there, and his cousin Rocco, and the handful of nieces, nephews and grandchildren who still lived in the area.

Zook did not attend. He told Rosa he did not like funeral homes, where caskets were open and the departed individual was like the centerpiece at a large feast, a big turkey on the Thanksgiving table. Rosa understood. She was not comfortable with the role of Arnie's corpse at the proceedings either, but they were Catholics; it was what they did and they did it primarily for others, people who deserved a chance to say their final goodbyes face-to-face. It was not, of course, Arnie's face, not the real one, the one he had worn when he died. But that didn't matter. In fact, it was an attraction, to look upon their late friend as he had appeared when he and they were so much younger, not a crease in sight---the days when many of these same people had danced to the same music as Arnie and Rosa. Those embalmers, they never got any credit for it, but they were artists, genuine artists. Artists of the gruesome.

Wednesday morning, Father Daniel presided over a mass at St. Veronica's. Zook was okay with churches, and made it a point to see the priest before the service began; he described Rosa as having "ice water in her veins," for which it was clear that he resented more than admired her. The priest told him not to be hard on the widow; different people reacted to grief in different ways. "Yeah," Zook said, he supposed so, but his beloved Statsy-babe had been dead for two and a half days now and his wife was still auditioning her face for Mount Rushmore.

Near the end of the service, though, she finally broke down. Zook watched from a few pews behind and to the side as her tears, quiet ones to be sure, began to fall without stopping, and without her making any attempt to blot them. They were meant to be, Zook supposed, and she had decided to let them flow.

Which they did all the more so when it came time for her to rise from the church's front row and proceed down the aisle behind the casket as six men carried it from the altar to the hearse waiting in front of the church.

Rudy Battaglia was one of them; she couldn't attach names to the others. Two more men, Vinnie and Rocco, both almost as unsteady on their feet as Rosa, accompanied her on either side, each holding one of their hands under an armpit and the other gripping a wrist. The men were not her escort; she was their burden, as Rosa was dragging her feet as much as advancing them on her own. Her tears had vanished, but she kept her eyes on her feet, apparently embarrassed to be seen in such a helpless state in public. Her rosary beads were wrapped in one hand, but they might have been an old bracelet for all the attention she paid to them. She had nothing to pray for now, no reason to plead with the Almighty for a better outcome. He had made his decision. It was up to her to live with it.

Zook stayed in his pew and watched Arnie and Rosa pass in their distinctive ways. He wondered whether he and the widow could ever be friends and, if not, whether that meant his ties to Arnie had been irrevocably broken. He knew an Arnie who was different from the one Rosa knew. There were similarities, of course, but were they enough to create a bond between his old friend and his long-time wife? He bit his lip. He didn't think so. Nor did he think he could bear it.

What was he going to do without Stats in his life?

When the church had almost emptied of mourners, the last of them buttoning their coats as they stepped outside, Zook stopped in the aisle. He had heard the dim echo of footsteps behind him. Father Daniel was hurrying from the altar to catch up.

"Are you going to the cemetery?" the priest asked.

"Yeah, except the whole thing makes me . . . I don't know, it's creepy. I guess *you* done it so many times it don't really get t' ya. An', a course, y' got such a strong faith. Me, I never been t' a funeral before, an' right now I don't even know 'bout my faith, whether I even got it. Day like this, though, I gotta admit, makes me think it's time t' start lookin' inta things. Y' know? Is there really life after death, Father?"

He chose to take the question as rhetorical. "When you lose your best friend, it's a real test, there's no denying it." The priest shoved open the church door and motioned for Zook to exit first. Before him, at the curb, was a line of the most stylish automobiles he had ever seen. The hearse was first, and then maybe half a dozen limousines. Caddys, Zook thought they were, but it was hard to tell the way they were parked so close to one another. Waiting to enter were several of the people who had, perhaps for the first times in their lives, gone to mass on a Wednesday morning.

The funeral director, holding a pen and small notebook, was talking to the ladies and gentlemen in the limo line, assigning cars according to the prestige of the passengers and measuring prestige according to proximity, either by blood, marriage, or friendship, to the decedent. As a person entered the car, the director made a check mark on the paper.

"You should be in the first car, Zook, you know that?"

"Get outta here, Father," he said, "Me, leadin' a parade a limos? That'll be the day. Besides, I'm dressed in my Sunday best an' I still don't stack up t' nobody else. Maybe you noticed before, I ain't exactly the limousine type."

"You're the limousine type for today, Zook. What Arnie meant to you is something that can't be replaced."

Zook didn't want to dwell on that now. "I was thinkin' that, an', I mean, I know it ain't none of my business, but a big do like this---two nights in the funeral home for viewin', the limos, an' all the other costs that go along with dyin' in style, like Statsy's doin'---it must cost a lotta money. Helluva lot more than he got."

Father Daniel did not reply. After a few seconds, he nodded once or twice.

"So who's footin' the bill, Father?"

Again the priest did not reply immediately. Then: "I'll tell you because you were Arnie's compadre through thick and thin. But you've got to promise me, swear on the building we're standing in front of, the home of the Holy Trinity, that you'll never breathe a word of this to anyone."

Zook solemnly held up his right hand. "Swear to God."

"Well," Father Daniel said, "Gibraltar Security is paying for half of it."

"Yer kiddin'."

"Matthew D'Imperio threatened to quit if they didn't kick in."

"Holy smokers," he said, probably for the first time in his life, although he had heard the expression more times than he could remember. "An' the rest of it?"

"This is something you've really got to keep quiet." He paused. "The Beaver Valley Colored People's Action Committee."

"Huh?

"They volunteered."

"But that's . . . that's Ronnie What's-'is-name's group."

"Mr. Washington and I worked out the details with the funeral director."

"I can't believe it!"

"Mr. Washington called a special meeting of the board Monday night. A secret meeting. As the chaplain, I'm automatically a member of the board, so I was there. Mr. Washington asked for permission to bring the matter to a vote at a special session of the full membership that he scheduled for Tuesday. He had calculated how much money each member of the B.V.C.P.A.C. had to chip in to pay half the bill, and didn't think it was excessive. The board gave him permission to bring up the matter Tuesday."

"So the whole group showed up then?"

Father Daniel shook his head. "There wasn't enough notice. A lot of people just couldn't make it. But we had ourselves a quorum; that was all we needed."

Zook didn't care what a "quorum" was. "Then what happened?"

"Well, as you might imagine, some people were for it, some were against it. Things got to be pretty heated after a while. I was afraid at one point that a couple men would start swinging at each other. But Mr. Washington got everything calmed down, and kept pleading for the donation. Finally they put it to a vote."

"Was it close?"

Father Daniel shrugged. "Not really. The ayes had it, and one of the people who had been most strongly against the motion at first asked that the vote be recorded as unanimous. It was."

"Holy Mother a Mary."

"Ronald Leander Washington is a hard man to resist, Zook. He can bring a tear to the driest of eyes. Anyhow, that's the story. You're the only person who's not a member of the B.V.C.P.A.C. who knows it."

"Y' can count on me t' keep it that way, Father."

"I know," the priest said. "Don't worry, I know."

Only two more limousines and five people remained, three of them older women.

Zook exhaled so powerfully that he ended up coughing.

"Are you all right?"

"Yeah. Yeah," Zook said.

The funeral director tapped his pen on the notebook and chatted with women, surrounding him.

"So, um, y' see any a the Super Bowl?"

"Every play of it. First time in my life I ever watched a whole football game."

"Then y' know that Namath was the MVP, right?"

He said he knew.

"Got himself the keys t' a brand new, 1969 Plymouth Roadrunner, any color 'e wants. An' 'e deserves it, nobody can say he don't. Seventeen for 28 for 208 yards, more than a sixty percent completion percentage. No TD passes, granted, but no interceptions either. The Colts only sacked him twice all day, an' I couldn't help thinkin'---"

The funeral director interrupted Zook by motioning for the priest and his companion to get into the back seat of the last limousine. Zook slid in first and shimmied all the way over. Less than a minute later the cars started their engines and the slow, silent procession to eternity began.

"So I was sayin'," Zook continued, as the cars started in so stately a manner up the hill to the St. Veronica's Cemetery, "well, I guess I was kinda wond'rin' if y' think, well, maybe this'll sound silly, Father, but yer the expert on these kinda things, so . . . so y' think there's any chance that Statsy, well---"

"Yes. Yes, I do," Father Daniel said. He reached over and gave Arnie's best friend a quick squeeze on the thigh. "I think he knows, I really do."

"Honest?"

"I don't quite understand how these things work, but I'm sure the Good Lord was looking down on Sunday the same way He's looking down on us now, and He made sure that Stats knew the numbers before the final whistle."

It was Zook's first time in a car with power windows, and when he finally figured out how the automatic switch worked, he watched the glass glide down as a breeze blew in that was a little too cold for comfort. He didn't mind.

"How's bout the car? Stats maybe even knows about knows about Joey's car, too?"

195

"My guess? He even knows what color Joe's going to pick, even if Joe hasn't decided yet himself."

Zook couldn't help but whistle at such a supernatural speculation. Then, after allowing a short spasm of coughs to burn his throat, he leaned his head out the window as far as he could, and without even a thought for his zygomaticus major, looked up at the sky and for the first time in his life, with no one but the Good Lord able to see him, flashed a smile into the heavens.

CPSIA information can be obtained
at www.ICGtesting.com
Printed in the USA
BVHW03*0919250718
522513BV00013B/9/P